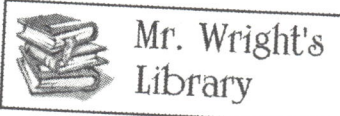

Books by Robin Brande

Evolution, Me & Other Freaks of Nature

Fat Cat

Doggirl

Parallelogram series

Secret Security Squad series

Replay

PARALLELOGRAM

Book 1: Into the Parallel

By Robin Brande

PUBLISHED BY:
Ryer Publishing, Tucson, AZ
Copyright 2011 by Robin Brande
Cover photo by Alexey Rumyantsev, Gail Johnson, and Corey A. Ford
Cover design by Robin Ludwig Design, Inc.
Layout by Cheryl Perez

ISBN-13: 978-1466487710
ISBN-10: 1466487712

All rights reserved. No part of this book may be reproduced in any form or by any electronic or mechanical means including information storage and retrieval systems—except in the case of brief quotations embodied in critical articles or reviews—without permission in writing from the author.

****

This is a work of fiction. Names, characters, places, and incidents either are the product of the author's imagination or are used fictitiously. Any resemblance to actual persons, living or dead, events, or locales is entirely coincidental.

To many people, science has become the new magic.

Walter "Skip" Whitfield, Ph.D.

One

They said it couldn't be done.

Well, that's not exactly true.

They said it couldn't be done by a 17-year-old girl sitting alone in her bedroom on a Saturday morning.

Well, that's not exactly true, either, since it's not like there's some physicist out there who specifically made that prediction—"A seventeen-year-old girl in her pajamas? Never!"—but the point is, no one is going to believe me even if I can prove what happened, which I'm not really sure I can.

But I know I did it. I was there. I didn't imagine it or dream it or go into some sort of altered state that confused me. I felt the wind. I smelled the dog's breath. I saw our mother. I drank some tea. It all happened.

So if she's real—and I know she is—I just have to prove it. Go there again and this time bring something back. Like a strand of her hair or a piece of her fingernail.

Something with her DNA on it. To prove that she is me.

Two

It's been going on for six months.

Six months of trying every day, sometimes twice a day, the big earphones over my head to block out any outside noise, while the voice on the CD says things like, "Imagine yourself into clouds. Be the rain. You are a flower—let the butterflies fan your face." An hour or more of that every day, with it never, ever working. And why should it? If you think about it, it's totally ridiculous.

But I knew I had to try something, and this was as close to an idea as I had.

It was all about the vibrations.

There's this theory in quantum physics—a really respected theory, even though a lot of physicists still disagree with it—that says the smallest building block of life isn't the atom or electron or quark, it's actually tiny, vibrating strings. Superstrings that change shape and speed and tone depending on whether they want to turn themselves into subatomic particles or elephants or galaxies.

And what turns them from amorphous, random strings into cotton balls or horny toads is the particular way they vibrate—

fast or slow, big waves, little waves, strings composing the universe the way violins create the sound of an orchestra. Strings in you and me. Strings in alien life forms, if there really are any. Vibrating strings as the basic building block of every single universe that might be out there.

So when my best friend Lydia mentioned one night that her yoga instructor had been teaching them all how to change their vibration, my ears shot up like a terrier's. I don't usually ask her too much about yoga—it's just too weird for me—but this time I had to know.

"What do you mean, change your vibration?" I asked her. Casually. Because I knew if I showed too much interest, she was bound to launch into one of her lectures again about how yoga will change my life and why aren't I coming to class with her and how can I keep living this way, and all of that. Ever since she got wrapped up in it a few years ago, she thinks it's the answer for everything.

Of course, she accuses me of thinking physics is the answer for everything, so I guess we're even.

"Raise your vibration," she repeated. "You know, take it from a level 200 to a 310."

"Oh," I said. "Uh-huh."

We were chopping onions for her mother, who was making dinner for all of us, and I waited a few more seconds, really concentrating on my onion, before asking Lydia some more.

"So . . . how does he do it?" I said. "You know, get your

vibration up."

Lydia scraped her choppings into a bowl and reached for the clump of garlic. "You meditate," she said. "An hour every day. He guides you through it until you can free your mind."

"This is . . . in class?" I asked. Lydia goes to yoga every day after school, and teaches there a couple of times a week.

She laid down her knife and gave me a critical look. "He's that visiting instructor I told you about—remember, the one I told you that you had to come see? But you were too busy reading Hawkins, or whatever."

It was true, I'd made up some excuse. Although I probably really was reading Hawkins.

Lydia went back to chopping. "I bought one of his CDs afterwards—the one with the same meditation from class. It's amazing."

I picked up a green pepper, ran it under the faucet, and pretended I didn't care. "So . . . do you think it worked? I mean, do you think it might have changed your vibration?"

"Definitely," Lydia said. "Can't you tell? Everyone else has really noticed it."

I wasn't sure what a 200 vibration versus a 310 looked like, but I was willing to take her word for it.

"So do you think I could . . . I mean, do you have it here?" I asked. "Could I maybe listen to it? Just out of curiosity."

Lydia gave a little snort. "Sure. You'll last about two minutes. It's not 'scientific' enough for you."

I shrugged. "Just to try. Out of curiosity."

Which is why I raced over to the yoga studio after school the next day before Lydia could get there, and secretly bought my own copy. Because I could tell right away, after listening to it for just a few minutes in her room, that this might finally be the key—the exact secret I'd been looking for.

Because here's the story: I need a miracle. Not some woo-woo, yoga-world kind of miracle, but a good honest scientific one. The kind of miracle that saves a girl in my position and sends her off to college so she can begin the rest of her life.

I know I'm good at physics. If it's not too braggy to say so, I'm great at it. It's been my life ever since I learned about it in fifth grade.

But there's a major, major problem, and everyone I've talked to about it—from my school counselor to my teachers—agrees: I suck at math. I mean, suck at it like people who can't throw a ball suck at that. Like, embarrassingly, humiliatingly suck at it. My brain just will not bend itself that way, no matter what I've tried.

And I've tried. Special books, remedial tutoring, instructional videos, even step-by-step comic books for little kids. I can do addition and subtraction pretty well, and multiplication if I'm not under too much pressure and have enough time, but I swear, there's something about algebra that makes my skin break out. And geometry? Forget it.

And there's no college that I know of that will let you into their physics program—or probably any program—if you can't at least pass Algebra I. So there's that.

Then there's the fact that it's not just any college I want to get into, it's Columbia University in New York City, where the greatest physicist in the world is currently a professor, and if he could be my teacher I would simply die from mental ecstasy, because I've read every single one of his books about ten times apiece, and I know if I could just get into his program and show him how I was meant to be a theoretical physicist and unlock all the secrets of the universe right alongside him, my life would be perfect in ways I can't even imagine yet. Well, that and this one particular guy falling in love with me, and then I'd be set.

But the problem is the great Professor Herbert Hawkins knows how to do math. He believes in it. He's a professor of both math and physics. And I doubt if he'd lower himself to even spit on an application like mine, with all my straight As in science and straight Ds in math. Not without something extra—a secret weapon of some sort. A miracle.

Which brings us back to vibration.

I was reading one of Professor Hawkins's books earlier this year—the new one he has out about parallel universes—and there was this one little line in there about vibration. He said that one of his colleagues threw out this idea at lunch one day about how we might be able to bridge the gap between our universe and any parallel one next door if we could just get the strings to vibrate right. Line them up somehow, get them all on the same frequency, then *oop!*, slip right past the barrier and end up in another world.

Everybody laughed at him, of course—that's what physicists do all the time, to spur each other on to even greater discoveries—but I wasn't laughing. I wasn't even sure if I got it. And then it was just a few days later when Lydia said the thing about her yoga teacher and the vibrations, and it all started fitting into place.

Because if it's true? And I'm the one who proves it? Won't Columbia University let me in *then*? Wouldn't Professor Hawkins see my name at the top of the application and say, "What? What's this girl doing in with the rest of the stack? Give her to me—I'm calling her this morning. I *have* to have Audie Masters in my lab."

Which is why every day for the past six months I've been applying myself to vibrations. Diligently turning myself into clouds and raindrops and wisps of air as the yoga teacher drones on in my headset, and trying as hard as I can to change my vibration from whatever it is to whatever it needs to be.

And then this morning it finally worked. I didn't even realize it until suddenly there was this cold wind blowing against my bare leg. I reached down to pull the sheet up over it, but there was no sheet. There was no bed. Just cold, hard ground.

I gently peeked open one eye.

And there I was. On top of a mountain somewhere, sitting on the dirt, the wind whipping over me something fierce.

And there she was. A young woman. Sitting just a little distance away from me on the edge of a cliff, her legs dangling over, hiking boots on her feet. Her eyes were closed, her face tipped into the sun.

She had long dark hair pulled back into a ponytail. I could only see the side of her face, but what I saw was enough. I drew in a breath.

She must have heard me, because she turned and her eyes got wide. We both stared at each other for one long frozen moment. Because of course we recognized each other—we *were* each other.

My brain was still having a hard time catching up. I'd *done* it. It had worked. The truth is maybe I hadn't really believed in any of it until that moment—a theory is a theory, and it doesn't mean it's right—but now there I was, in a parallel world, staring at a parallel version of me.

I didn't know what else to do. I gave her this little dorky wave and started to say, "Hi. I—"

But that was it. Whatever I thought I was going to say—"*Hi, I'm Audie. Hi, I'm from another universe. Hi, I think you're me.*"—I never got it out.

Because right about then her dog decided he'd better kill me.

Three

He was a big boy, maybe a hundred pounds of yellow, snarling Labrador, and even though I've always heard those kinds of dogs are supposed to be friendly, apparently that was only in my own universe and not this one. In this one he looked ready to rip my throat out.

"Easy, Red," the girl said, but she didn't seem all that concerned. The dog maneuvered in front of her, his legs rigid, ears back, hackles mohawking down his spine. Meanwhile the girl still sat there looking at me curiously like I was some new kind of animal that had just appeared.

The dog started edging toward me, growling so loudly now I could actually feel the vibration of it in my stomach. This wasn't what I expected just from listening to a meditation CD. Where were the fluffy flowers? Where were the happy clouds?

"Red, relax!" the girl said. "It's just a holo." She picked up a rock and flung it at me. She was just starting to say, "See—" when the rock hit me and bounced off.

Her eyes narrowed. She picked up a second rock and pitched it at my chest.

"Ow! Can you stop?"

The girl sprang to her feet. She pointed at me with an outstretched arm and started shouting.

"What are you? Did Ginny send you? Where did you come from? What do you want?"

It was hard to make myself heard over the dog, who was now more worked up than ever, slavering and barking, just inches away.

I held up my arms in front of my face. "Can you call off your dog? *Please?*"

"What are you?" the girl demanded. "Who sent you? Are you real?"

"Yes, I'm real! Nobody sent me—I sent myself. Now PLEASE!"

And then suddenly everything changed.

The wind shifted direction and blew over me from behind. The dog tilted his head and sniffed. It was like he'd finally just gotten a good whiff of me.

And instantly his whole body relaxed. His ears came up, his mouth popped open, his tongue hung out, and his tail wagged. He went ahead and tackled me, just like I'd been afraid, but he was licking me and wiggling all over like he'd never been so happy in his life.

"Red—" the girl said, but her dog was too busy wrestling with me to notice.

Finally I got control of the situation and was able to sit up again. "Good boy," I said, patting his head, and that was enough to make him plop down in front of me, chin on my lap, tail swishing happily in the dirt.

The girl stared at me in wonder. "I don't understand." But I was pretty sure she did. Whether she was ready to believe it or not, her dog had just confirmed our matching DNA.

Although the truth was, we weren't *exact* duplicates. Not exactly. She looked a little taller than I am, definitely *way* fitter—or maybe just more outdoorsy, although the way she carried herself made it look like her arms and shoulders were a lot more muscular than mine. But aside from that, same square face, same nose and mouth and blue-gray eyes—same overall everything.

Except for our hair. That was the only real difference. Same exact color, but mine is limp and scraggly and sad, whereas hers was long and thick like a horse's tail. You could have pulled a tractor out of the mud with that hair. Mine breaks if you even try to comb it.

And we were dressed differently, of course. She wore gray pants, hiking boots, a navy blue sweater. It all looked pretty regular—like something I could have bought at an outdoor clothing store if I wanted to. No weird fabrics made out of negative-ionic pulsating supercharged atoms or anything. It just looked like regular fleece and cotton.

Whereas I sat there in the dirt still wearing what I'd had on five minutes before: just my sleep shirt and boxers. No socks, no shoes, nothing else. Thank goodness for the warm dog draped over my lap. He was the closest thing I had to pants.

"I don't understand," the girl said. "Any of this."

"It's kind of hard to explain," I said.

"But you *can* explain it?"

"I think so, maybe if I start at the beginning—"

But that would have to wait. Just then a huge gust of wind came up and blasted right through me. I shivered so hard the dog had to lift his head off my lap.

Despite everything, the girl was practical. "You're going to freeze out here. Come on—I need to get you some clothes." She headed toward the trees behind her. "Hurry—we have to get to my camp."

She took off at a trot, and the dog and I jumped up to follow.

But as the three of us made our way through the pines, I couldn't help having a few random thoughts: like, how did I know it was safe?

And for that matter, how did the girl know *I* was?

Because, really, what did she know about me? I'd just shown up, suddenly out of nowhere, wearing her same face and body and totally inappropriate clothing, and yet she was trusting me enough to take me back to her camp? How did she know I wasn't dangerous? How did she know I wasn't some alien or clone sent to harm her?

And same question for me—how did I know I could trust her?

Because when you thought about it, I had no absolutely idea where I was. Not just where in the world but in *what* world. The place looked a lot like Earth, but it could be completely different. There might be creatures on it I had never heard of or seen. The girl looked human, but how did I know she didn't eat her own kind? Maybe she was leading me back to her people, who were going to throw a big party in my honor and then roast me alive.

At least the dog was on my side. He stayed so close I could feel his breath against my bare leg as I hurried down the trail, trying not to jam my bare feet against every rock and twig.

At one point the girl got a little too far ahead of me. I was afraid I'd lost her.

"Audie?" I called out, wondering if it was possible she had my same name.

She didn't, but she did come back. And she understood.

"Halli," she said, pointing to herself. "I'm Halli."

I introduced myself and we both shook hands.

Which, considering the science of the whole thing, might be the weirdest thing I've ever done.

Four

Frequently Asked Questions:
What is Columbia looking for when evaluating students for admission?

In the process of selection, the Committee on Admissions considers each applicant's academic potential [*uh-oh*], intellectual strength [*got that*] and ability to think independently [*yes*]. The Committee also considers the general attitudes and character of the applicant [*Dear Sirs/Madams, I have a great attitude*], special abilities and interests [*able to eat, sleep, and breathe physics; 100 % interested in becoming Professor Hawkins's best friend and protégé*], maturity [*decent*], motivation [*HIGH*], curiosity [*HUGE*] and whether he or she is likely to make productive use of the four years at Columbia [*I swear, I won't even watch TV*].

In its final selection, Columbia seeks diversity of personalities, achievements and talents, and of economic, social, ethnic, cultural, religious, racial and geographic backgrounds [*I have a great personality, am working on a big achievement, and my economic background will balance out all the people there who have money*]. Each applicant's academic record is examined [*please overlook the math grades—the famous physicist Michael Faraday couldn't do math, either, and he still discovered electromagnetism*] [*I'm not kidding—you can look it up*], together with reports on personal qualities that have been supplied by the principal, headmaster or counselor and by teachers [*my physics teacher is working on a letter. I know it's going to be good*]. The student's record of participation in the life of his or her school and community [*does working for my mother's non-profit organization count?*] is also important, as is his or her performance on standardized tests [*again, please excuse the math scores. Remember: electromagnetism*].

Deadline for Admission: November 1.

Number of days remaining to come up with some huge discovery that will convince them to let me in: 40.

Five

Halli led me into a small clearing. And there it was: a normal-looking campsite with a tent and a campfire and all that. Not that I've ever camped, but it sure looked like any picture of it I've ever seen. No human skulls lying around, no scraps of flesh where maybe the dog had tricked someone else into thinking he was friendly, then ripped the intruder to shreds.

Halli opened the door to her tent and dove in. She backed out again holding an armful of clothes. "Here," she said, "put these on. Right away."

Warm black pants, fuzzy red jacket, thick gray socks. All in my size, of course.

While I pulled on her extra clothes, Halli hefted over an armful of logs and then coaxed her campfire back to blazing.

"There," she said, sitting down across from me and stretching her fingers over the flames. "Warm yet?"

"Almost." The dog was certainly doing his part. As soon as I finished dressing, he lay down as close as he possibly could to me, rested his chin on my lap, then closed his eyes and sighed deeply.

Halli shook her head. "He doesn't do that with anyone except me." She looked me straight in the eye. "But I guess it's obvious, isn't it?"

"I think so," I answered.

"Then would you explain to me how?" she asked. "And who—or whatever—you are?"

"I'll try in a second," I said. "But can you tell me something first? Is this . . . Earth?"

"Yes." But from the look on her face she obviously thought the question was strange.

"Where are we? I mean, specifically, on Earth."

"It's called Colorado."

"We have Colorado, too," I said excitedly. "I mean, I've never been there, but we have it."

"Who's 'we'? What exactly are you?"

It was kind of a rude question to keep asking, but I couldn't blame her. "I'm just a girl," I said. "Like you. We have Earth, too. I think it's just . . . a different one."

She started to say something, but I cut her off.

"I promise I'll try to explain in a minute, but can you just tell me what the date is? Please?" I wanted to make sure I hadn't gone backward or leapt forward somewhere in time— because that would open up a whole new set of possibilities. And a whole other set of problems. Not that this set was going to be easy.

September 22nd. Same date and year as when I'd left this morning.

I let out a breath. My brain was going a billion miles a minute. But it all boiled down to this: Professor Hawkins was right. Parallel universes really do exist. And I'd found one. Same Earth, same time, same identical features.

Except for one thing.

"But you're not Audie Masters," I said.

"No, I'm Halli Markham. And now it's your turn," she said. "Tell me everything you know."

Six

"There are two theories," I began. "Well, really three. Well, really there are *lots* of theories—" I stopped myself. *Keep it simple.*

Lydia always makes snoring sounds whenever I talk about too much about science, so I've learned to keep it short. People don't have the patience for it the way I do.

What I needed was a visual aid.

I untangled myself from the dog, stood up and found a stick. Red immediately got up, too, tail wagging, obviously thrilled I was going to throw the stick for him. Instead I used it to draw two lines in the dirt.

"Let's say this line is my universe," I began. "Everything in the universe—all the stars and planets and everything on them—humans and everything else—we're all confined to this one membrane. A three-dimensional membrane—they call it a 'three-brane.' " I stopped for a moment. "Is this . . . too much?"

"No," Halli said. "Go on."

I pointed to the second line. "Over here is your three-brane. Your whole universe."

I dug both lines a little deeper. "Usually we just exist side-by-side—maybe even a fraction of a millimeter apart—but we never actually touch. We never communicate or even know the other one exists. Then every trillion years or so, the membranes collide and they blow each other up and we start the whole cycle again."

"Is that true?" Halli said. "I've never heard anything like that."

"Well, right now it's just a theory. It's called cyclic cosmology. There's a lot of math and physics to support it, but so far nobody's really been able to prove it."

Until now, I thought. I was going to be the youngest Nobel prize winner for physics ever.

I drew five more lines in the dirt. "There are other scientists who say there are multiple universes, not just two. It's the *multiverse* theory—a different universe for every possibility. So maybe in Universe X your parents meet and have you, but in Universe Y they meet and hate each other and marry other people and have Child Z, not you. Does that make sense?"

"I think so," Halli said.

"Okay, so back to our original two universes and their membranes. Whether there are two parallel universes or five million, the fact is none of us knows the other ones exist. We might guess they're out there, but we can't prove it. We can't communicate with each other."

"Until today," Halli said.

"Exactly." I was happy she caught on so quickly. I figured she was ready for the next step.

I drew some squiggly lines in the dirt. "And that's where string theory comes in."

Halli blew out a breath. "I'm going to need some tea for this."

I'd done it again—lost my audience. At least Halli hadn't made snoring sounds yet.

"Sorry, I'm not very good at explaining—"

"No, you're great," Halli said. "It's just a lot to take in. Without tea." She smiled encouragingly. "But this is really helping. Don't stop."

It was amazing how good that made me feel. Even though technically it might look like it was me telling myself—like I was giving myself a pep talk in the mirror.

But this wasn't a mirror and she wasn't me. Halli was a different entity. We might *be* the same, but we weren't the same.

Maybe I needed some tea, too.

She quickly brewed some up, first crushing some seeds into the bottom of her cookpot, then adding some sort of ivory-colored liquid on top. The steam from it smelled rich and spicy—something like cinnamon, but not quite.

She poured half of it into a mug for me and the rest into a bowl for herself. Which made sense, I thought, since she wasn't really expecting company and wouldn't have brought along a second mug.

But then I did something really stupid. I waited until Halli looked away for a moment, then quickly wiped off the rim of the mug with my sleeve. And instantly felt ridiculous. Because if she had any cooties, weren't they my genetic cooties, too? We could probably share the same toothbrush and it wouldn't hurt me. Not that I ever would.

"Okay, so string theory," I said when she'd settled back down again. I gave her the shortest version I could.

At the end of it she pulled her sweater away from her shoulder. "Strings?"

"Strings," I confirmed.

Halli pointed at Red. "Different strings?"

"Well, same strings, just like atoms are all the same, but let's just say they're vibrating differently to make up the particles that make him."

Halli considered that a moment, then nodded. She pointed at one of the pines. "Tree strings?"

"Sure," I said, just to keep it simple. "We can call them that."

"Fine," Halli said, "go on."

The last piece was the meditation CD. And how I've been trying to vibrate differently all these months.

"I thought maybe I could do it if I just concentrated really hard."

"Or maybe if you didn't concentrate at all," Halli said. "That's what I try to do when I meditate—just completely empty my mind."

"Sure. Okay." I was too into my own story at that moment to follow up on what she'd said, but I was going to find out more soon enough.

"So I had this idea," I said, "that in the same way there are gravitational and electromagnetic and other kinds of fields, maybe there's also a vibrational field that no one's ever discovered. Maybe they just haven't been looking for it. And I thought maybe that could be the way to bridge the gap between the two universes."

I drew a short line in the dirt connecting two of the longer ones. "If I could vibrate past the field, across one three-brane into the other, maybe I could contact that other universe. Your universe. And this morning it finally worked."

Halli had lifted the bowl to her mouth, but now she paused mid-sip. "Oh." And then she smiled mysteriously.

"What?" I said.

"Now I understand," she said. "It happened because of me."

"What? No—" Hadn't she been listening?

"I'm saying it wasn't just you," Halli went on. "It had to be me, too."

"I don't know what you mean."

"How long did you say you've been trying to do this?" she asked. "Six months?"

"Right."

"And it never worked."

"I was always too distracted," I said. "I'm not good at settling down and just meditating."

"Well, I am," Halli said. "I'm actually quite good at it. I've been doing it since I was little. But do you know when I haven't been doing it? These past six months. Not until today."

She sipped her tea and studied me over the steam. Like she was waiting to see the moment when I finally got it.

And then I did.

"You think it's two-way," I said. "Sender and receiver."

"Yes."

"I've been calling out, but there was no one listening at the right frequency—until this morning."

"Right," Halli said.

"And no one else was ever going to answer because she wasn't you. She wasn't like me. It had to be you because our brains are made the same."

Halli smiled. "And look how smart we must be."

I closed my eyes. My head was feeling spinny.

"Why today?" I asked her. "Why today and not the last six months? If I've been calling and calling to you, why haven't you answered?"

Halli paused. She set down her bowl. I could tell she was stalling.

Finally she looked me in the eye. "It's because I haven't wanted to meditate for the whole past year. My grandmother died a year ago today. She's the one who taught me to do it, so I guess it's been my own personal protest not to meditate anymore. I thought it would be too intense—I'd be too sad. So I just gave it up.

"But yesterday I thought I should honor her. So I came up here to camp, and this morning went out on that cliff to meditate. And I called to my grandmother and asked her to come to me.

"But then you showed up instead."

Seven

Before I could ask any of the obvious questions, like, *Why would your grandmother come if she was dead? Do you believe in ghosts? Do the dead come back to life here?*—Halli saved me the trouble and went ahead with her own explanation.

"Do you know my grandmother?" she asked. "Virginia Markham. Ginny."

So that's whom Halli had been asking about when I first showed up.

It seemed like I *should* know her grandmother. If Halli and I were exact genetic duplicates of each other, each living in our own universes, then it made sense that our parents and grandparents and every other relative down the line should also be exactly the same. Like I told Halli, all it would take was one person in our ancestry deciding no, he or she would rather go out with this person instead of that one, and the whole gene pool would have been different, meaning Halli or I would never have been born.

So I had to assume that Halli and I had the same grandmother. I also had to assume, based on the fact that Halli was called Halli instead of Audie, that her grandmother would have a different name, too.

"Do you have a picture of her?" I asked.

Halli ducked inside her tent and emerged with a rolled up scroll-looking thing. She unfurled it and laid it flat on her lap. It turned out to be a kind of computer-like screen about the size of a sheet of paper, and practically as thin. Halli pressed the surface of it in a couple of places, then passed it to me.

The face looking up at me was definitely my grandmother's. My mother's mother, to be exact. A sweet old lady my mom and I both affectionately refer to as "it's for you" whenever we see her number on Caller ID, because conversations with her can definitely be . . . less than fun. My grandmother doesn't really approve of how we run our lives. We're too poor for her compared to my Uncle Mike and his family, and my grandmother just can't help bringing it up all the time.

"Did your father send his child support this month?"

"Mom, it's for you . . ."

"Is that her?" Halli asked once I'd looked at the screen.

"Yes, but her name's Marion Fletcher over . . . " I gestured vaguely to my left. " . . . there."

"But you're sure they're the same."

"Yes," I said.

A beeping sound came from the screen. The photo on it disappeared, and in its place came a swirl of lights. They lifted off the screen and twisted in the air right above it.

Halli groaned. "I shouldn't have turned it on."

"What's—"

But Halli held her finger to her lips and motioned for me to get inside her tent.

A voice came from the swirl of lights. "Halli? Where are you?"

I knew that voice. It was my mother's.

As soon as I was safely in the tent, peeking around the edge of the flap, Halli pressed something on her screen.

"What," she asked dully.

Suddenly a head appeared. My mother's head. Also her shoulders and a little of her upper torso. Maybe at three-quarters their regular size, but otherwise looking fully real in three-dimensional color. It looked like she was there in person—or at least her upper body was. She hovered over the top of Halli's screen, talking to her as if they were in the same room.

"We were worried," my mother—technically, Halli's mother—said.

"Why?" Halli asked. "I'm sure my dot moved."

"You shouldn't be out there alone," her mother said.

"I'm not alone—"

Halli glanced my way. I ducked back inside the tent. I thought I was supposed to be a secret.

"—I'm with Red," Halli finished. Then she slowly started edging toward the tent.

She knelt down in front of the door, held the screen high over her head, then coughed. The screen jiggled and the three-dimensional image of my mother lost focus—sort of like bad TV reception. And in that moment, Halli passed the screen to me.

"No!" I whispered.

"Yes," Halli mouthed.

She quickly skittered away from the tent. I was alone with just her mother.

"Uh . . . hi," I said as soon as her face came back. I couldn't resist poking my finger through her cheek—she just looked so real. But of course my finger passed right through. It was just a hologram.

"Red, relax! It's just a holo," Halli had said when I first showed up. Now I understood. No wonder she was so confused when that rock she threw at me bounced off.

" . . . traveling with your *dog* isn't the same as being with other people," Halli's mother was saying. "Your father and I worry about you."

When I didn't answer right away, she said, "Halli, are you listening?"

"Oh, sorry, Mom. Go ahead."

"Mom?" She seemed a little flustered by that. Halli shook her head at me. Her mother cleared her throat and continued.

Meanwhile I stared at her face.

That woman was definitely my mother. And definitely not.

She looked older. More tired. Heavier, too. Not healthy and energetic-looking like my mother. Just generally puffy and worn out and old.

"Are you listening?" she asked again.

"Yes," I said. "Sorry. How are you?"

Halli waved for my attention and shook her head again. Apparently I wasn't handling this right.

Her mother seemed confused by my question, too. "I'm . . . fine. I wish I didn't have to track you down all over the world—"

Halli gestured for me to wrap it up.

"Um . . . I have to go," I told her mother.

"When are you going home?" she asked.

"Uh . . ." I looked to Halli for the answer. She shrugged like she didn't care.

"I might stay out here a while," I told her mother.

"Why?" her mother asked. "How much longer?"

Halli came to my aid. She motioned for me to lift the screen high, then she rushed in smoothly and did the coughing thing again. She jiggled the screen and retrieved it from my hands. I took the hint and ducked back into the tent.

"I have to go," Halli told her mother as soon as the screen was back in front of her and the hologram focused again. "Watch my dot. I'll probably be up here a few more days."

"Will you call me?" her mother asked.

Halli coughed again. "Need water. Goodbye."

Then she pressed the screen and her mother's head disappeared. Halli sat back on her heels and blew out a breath. Then she smiled at me.

"Very good," she said.

"I'm sweating," I pointed out.

"Was that her?" Halli asked. "Same mother?"

"Mostly."

"Well then," Halli said, "I'm sorry."

Eight

Not really the same mother, I wanted to tell her, but I was afraid it might hurt her feelings.

Because even though the face generally looked the same, the tone—the vibe of the woman—was definitely different.

Or maybe what was different was how Halli treated her mother. Maybe that was the whole wrong thing. Because I would never talk to my own mom that way.

We've been a team, my mom and me, since I was ten. Before that we were part of a triad, a trio, a family—but she and I don't really talk about that anymore. There are no pictures of him on the wall. If there are still photos of the three of us in albums, they're tucked away in my mom's closet. When he left, he left us for good, as far as my mom was concerned. If he sends checks now and then the way he's supposed to, she deposits them like she would any donation she gets at work. We never talk about him. And I'm kind of okay with that.

I used to feel so sorry for Lydia and her twin brother Will. They lost their dad for real—as in dead—back when they were little. I thought it was so sad they'd never know what it was like to have him around as they grew up. But people adjust. I've adjusted. Now it would feel weird to have him back.

So whatever weird thing there was going on between Halli and her mother, it wasn't anything I shared or understood.

But it made me curious about something.

"Are your parents divorced?"

"Divorced?" she said. "No."

Wow. What an interesting thing. She must have had a whole different life, growing up with both parents. I wanted to hear all about that at some point, but first there were other things I was more curious about.

"What did you mean when you said to your mother, 'Watch my dot'?" I asked.

"My location on the map," Halli said. "You know . . . the tracking."

She could see I didn't have a clue.

"You don't have that?" she asked.

"I mean, sure, we have maps . . ."

Halli pulled her shirt down on one side and bared her shoulder. She pointed to a spot beneath the left side of her collar bone. "Don't you have one of these?"

"One of what?"

"An identifier. A tracking cell embedded under the skin. We all have them."

I know sometimes pet owners microchip their animals, but I've never heard of doing it to humans.

"Does it . . . hurt?"

"Probably," she said. "But you get it when you're a newborn, so I don't really remember."

I thought about what that must be like: Here's your new baby, Mrs. Jones, let's just weigh her, measure her, microchip her—good to go.

"So that means your mom can track you wherever you are?"

"Unfortunately," Halli said. "But only for another few months. Then I'm taking her off the list—taking both of them off."

I felt like I should understand—she was speaking clearly, and not only in English, but actually in my own voice. Yet I still didn't get it.

"I'm sorry—take who off what list?"

"My parents. Off the list of who gets tracking information. Once you turn eighteen you get to decide."

"Oh, sort of like a friends-and-family plan."

"A what?"

"Never mind," I said. "So you're saying no one can track you once you're eighteen? I mean, unless you want them to?"

"The government still can—everybody has to register with them. That way if you commit a crime, or you're lost up on Everest, they can find you."

"Wow."

"So you don't have that?" Halli asked.

"Not at all."

But it was an interesting idea, for sure. I started thinking about who would be on my list. My mother. My father. Lydia and Will and their mom Elena. And . . . that was about it. Those are the only people I care about and the only ones who probably care about me.

Kind of sad.

"How many people are on your list?" I asked Halli.

"Three. Two now, with my grandmother gone. And soon, zero."

I was practically sociable compared to her.

I heard a beeping again. More of a ringing, really. I waited for Halli to answer her screen. She didn't even seem to notice the noise.

Because it wasn't her noise. It was mine. My phone, my world.

And thanks to that, me back in my own bedroom.

Nine

It took at least three more rings before I felt oriented again. Then I reached over and answered my phone.

"Hey," Lydia said, "what took you so long? Were you sleeping?"

I checked the clock. It was 11:30. I'd been gone three hours.

"No . . . I . . ." I rubbed my hand over my face, like I could dry-scrub it back to reality. Then I noticed my clothes. Not my warm, cozy camping outfit anymore. Back to my own boxers and sleep shirt.

"Audie?"

"What?"

"What's going on? Why are you acting so weird?"

"I'm . . . ." Another dry scrub. "Okay. Sorry. Hi. What's up?"

"Mom wants you over here tonight for a barbeque."

Lydia and Will's mom Elena always tries to keep me fed whenever my mother's out of town. Since my mom and I hardly ever cook for ourselves, I'm always happy for the invitation.

"Okay, sure," I said. "What time?"

"Six. I'm teaching until 6:30, but she says come early."

"Is . . . Will going to be home?" I asked as casually as I could.

"Yes, and Hairball, too, of course."

Great. "Okay, I'll be there. Tell your mom I said thank—"

But Lydia was already off the phone, on to the next thing.

I turned my phone as off as I could. Off OFF. Stupid thing. I had been having the greatest experience of my life, and that idiot phone had to ruin it.

I sat there in bed and caught my breath. Caught up with my brain, is more like it. Three hours in another dimension, another universe, another life.

In-freakin-credible.

I needed to get back there as quickly as I could. I popped the earphones back on and rewound the CD and prepared to go back to some campfire discussion and a big warm dog curled beside me.

And I waited. And I tried. And . . . nothing.

I tried for a whole hour. Kept looking at the clock, then closing my eyes again and trying some more. Which might have been the problem—I wasn't in that relaxed, meditative brainwave state like before. If I had a vibration, it was an agitated one—not the kind that had broken me past the barrier before.

Or maybe, I thought, Halli had moved on. She wasn't sitting there trying to reach me—or reach her grandmother—like before. Maybe it really was a two-way connection, and unless we were both exactly set up to match our vibrations, it wasn't going to work.

Which was SO frustrating. I couldn't get her a message, like, "Hey, turn on your brain at 2:00 this afternoon—meet you back at the cliff." I had no way of letting her know when or if I was back in my meditative groove. So I'd just have to use the same trial-and-error as before—putting myself in the right frame of mind as often as possible, and hoping one of those times worked.

For now, the best I could do was sit down and write up my notes about everything that had happened.

Because *if* I ever ended up there again, I was going to need to ask a *lot* of questions.

Ten

"Heeeey, Audie girl, whatcha up to?" (Wink.) (Plump up the hair and toss it.) (Annoy me.)

"Hey, Gemma. Hi, Will." I gave him a little wave. Even though I was standing right in front of him. Because I am a dork.

The three of us hung out in the back yard while Will's mom worked the grill, and even though Elena was only two feet away, Gemma still felt perfectly fine pressing her padded English bra right up against Will's arm and trying to slip her hand down the back of Will's waistband while he and I talked as if THAT WASN'T THE MOST IRRITATING THING EVER. And embarrassing. As in must-look-away uncomfortable.

And Will didn't even seem to notice.

But Elena did. I glanced over and caught her eye. She scrunched her face to the side and stuck out her tongue. She's not a big Gemma fan, either.

"So I was hoping you could take a look at the program," I told Will, after explaining the problem I've been having with the computers at work. "Maybe sometime in the next couple of days?"

"Sure," Will said.

"You can fix that, cahn't you, babe?" Gemma asked him with a wink.

(Here, how's this hot coal from the barbeque feel on that eye?)

"I'm sure he can," I said, refusing to look at her or the hand wedged down his backside.

"I'll come in tomorrow," Will promised.

Me, too, I thought, even though I hadn't planned on going back in until Wednesday.

Gemma made a pouty face and plunged her hand down a little further and tossed her hair and pressed her bra against Will's arm (a very complicated sequence, but no problem for a pro like her), and said, "I thought we might see a show tomorrow."

(We call them movies here, Gemma.)

Will didn't seem to notice the boob against his sleeve. Or maybe he's immune to it after so many repeated applications. "I'll probably have to work all day," he told her. "I've already got four clients lined up—five, now. I'll try to fit you in around noon," he told me.

"Great," I said. "Thanks."

Will has his own computer consulting business—*Computer ER: Emergency Repair*. He used to work for just our moms at their non-profit organization, but then word got around, and pretty soon he was running his own 24-hour tech support for people willing to pay a hefty price for a house call. He's come a long way since the days when he and Lydia and I thought we might make our fortune on a lemonade stand.

"Babe, it's our eleven-month anniversary." Gemma winked at me. "Audie girl, couldn't you spare him?"

(Could, won't.)

Will's dark eyebrows wrinkled. I could see he was already thinking through the software problem I'd described. He mumbled to himself as much as us, "I thought I fixed that problem."

Gemma offered me a tight smile. She thought she had fixed it, too.

Eleven

Lydia didn't show up until after nine. Turns out there was some guest yoga instructor in town, and after Lydia taught her Saturday afternoon class she and the other yoga teachers at the studio got to sit in on a special session with him.

Since we were all in the living room by then, Lydia pushed aside the coffee table and demonstrated one of the new, advanced poses the yoga instructor taught them. It involved twisting her body one way, legs another, head a third way, if that's even possible, which, apparently, it is. I couldn't have gotten my body to do that even if someone took it apart and handed the pieces to me separately.

Lydia is . . . amazing. I've never understood why she doesn't have a million guys after her all the time. She's clearly the most beautiful girl at our school. She has all her mom's dark exotic features—the long black hair, the dark eyes, the olive-toned skin—Will has them, too, except his hair just brushes the top of his collar, and by late afternoon his face always has the shadow of stubble—even more on the weekends when he doesn't always have time to shave—and man, that guy is incredible-looking, but he's never seemed to know it. Which only makes him even hotter, if that makes any sense.

But back to Lydia. And me. I'm sure a lot of people look at us and have no idea why we're even friends. We have none of the same interests. In fact, to be truthful, a lot of our interests actually bore each other. She doesn't care a thing for science, and until the vibration issue came up, I thought all of her yoga stuff was just weird and pointless.

But whether or not you have a lot in common with someone, when you're thrown together with that person from the time you're little, you can't help but grow attached. Our mothers became best friends years and years ago when they started their non-profit company, *Build a Fund for Good*, and somehow the three of us kids just assumed we should all be best friends, too.

Or more than that, if a certain someone would ever open his eyes.

Which I've never told Lydia about. I have my reasons, mostly involving the fact that she's not that great at keeping secrets—except her own—plus she'd probably laugh in my face if she knew how much I loved her brother. And even though they're not that close, she might feel some sort of twin-inspired compulsion to tell him, which means I'd either have to die of humiliation or flee the state and live under an assumed name and never get to eat Elena's food again. It's just not worth the risk.

"How's that bloke?" Gemma was asking Lydia. "What's his name—Davey?"

Lydia narrowed her eyes. "How do you know about him?"

"Will told me."

Lydia transferred her Evil Eye to her brother. "Thank you. You are now officially cut off."

Will laughed. "Oh, come on. Big secret. You've been stalking him all month."

Elena looked up from the button she was reattaching to a shirt. "Big secret to me."

Lydia shrugged. "Guy from the yoga studio. Total loser. Move on."

That's about all I knew about it, too. One day he was the extreme object of her affection, the next day he was out.

Which seems to happen often with Lydia.

"If you need some advice—" Gemma started to say, and I immediately stifled a smile. Because I knew exactly what Lydia was thinking.

HAIRBALL.

But Lydia smiled sweetly. Fakely sweetly. "Yes, Gemma, please. Give me all your best advice. I'm sure my brother would love to know how you landed him."

Gemma winked. "We'll talk in private."

And Lydia actually went along with it. She got up and the two of them went into Lydia's bedroom and closed her door.

Will and I exchanged a look.

"Aren't you curious?" I asked. "How she 'got' you?"

Big mistake. Because the last thing I wanted to see was the sly smile that brought to Will's face. Or hear him say, "I know exactly how she got me."

I wished I were back on a mountain.

Twelve

Frequently Asked Questions:
What does Columbia look for in a candidate?

We use a holistic review process when evaluating applicants for admission [*so if you happen to be a total loser at, say, math, we might be willing to overlook that if you have other, spectacular qualifications. Like discovering a parallel universe. That just might do it*]. That means admission to Columbia is not based on a simple formula of grades and test scores [*this better be true*].

Instead, we consider a variety of factors: the student's academic record, extracurricular interests, intellectual achievements and personal background [*Dear Professor Hawkins: If I can prove I really did it, and I can figure out all the physics so that you or anyone else can duplicate it in your lab—*

[*I'm working on it*].

Thirteen

I left Lydia and Will's house pretty soon after that. No point in sticking around just to torture myself. Plus I really wanted to try to see Halli again. Maybe I could reach her before she fell asleep.

I set up everything the way it had been this morning: same clothes, same lighting, same position in my bed with the sheets pulled up over my legs.

But I knew the key was going to be relaxing my brain. Because if I couldn't do that—couldn't be as nonchalant about it as I had been this morning—I was never going to recapture those particular vibrations again. Even if Halli were on the other end of the line waiting for me.

And that was the big question: was she? It depended on a couple of things.

First, did she like me? I know that sounds sort of first grade—"Can I play with you? Will you be my friend?"—but I had to factor it in. Because I knew that I definitely wanted to spend time with Halli again, but if she didn't feel the same way, why would she ever go to the trouble of inviting me back?

Second, if she did want me there, would she remember the steps she went through that brought me? Would she have to sit back on that exact same ledge—which might be unlikely there at 10:30 at night—and free her own mind the way I was going to try to free mine? What if she was as tense as I was, and couldn't get the same vibration as before?

And last, even if she did want me, and she could tune her mind the way she had before, there was still the question of whether that was really the secret behind it all. So far that was only a hypothesis. What if my being there this morning had nothing at all to do with my particular methods or hers, but instead was just a random, unrepeatable event?

"Come on, Halli," I mumbled as I settled into my pose. "Calling Halli . . ."

And eventually, there she was.

Fourteen

I was so friggin cold again. I have to figure out the clothes thing.

But Halli was ready for me, my same outfit laid out.

"You just disappeared," Halli told me. "Left your clothing in a heap."

Red was beside himself to see me. His whole body wagged, from shoulders to tail. I kneeled in front of him and gave him a big hug.

"Happy to see you, too, boy."

It was nighttime there, same as at home. Clear sky, brilliant stars. I tried to find the constellations I know—Orion's belt, Cassiopeia, the Big Dipper—but either I wasn't looking in the right places or they weren't there.

Which was an interesting thing to think about—did they have a completely different star system? I'd have to add that to my list of things to investigate.

While I pulled on Halli's warm layer of clothes and wrapped myself in the thick sleeping bag she'd brought out from the tent, Halli boiled water and made us hot chocolate.

"Did you know I'd come back?" I asked, gratefully accepting the mug.

"I hoped."

What a nice thing to hear.

We were by the campfire again. So she didn't have to go back out to that cliff to duplicate the experience.

I asked her what she did.

"I meditated a couple of different times today," she said. "First right after you left—"

"I tried that, too! Why didn't it work?"

But I knew why: I was too agitated.

Halli was more generous. "Maybe it was too soon. Maybe we both needed a little time."

I petted the dog, who had cozied up right beside me again. I could get used to that. I've never really been a dog person—or a cat person or any other kind of animal—but if this is what it was like, I was all for it.

I took a sip of cocoa. It was better than any I've ever tasted in my life.

Or maybe the whole experience made everything better. It's hard to express just how happy I was to be back there. I had done it again. And Halli had, too.

On purpose.

Maybe it should be obvious that a parallel version of me would want me around, but it wasn't obvious to me. I've gotten used to the kind of friendship Lydia offers: Fine to have me around, also fine not to. We don't hang out every day. We don't even talk every day. She and her family live about two blocks over, but unless Lydia and I are at school or doing something like the barbeque earlier tonight, we don't really make the effort to see each other.

I don't know how other friends do it, but that's what works for us.

So to have Halli actively want to hang out with me—twice in the same day—well, that was something new. And very special to me.

"I feel like I should ask you a million questions all at once," I said. "In case I disappear again."

"Why did that happen before?"

I explained to her about the phone, and about the steps I'd taken this time to make sure nothing would interrupt me.

"A noise was all it took?" Halli asked. She stared into the fire for a moment and considered that. "Interesting."

"Well doesn't it make sense?" I said. "If I was in a deep meditation before, then anything that would bring me out of it had to interrupt the signal."

"What did it sound like?" Halli asked. "The phone ringing. Was it loud or did it sound more muffled, like it was far away?"

"It sounded . . . I don't know, regular. Like it was right beside me, which it was."

"And when you woke up," Halli said, "what were you wearing?"

"Same thing as when I got here."

"Interesting," she said again.

Obviously I wasn't the only one trying to puzzle through how the whole thing worked.

"Do you have a theory?" I asked.

"Maybe. Let me add a little wood first."

She built up the campfire while Red and I sat watching. Sparks danced from the center as Halli plopped on a nice fat log. She used a stick to stir the coals underneath.

"I told you I'd been trying to contact my grandmother," Halli said. "You probably thought that was strange."

I saw no reason to lie. "Yes."

"She is dead," Halli said. "I saw the body. I know she's not coming back."

"Then why?" I asked. "How did you think you could speak to her?"

"Do you know anything about the ancient yogis? In India?"

"Not really." Lydia may have talked about that here and there, but it was never anything I paid attention to.

"If you read the histories," Halli said, "you find all sorts of reports of yoga masters—the saints and gurus—who reappeared to their students after death. I thought maybe . . ."

She stirred the fire again. "I don't know. It was worth a try."

"Was she a teacher?"

"She was my teacher," Halli said.

I didn't feel like I really had a grasp on our conversation. One minute we were talking about why I kept showing up places wearing just my boxers and a shirt, and the next we were talking about Indian saints and gurus reappearing after they were dead.

"You don't understand," Halli guessed.

I smiled and shook my head. "Not at all."

"We were in India, Ginny and I. We used to go there every year—I was born there. In a little town called Halli."

That explained the name. Mine would have been Yuma.

"So what were your parents doing there," I asked, "in India?"

"Saving the world, of course. But then they came to their senses and went back home and left me with Ginny."

"They just . . . left you?"

"Yes."

Wow. I *really* didn't get her life.

"So Ginny and I lived there for a while, and then we started moving around a lot, but we always came back to India once a year. She loved it there—we both did."

"I've only been to two other states in my whole life," I told Halli, a little embarrassed at my lack of adventurousness.

"And another universe," she pointed out.

"Oh." I smiled. "Yeah."

"I love traveling," Halli said, "but I also think it's good to stay in one place sometimes. That's what I've been doing lately."

She added another log to the fire. The thing was blazing now.

"So, there we were last year," she continued, "enjoying our month in India, and one day Ginny went off to her early morning prayers and she never came back. I didn't know she was dead until someone came to tell me that afternoon. And I was too sick to go see her body until the next day."

"Sick? What was wrong with you?"

"Oh. Ginny poisoned me. So I wouldn't follow her."

Fifteen

"She poisoned you?" My Grandma Marion might be critical, but she's not homicidal.

"Not enough to kill me," Halli said. "Just enough to make me sick so I'd have to stay home that day."

"Why did she want you at home?"

"Because she was going to die."

"You mean she did it on purpose?"

"No," Halli said, "but she knew. Otherwise she wouldn't have poisoned me."

Parallel universe or not, the story didn't make any sense. People didn't act that way. Unless I was right about what I thought before: maybe the humans on this planet behaved in ways completely different from what I knew.

"I'm sorry," I said. "I just don't . . . "

"Understand?" Halli finished. "Believe me, it's taken me a year to even begin to *think* I understand. I still don't know if I do. Ginny left me in a hard position. She's all I think about, sometimes."

All this time I thought it would be about me. Me making this great scientific breakthrough. Me traveling to another universe. Me meeting my alternative self. I never considered that the other me might have a whole life of her own, with her own unsolvable problems. And so far, a grandmother who tried to poison her to keep Halli from being there when the grandmother died beat out any of the petty problems I had at home.

"But," Halli said, "that's enough of all that."

"No, really, it's fine—"

"No, really," Halli said, "it's not. I've already spent too much time thinking about her. I need to think about other things."

Which pretty much meant I could forget any of my followup questions, of which there were many. Starting with, "*How did she poison you?*"

But Halli was back to figuring out me and my boxers. "Have you ever heard of bilocation?"

"Bilo . . . no, I don't think so."

"It means the ability to be in two places at once. To be there in body—in full physical form—in both locations."

"You mean like the way someone can split photons?"

"I don't know," Halli said. "Maybe. How does that work?"

"You shine a photon—it's a particle of light," I explained, "through a slit, and you split the light into two locations. They're both still part of the same photon, but now that photon is in two separate places. It's more . . . complicated than that, but that's sort of generally it."

"Okay," Halli said, "now think about doing that with your body."

I did think about it. For about five seconds. And then dismissed it. "I don't see how that would work. There's too much mass involved—no one has ever done that before."

"The ancient yogis did it," Halli said. "All the time."

She told me that according to some of the histories she's read, ancient yoga masters could appear in two places any time they wanted. Their bodies would be in meditation in one town, and would appear in front of a student in another town miles away.

"As a spirit or something?" I asked.

"No, as a full physical form. Their students could hug them, eat with them—no different than if the master was there in the room. Which he was. While he was also in deep meditation somewhere else."

Now I thought about it for more than five seconds. A campfire is good for helping organize your thoughts. I stared into the flames for a good long time and let what Halli said percolate in my brain.

"So I'm in my bedroom at home right now."

"Possibly," Halli answered.

"And I'm also here—you can see me, Red can smell me and feel me—his head isn't just passing right through my lap onto the ground."

"You're here," Halli confirmed. "You drank my cocoa."

"Wow."

"Yes, wow," she agreed.

I couldn't help but grin. "This is *way* better than I imagined. No one has *ever* done experiments like this."

"But what about what you were telling me before?" Halli said. "About the three-branes, and bridging the gap between the universes and all of that? Does this still mean you did it?"

I had to think about that. "I'm not sure. I've made contact—obviously—but I don't know if that's the same as leaving one dimension and traveling to another. That's a good question."

"Or staying in one dimension and still traveling to another," Halli pointed out.

"Wow," I said again.

"I think the next question is," Halli said, "can we make it happen both ways? Can you send yourself here, and I send myself there?"

Chills went through me, and not just because of the cold night air.

"I don't know—do you want to try?"

"Maybe you should go home first," she said. "Then we'll wait a little while and we'll try to contact each other again.

"But then you have to try to stay where you are," Halli added. "I'll focus on coming to you."

"I can't believe we're even talking about this."

Now it was Halli's turn to grin. "Fun, isn't it?"

Sixteen

The first thing I had to do was clean my room. It's one thing to let Lydia see it the way it normally is, but let my genetic double from another world see what a slob I am? No way.

I did what I could in half an hour, which is when we agreed we'd try again. Even though I told Halli it might take me a while to get into the meditation. It seems the harder I try to relax my brain, the harder it is to do.

But finally, sometime after midnight, I felt a pinch on my left big toe. I opened my eyes.

"Heya," Halli said.

She looked around my room. The lighting was low so I could get in the meditative mood, but even with bad light you could still see the place was pretty shabby.

Halli wore the outfit I'd last seen her in at the campfire—her gray hiking pants, the blue sweater, and her dusty boots.

"Where's Red?" I asked.

"If we're right about this," Halli said, "he's still curled up on top of my sleeping bag, right next to me in the tent. He shouldn't even know I'm gone."

"It's stupid, but I was kind of hoping—"

"I could bring him?" Halli said. "I know—I actually tried. I thought about him the whole time. Obviously that's not enough."

It's amazing how disappointed I was. "Oh, well. Maybe we can try again."

"You don't have a dog?" Halli asked.

"Never really wanted one before."

Halli got up from my bed and started looking around.

I cringed a little. "It's pretty messy."

"Don't worry," she said. "I've seen a lot of places."

She tilted her head to read the spines of books above my desk. "*Physics I, Physics II, Phun With Physics, Physics is Phun*—I can see why you know so much."

"Oh, those are from when I was a kid." I pointed to the bookcase in the corner, its shelves sagging under all the newer books by Professor Hawkins and a bunch of other quantum physicists. "That's mostly what I read now."

Halli gave me a look like she was impressed.

"What do you read?" I asked.

"Mostly the explorers," she said. "Savage, Thayer, Shackleton, Monroe—that's all I've ever really been interested in. I've probably read hundreds of them by now."

The only name that sounded familiar was Shackleton. And I wasn't sure why. Had he discovered some island? I'd have to look it up.

But it couldn't be the same guy. Just a similar name in a different universe.

Halli made a half-turn toward my closet, then very generously pretended she hadn't seen it. It's gotten so bad I can't even close the door on it all the way. It's crammed with every piece of clothing I've worn since probably fourth grade. I have to get around to weeding that out one day. It's just never been a priority.

"Can I see the rest of your house?" Halli asked.

"Sure! Of course!" I said with false enthusiasm. Of course she wanted to see more—wouldn't I, in her place? And of course that hadn't occurred to me before. The house was a total wreck.

I just hoped she lived in a place not so different from mine. Because mine was kind of a dump.

It's not my mom's fault—or mine. We've just had to make do. We've lived in this same house since I was little—since the year my mom and Elena started working together, when Will and Lydia and I were four. My parents moved to Tucson because of my dad's job at the time, and even though that didn't last very long, they decided we should stay.

We've kept the same furniture since then. For thirteen years. My mom's pretty good at sewing, so everything gets fresh slipcovers every now and then. She and I also go through these periods where we feel like repainting everything, including the walls and the cupboards and tables and chairs and anything made of wood—but generally the house looks like what it is: a two-bedroom, one-bath place where a mother and her daughter live together and hardly ever invite anyone to visit.

But Halli was very nice about it. "This place is really sweet. I like how cozy it is. Do you live here alone?"

That was sort of an odd question. "No, my mom, too." And then I remembered something Halli's mother had asked in their quick conversation: *"When are you going home?"* Not "coming" home, but going.

Halli lowered her voice to a whisper. "Is she sleeping? Can I see her?"

"Who, my mom? No, she's away on business right now."

Halli's mood immediately darkened. "Oh. Of course. You said she was like mine."

"No—I mean, she does live here, she just has to travel a lot lately. For her work."

"Of course," Halli said. "Right."

I felt like I should have done a better job of defending my mother. But the truth is she has been traveling a lot lately—what else was I supposed to say?

I changed the subject. "Do you live alone?"

"Now," Halli said. "Before I was always with Ginny."

"Where do your parents live?"

"In Seattle."

"Where do you live?" I asked.

"Colorado. A little town called River Grove. It's not far from that mountain where I'm camped right now."

Which only served to remind me of how other-worldly this whole situation was. Halli was here with me, but not really. Or yes really, but also someplace else.

"What about you?" Halli asked. "Where are we?"

"Tucson. Arizona."

She smiled. "Ginny and I went to Arizona once. It was hot."

"Yeah," I said, "that's basically it."

Halli kept on wandering through the house. At the far end of the living room she paused in front of our wall of pictures. Five framed collections of a bunch of snapshots from when I was little up until a few years ago. My mom and I haven't gotten around to adding any of the new ones. Not that there are too many exciting photos to add. Most of them are the same old stuff—us over at some barbeque at Lydia and Will's, us opening a few gifts on our birthdays or at Christmas—the usual. Yawn.

But Halli was fascinated.

She spent time in front of each picture. She especially studied the ones with my mom and me.

She pointed to a snapshot of the two of us standing outside our house. I was probably around eight or nine.

"They look almost exactly alike," Halli said, peering closely at my mother. "Maybe a little different around the eyes?"

"Yeah, maybe," I said. I didn't want to insult her mother, but the truth is I do think mine is prettier.

Halli continued to study the photos. "Who are they?" she asked, pointing to a picture of Lydia and Will and me at one of our moms' fundraising events when we were in junior high.

I gave her the brief rundown—best friend, best friend's twin brother—just the basics. I didn't feel like I should really get into the personal stuff. Not because I didn't trust Halli, but just because I didn't really know her. Which is a weird thing to say about your exact parallel self.

Halli worked her way through the rest of the photos. When she came to the last set she said, "You don't have any of your grandmother?"

"Um, not up there." Because really, my mother and I don't need reminding. We know she's out there. Her phone calls are intrusion enough—we don't want to have to look at her every day on top of that.

But of course Halli would want to see her—it reminded her of Ginny. I pulled out a couple of photo albums where I knew Grandma Marion made an appearance.

"Here." I pointed to a picture of her wearing a bathing suit and big sunglasses. Her hair was all puffy and hairsprayed. That's why she always refuses to go in the water—doesn't want to ruin her hair. Or her makeup. Or her jewelry.

"Where is this?" Halli asked.

"My grandmother's community pool."

"Oh." I wasn't sure if she understood what I meant, but she was already flipping the page to other photos.

"And where's this one?"

I looked over her shoulder. "This dress store she really likes. She was trying to get me to try stuff on." I quickly flipped the page. I didn't need reminding of that particular trip. Grandma Marion made my mom and me shop with her practically every day.

Halli pressed her hand against the new page. "My father," she said, smoothing the plastic over the photo so she could see him better. "How old are you here?"

"I don't know, maybe eleven?" I was surprised that photo was in there. My parents were divorced by then. It was my first summer visitation—two weeks with him and the girlfriend he had at the time, at my dad's new house in San Diego.

The picture was of my dad and me at the zoo. We were in the bird display. I had some birdseed on my open palm, and a big bird of some kind sat on my shoulder ready to hop down and peck my fingers off. I didn't look very happy. But my dad gave the camera his best charmer smile while his girlfriend took our picture.

"It's so strange," Halli said, studying my father. "I know our parents are the same, but still . . ."

"I know," I agreed. "It's weird."

"Do you like him? Your father?"

"Yeah, I guess. Sure." Aside from the string of obnoxious girlfriends and the fact that he never pays child support on time. But I didn't feel the need to say that to Halli.

She flipped through both albums, searching for any photos of my Grandma Marion. There weren't many. And I'm pretty sure that the more Halli saw of my grandmother, the less she was reminded of her own.

Finally Halli closed both books. She seemed a little deflated.

"Do you have anything to eat?" she asked. "I'm starved."

Snacks are something we always have. My mom and I live off of Doritos.

I took Halli into the kitchen and pulled out a fresh bag of them from the cupboard.

"What's that?"

"Tortilla chips."

"What's the . . . orange on them?"

"Cheesy . . . something," I said.

"Oh." Halli gazed past me into the cupboard. She shifted a few things around to see the stuff in the back.

"Do you mind if I make pancakes?" she asked.

Uh, did I mind if someone actually cooked real food? Our kitchen might never recover from the shock.

While I sat at our yellow table (my mom's and my most recent repainting project), Halli measured and mixed, heated and poured, cooked and flipped.

"Would you grab that peanut butter I saw in there?" she asked. "And the syrup?"

Peanut butter and syrup? She was from a different universe.

She rooted around in cupboards and drawers until she found plates and a supply of utensils. I loved how comfortable she felt in my kitchen—I never would have been able to do that in someone else's.

Finally she sliced up two bananas, and then laid out our whole feast.

"Do you have anything hot to drink?"

"Um, there's coffee," I said. I showed her the giant can of instant my mother buys at the warehouse store.

Halli lifted the lid and gave it a sniff. "Eck. Disgusting. We're better than this."

That made me laugh.

"What?" she said. "It's true."

She sat down across the table from me, then forked the first three pancakes off the stack for herself. She smeared each one with peanut butter, dotted them with banana slices, restacked them, then poured syrup over the whole concoction.

And before she could take even one bite, she completely disappeared.

Seventeen

I tried to get her back for the next hour, but eventually I couldn't keep my eyes open any longer. I fell asleep sitting up in bed.

By the time I woke up this morning, there were already four messages on my cell phone. Which made me feel a little guilty, since they were all from my mom, but also a little pleased with myself, because not one of them had interrupted my session with Halli last night.

"Hi, honey," she said when I called her back. "I've been trying you since last night—"

"I know—I'm sorry. I shut off my phone early. I was just really, really tired."

"How are things?" she asked.

"Good, good. I went over to Will and Lydia's last night . . ." and then I filled her in on the rest. Minus any of the juicier parts, like having to resist stabbing Gemma in the forehead with Elena's sewing needle, and the fact that I'd had a huge scientific breakthrough that involved my body appearing in two places at the same time.

Some things are just too weird to say over the phone.

When I finally hung up, I had to ask myself: When am I going to tell her? And what am I going to say?

But the answers were *not today*, and *I'll figure it out later*.

For now I had more important things to worry about.

I took a shower and then put on my robe while I tried to decide what to wear. I couldn't keep relying on Halli to dress me. Somewhere in that closet I had to have something that was suitable to wear on a mountain top.

I changed into jeans, a long-sleeved flannel shirt that used to be my dad's (how long had that been in there?), the thickest socks I could find, and some old tennis shoes. At the last minute I added my only winter coat—I wasn't sure what the weather was going to be like over there today. It would be better to come prepared.

And then I assumed the position on my bed, headphones on, and tried to slip back into the groove.

When I got there, Halli's camp was in shambles.

Eighteen

"What happened?"

"I'm hoping you can tell me," Halli said.

The door to her tent had been shredded. The whole thing hung there in ribbons.

"Hi, boy, happy to see you, too," I said absent-mindedly as the dog whirled and jumped in pleasure. "Who did this?" I asked Halli.

She pointed at Red.

"What? Why?"

"All I know," Halli said, "is I was sitting with you there in your kitchen, and the next moment I hear this poor dog howling his lungs out, tearing around the camp like a wild thing."

"Why?" I asked. "Do you know?"

"The only thing I can figure out," Halli said, "is that Red woke up at some point last night and realized I was gone. Which means maybe it isn't really bilocation—maybe we both traveled with our whole bodies yesterday."

I sat down next to the waning coals of the fire. "Wait a minute—I have to think."

"Well, think about this, too: ever since Ginny died, Red can't stand to be away from me. I think he feels his pack went from three to two, and he's not going to lose another one."

"Do dogs really think that way?" I asked.

"Sure they do," Halli said. "They can count. At least to that extent."

"Has he ever done something like this before?"

"Twice," Halli said, "before I learned my lesson. I left him alone in an apartment once while I ran out to talk to someone on the street, and by the time I got back—maybe five or ten minutes later—he'd completely ripped through the whole apartment, knocking things over, digging into the carpet, and I could hear him howling as I came up the stairs. Just like last night."

"So wait," I said, trying to get a grip on the whole thing. "So you heard him somehow—from my house. From my universe."

"No, I didn't. Not until I came back."

"But then why did that make you disappear from my house? How did it break the connection?"

"That's what I'm asking you," she said.

Halli went back to packing up her things. I noticed she'd already put all the cookware away, probably somewhere into her backpack. We wouldn't be enjoying a leisurely cup of tea this morning.

I also noticed that I'd been successful in showing up with all my clothes—all the way down to the heavy coat. But once again, just like the previous two times, my headphones never made it.

I wondered if that was because they had metal in them. But why should that matter?

I had a lot to think about. Starting with Red's reaction.

"It just doesn't make sense," I told Halli. "You must have heard him somehow. It's like when Lydia called me on the phone yesterday—I thought I heard it ring while I was still here. In fact, I'm sure I did—didn't I?"

Now that I thought about it, I couldn't really remember.

"Like I said," Halli repeated, "maybe I was wrong. Maybe we didn't bilocate. Maybe each of us came all the way over."

I stood up and started pacing. "But that's so much mass!" I told her. "Do you know how hard that would be? You're talking about taking a whole human body and somehow transporting it across two separate three-branes—"

"Maybe there aren't really three-branes," Halli pointed out. "Didn't you say that was just a theory?"

"Yeah, but . . ."

Yeah, but what? Wasn't that the whole point of theories? You throw them out there for other scientists to pick apart and prove whether you're right or wrong.

But it couldn't be. I wasn't going to be the person to prove Professor Hawkins wrong. As between the two of us, who was more likely not to understand the intricacies of parallel universes and cyclic cosmology? Obviously I was the one who was confused.

Red had been watching me, nervously, the whole time I paced around. I felt bad for the guy—he'd already been through enough. I sat back down and let him snuggle up to me while I petted his fur and thought.

And one of the thoughts was random.

"Why does he act this way toward me, do you think?"

Halli shrugged. "New toy. Another member of his pack—could be a lot of different reasons. Red is his own dog."

"Did he howl yesterday when I disappeared?"

Halli thought about it for a second. "No."

I tried not to let that hurt my feelings.

"Did he look for me?" I asked. "Act like he even noticed I was gone?"

"He did look for you," Halli assured me. "But he seemed to take it in stride."

"Huh." I wasn't sure what that meant, either, or if it were even connected. The whole thing was a puzzle.

I finally realized I'd been sitting there or pacing around instead of helping Halli pack up. "Can I do anything?"

Halli paused and rolled her shoulders. It gave me a chance to notice how much wider than mine they really are. Her whole body is like Audie 2.0—like she popped out of a larger, more muscular mold.

"Just talk to me, I guess," she said. "It's nice to have the company."

I stayed there for a couple of hours, throwing the stick for Red, batting around ideas with Halli. Even when someone doesn't know physics, it can still be helpful to brainstorm with them. So much of physics relies on practical questions about how the world works. And Halli had a great one.

"Why did my clothes stay here?" she asked.

"Huh?" I picked up the stick where Red had dropped it. That dog was tireless in the pursuit of fetch.

"The clothes I let you borrow yesterday," Halli said. "When you left—both times—they stayed here."

"Huh. I don't know. That's a good point." I told her about my headphones. Neither of us understood why.

But the main question—the one we kept going around and around about—was why Red reacted the way he did. The only possible conclusion was that Halli had disappeared. Or had changed in some way that radically upset the dog.

"Maybe you glowed or something," I guessed. "Or made some sort of vibrating noise."

Nothing seemed too implausible.

"Is there any way we can test it?" Halli asked.

"I could film myself," I said. What a weird thing that would be to see—me sitting there on my bed one moment, then *blip*, gone the next. I had the feeling that might just freak me out.

"Or I can," Halli said. "Set up a holonet. But that would still only answer it from my side—we should both probably do it."

"But what about Red?" I said. "If you really disappear—"

"You're right," Halli answered. "I can't put the poor boy through that again. Can I, Red?" She pulled the dog into her side and gave him a hearty pat. Red looked up at her with what can only be described as joy. That dog loved his girl.

I couldn't take her away from him—even for science. Not until we really understood what was going on.

We made a plan for later in the evening. Halli was done packing up her camp, and seemed anxious to go.

"It's four or five hours down to the base," she explained. "Then the drive. I'd like to be home before dark."

"What time do you think it is right now?" I asked.

Halli looked up at the sky. "Around 11:00, I'd say."

"You don't have a watch?"

She shrugged. "Don't need one."

"You can tell the time from the sky?" I asked.

"Usually. Within about half an hour. Unless it's overcast—then I have to try a few other tricks."

"Does your screen tell time?"

"My screen?" Halli thought for a moment, then said, "Oh, the tab—the tablet. It has a time feature. But I'm not really keen to turn it on. You saw what happened yesterday."

"Oh. With your mother."

"I usually try to stay off the comm field."

"The what?"

"Oh, sorry," Halli said, "communications. I keep forgetting you're not from here."

"Communications field," I said. "Is that anything like the Internet?"

"The what?"

"I should make up a dictionary," I said. "Cross-reference some of our words." The idea suddenly sounded great. "Wow—I could do a whole anthropological study over here." Wouldn't Columbia love that?

"You should read the histories first," Halli said. "Save yourself some time."

There was so much to do, so much to figure out. My brain felt fuller than it ever has.

"So I'll see you, then?" Halli asked, shouldering her pack. She whistled for Red. Instead of coming, he sat down in front of me and waited patiently for me to throw the stick.

"Maybe you should leave first," Halli said. "Make it easier."

"I'm not sure if I know how," I said.

"You did it last night," Halli pointed out. "When we decided to meet back at your house."

I hadn't even thought of that. At the time I'd been so excited about the prospect of her coming to my universe—and wondering whether that would actually work—I didn't even notice how I got home. It felt as natural to me as saying goodbye to Lydia or Will and walking or driving away.

So I decided to go with that.

"Okay, then, see ya," I said, trying to act and feel casual. La-dee-da, going back to my own universe now.

"Say goodbye, Red," Halli said.

The dog held up a paw, and I was gone.

Nineteen

Halli was right about the time. It was a little after eleven when I got back.

Just enough time to shower, change into something special, and get to the office by noon.

Where a certain computer programmer was scheduled to be.

"Hey," I said as I walked in.

"Hey." Will didn't look up. He sat there in his dark khaki cargo shorts and plain black T-shirt furiously typing in code. His hair was all messy and his face was shadowed with stubble. He looked *so* good.

"I brought you some cereal," I said. Will's favorite food. Day or night.

He leaned back in the chair and stretched his neck and shoulders. I handed him the supplies I'd brought from home: bowl, spoon, Cap'n Crunch, milk.

Will sighed deeply and dug in.

I forced my eyes away from him and onto the computer screen. "How's it looking?" I asked.

"Like they should have believed me two years ago and bought new computers back then."

"Ugh. Don't say that. We can't afford it." As *Build a Fund for Good*'s resident bookkeeper, I knew what I was talking about.

"There comes a point when you just have to put them out of their misery," Will said. "Face it, Aud, the time has come."

I love it when he calls me Aud. Even if it sounds like Odd.

"Don't worry," he said, chewing a mouthful of sugar and crunch, "I'll get 'em cheap for you guys."

"Thanks, Will."

"Thanks for the cereal."

Two more massive spoonfuls, then he handed me back the bowl and got back to work.

And as I stood there behind him, I don't think it's unreasonable to say I wanted more than anything to kiss the back of his neck where the tips of his black hair were curling ever so slightly, and then throw the bowl aside, twist his chair around, and plant my mouth against his and maybe not come up for air until we both turned 21.

Instead I settled for this: I walked into the kitchen to rinse out the bowl, but didn't quite rinse out the spoon. Instead . . . I licked it.

I KNOW! SHUT UP! Completely gross and unsanitary and pathetic, and if the Columbia admissions people ever found out about it, they'd ban me for life. But I'm sorry, it's the closest I might ever come to kissing Will. I've been doing stuff like this for years—licking around a cup I know he drank from, reusing a fork I know was his—all these sad, ridiculous attempts to be closer to his lips.

It's so humiliating I can't even believe I do it. If he ever caught me, I'd shrivel up and die. But I still do it. It's worth the risk.

Because here's the thing about Will:

No, here's the thing about me:

I have been in deep, desperate love with that guy since he was a four-year-old boy riding his Big Wheel around his driveway. And not just because I wished we could have afforded a Big Wheel.

He's amazing-looking, yes. Lots of guys are. The thing I love about Will is his heart.

He hasn't taken a paycheck from our mothers for years, even though he's always done all the computer programming and maintenance since we were in sixth grade. He says he doesn't need their money—he makes enough from his consulting business. Besides, whatever he made from our moms, he'd probably feel compelled to give back at the end of the year as part of his annual Day of Philanthropy.

Will doesn't just set aside ten percent for charity, like many generous people. And not just twenty percent, like *really* generous people. Will is a fifty-percenter. He keeps half for himself—for fast food, the occasional item of clothing, and now dates with the wonderful Gemma—and gives all the rest away.

He opened his first checking account when we were eight. And ever since then, he accumulates whatever money he receives during the year—whether from birthdays or Christmas or neighborhood yard work or now his thriving business—and every December he writes out three huge checks to the charities of his choice.

He's helped establish schools for girls in Niger. Paid for a water and sewage system in a small village in India. Helped equip a medical facility in Guatemala. Sent an Albanian widow to nursing school.

And the best part—or the worst, depending on whether you agree with him (Lydia does not)—is that Will does all of it anonymously. He had our moms set up a private account for him through *Build a Fund for Good*, and the checks come from that account without Will's name on them. So every year three lucky people or organizations get checks for them ranging from $40 (when Will was eight) to $6,000 apiece (last year), with an anonymous note asking them to continue doing good in this world.

How could you not love a guy like that?

I have the feeling Gemma doesn't know. And I have a pretty good feeling if she did, she'd think it was stupid. Which is another reason I hate her. She doesn't even know how great of a guy she has.

Will's one of those people you wish could be in charge of the world. He's also the kind of guy who would never want to put himself in that position. He likes doing good in secret. He's like that old man in Cincinnati or wherever who dresses up like Santa every year and goes around handing out cash to homeless people.

Thanks to the invention of fire, no one will ever know how many notebooks I've filled over the years with stupid, pathetic love notes and poems and even songs (they are so, so bad) about William Aristotle Stamos-Valadez. Or how many thousands of times I've written "Audie Stamos-Valadez. Mrs. Will Stamos-Valadez. Dr. Audie Masters Stamos-Valadez." That takes up a lot of paper, let me tell you.

But if Will were ever doing that—ever matching my name to his—he'd probably think of it as recognizing me for who I am to him: another sister. I'm smart enough to see me versus Gemma. Me versus Lucy, the girl he dated before Gemma. Me versus any other girl in the universe.

Which makes me wonder: would he feel the same way if he ever met Halli? Would he be like Red is with me—just give her a sniff and accept her, and right away start treating her as if she were me? Or would he see her the way I wish he would see me?

So many questions. So many possibilities. That's why I love science.

Too bad science can't really love me back.

But then it's not like I've been writing "Mrs. Audie Masters-Science" in my notebooks all my life.

Will glanced at his watch. "I gotta go. Got a client on the east side."

"So they're . . . still not fixed?"

"I'll get you some new computers by Tuesday," Will said. "Promise. Cheap," he added before I could ask.

"Okay, thanks." *Thanks and I love you. Thanks and please dump Gemma. Thanks and did you notice I'm wearing your company shirt? The one with the sick computer with the thermometer in his mouth, next to the strong computer flexing his big computer muscles?*

"I'm wearing your shirt," I said, pointing to it. *Because I am a DORK.*

"Oh, yeah," Will said with a smile.

"How come you never wear yours anymore?" I asked. "When you're out on repair calls?"

"Gemma said it looks stupid."

HAIRBALL.

Twenty

Halli and I planned on meeting at 7:00 tonight. I had a few hours before that, and decided to spend them as productively as I could—diving back into Hawkins.

So much of what I'd read in his new parallel universe book had just seemed academic at the time. Interesting, but not specifically relevant to my life.

Now I read it like it was an instruction manual.

I went back to the section that had started me down this path in the first place—the part where his colleague had made that comment about vibrations.

Here was the section:

"After a long morning of listening to various presentations at the conference, several of us decided to go out to lunch to relax and discuss what we had heard. The mood was rather jovial; it might surprise people to learn that physicists can be a fun lot when we decide to let down our hair.

"Among the group were my colleagues from Columbia University, Drs. Anspaugh and Steglow, and a rather humorous fellow from a little college out west, a Dr. Whitfield, a man to whom I had been introduced several years before, and whom I knew always to be good for a laugh.

"And once again, Dr. Whitfield did not disappoint.

"As our quartet discussed some of the ramifications of the current research on superstring theory, M-theory, and three-branes, Dr. Whitfield suggested that we look for a solution to all three by attempting to coordinate the vibrational pattern of the superstrings with that of any vibrational field that might divide one universe or one dimension from the next.

"After all of us had a good laugh I asked him, 'And how would you propose to do that, Skip?' He said he would leave it to 'the greater minds of my colleagues to the east,' and asked if we would mind paying for his lunch since he had forgotten his wallet back at the hotel. As I said, the man never disappoints."

And that was all Professor Hawkins had to say about Dr. Whitfield.

I flipped to the index on all the rest of all of Professor Hawkins's books, but couldn't find any more mention of Dr. Whitfield. I did a quick Internet search, and found him: a physicist and neuropsychologist with degrees from the Universities of Montana and Colorado and also Yale, and currently teaching at a tiny little college called Mountain State in what looked like the equally-tiny town of Bear Creek, Colorado.

There was a photo of him on the college website. He looked about my mom's age, and more like a lumberjack than a physicist with his red flannel shirt and short brown beard. His faculty bio said in addition to teaching physics, he also taught a course on backcountry skiing.

What was a guy like that doing hanging out with Dr. Herbert Hawkins—one of the most famous and respected physicists in the world? Maybe it was like Professor Hawkins said: he invited Dr. Whitfield along as comic relief.

But the thing is, Dr. Whitfield had been right—the secret really did lie in vibrations. Was that just a lucky guess?

By now it was almost 6:00, and I needed to get ready for the evening.

I had a little dinner, checked in with my mom, and then dug out our old camcorder from the closet. Last time I checked it still worked, although the battery life has always been pretty iffy. The most I could really count on was about thirty minutes of recording. Which meant I had to wait until the last possible minute to turn it on, and then hope I could quickly relax and get to the right vibration before time ran out. No pressure there.

Next came dressing for the evening. I wasn't sure how cold it would be where Halli lived—it was still in the mountains—so I donned my same outfit from the morning: flannel shirt, jeans, big coat, thick socks, the whole business.

At about 6:50 I set up the camcorder on my desk and aimed it at my bed. Then I stuck my headphones on, took a deep breath, and pressed Record to start the filming. I sat back against my pillows, closed my eyes, and tried to relax into the proper wavelength.

I was so deep into meditation I didn't notice I was there until I heard her snicker.

"Warm enough?" Halli asked.

She was dressed in purple flannel pajamas and red fuzzy socks. And sitting on a celery green couch with a white blanket and a big yellow dog draped over her lap.

She lost the dog right away.

"I missed you, too, Red!" I laughed as he tackled me flat on the wooden floor. Somehow I had landed there instead of on the really soft, cushy-looking lavender chair right next to Halli. I have to work on that.

But the floor actually felt heated, which I didn't even know was possible, so it really wasn't bad at all. If you didn't count the hundred pounds of wagging, licking dog on top of me.

"Red, that's enough," Halli told him. "Off."

And off he went. He sat in front of me instead, just panting and wagging.

Now that I was free again, I could look around. I got up and brushed the dog hair off my chest.

"You can take your coat off," Halli said. "You probably won't need it."

I left it on the lavender chair, then kept on wandering.

It was a large wooden cabin, two stories high, sparsely furnished and exactly the kind of home where I'd love to live in my own or any other universe.

"This place is amazing," I told Halli.

"Thank you. But really, it's Ginny's. She left it to me."

"She left it to you? You mean you own it?"

Halli nodded.

I almost said, "You're lucky!" but then realized how awful that would sound since the only reason it had passed to Halli was that her grandmother had died. I swallowed that sentence and instead went with, "Can I look around?"

"Sure," she said. "I did at your house."

As if there were any comparison between her house and mine, other than the fact that they both had floors and ceilings and walls.

Start with that—the walls. Every available inch of them covered in maps: maps of cities, maps of countries, hiking maps that looked like they'd been rained on and stepped on and stuffed into pockets.

"Have you been all these places?" I asked.

"Ginny and me."

Over between the twin bookcases there was a huge map of the world, and it had colored dots all over it which I assumed must be places they'd been. The map was so covered with them, it would have been easier to figure out where they *hadn't* been.

I dragged my eyes away from the walls and took in the rest of the place. The bottom floor was one continuous room, living room on one end, kitchen on the other. There was a staircase about midway through the room, and a short hallway leading away from the base of it.

There wasn't much furniture in the living room. Just the couch, the chair, a low table, two large bookcases filled to capacity, a few rugs, a few lamps. In the kitchen there was one long counter with all sorts of shiny silver boxes sitting side by side, and a small square table with two wooden chairs.

I started down the hallway, but then turned to Halli to make sure it was okay. Red was back on her lap. She scratched him behind the ear and waved me on.

There were two doors, one on the right and one on the left. I chose the right door first: a bathroom. But really, heaven.

The room was huge—almost as big as the kitchen. And she needed all that space, because inside that one room there were: a claw-foot bathtub, a separate glass shower the size of an old-fashioned phone booth, a chaise lounge-looking chair with a reading table next to it, a bronze sink balanced on top of a log (the faucet was shaped like a swan. Water poured out of its beak. I checked), a little garden patch with a fountain and ferns and some plant I've never seen with heart-shaped leaves, two hooks holding a white terry cloth robe and a blue satin one, and two more hooks holding the softest, thickest towels I've ever touched.

"Can I live in your bathroom?" I shouted.

"Sure," Halli shouted back. "I'll stock it with food."

I could eat her pancakes while I floated in the tub. Our tub at home is so small I can only lie down with half my body in the water. I have to switch off between shoulders and feet. So yeah, I'll probably be moving into Halli's bathtub just as soon as I can figure out the logistics.

I left my future living quarters and strayed across the hall to the other room. A bedroom—Halli's, I guessed, based on the yellow hair on top of her dark red bedspread.

Not much furniture in there, either. Just the bed, a short bookcase beside it, a lamp on top of that, and a wooden desk and chair. Halli's screen—her tablet—was sitting on top of the desk.

Halli and Red appeared in the doorway.

"I love this whole house," I said. "It's so clean and beautiful."

"Thanks. I really love it here, too. I think it's my favorite out of all of them."

"All of what?" I asked.

"Ginny's houses."

"Hold on," I said. "There are others?"

"Five," Halli answered, plopping belly-down on her bed. Red hopped up to join her.

"Five more? You have six houses total?"

"And some apartments," Halli said. "Ginny lived all over the world even before I came along. It made it easier for her to have someplace to live in the places where she went the most often."

"India?" I asked.

"Yes, and Switzerland, Iceland, Germany—a few other places."

Something had been bothering me for a while now. It was time to solve at least one mystery.

"Yesterday when you were telling me about your dot, and how people can track you, you said the government keeps track in case you commit a crime or you're lost on Everest."

"Yes."

"Why is it called Everest here? Why do you have an India and an Iceland and a Switzerland, same as us? If the people's names here are different, why aren't the places, too?"

"I don't know," Halli said. "That's a good question."

"And Colorado," I added. "We have that."

"Do you have a River Grove?" she said, naming her town.

"I don't know," I answered. "I'll have to check." I should have thought of that before. "Hey, do you have someplace called Bear Creek here? Or Mountain State College?"

"No, I don't think so. I haven't heard of either of those."

I was about to start going down a whole list—"Do you have Yale? Do you have Columbia? Is there a New York City? Is there a Herbert Hawkins?"—but Halli held up her hand.

"Food," she said. "We need food first. Did you have dinner yet?"

I thought of the bowl of Cap'n Crunch I'd had at home, in honor of Will. I don't even like that cereal. I'm more of a Cocoa Puffs kind of girl.

"Um, not really," I said.

"Good," Halli answered. "I'll make us something nice."

I was just about to follow her out when I noticed the door inside her room. "Is that your closet?"

"Yes."

"Can I look?"

Halli shrugged. "Sure."

I slid open the door and looked inside. Wow.

One dress. One skirt. Two blouses. Three pairs of shoes—including the hiking boots I'd already seen her in. One shelf for T-shirts, one for pants and shorts. That. Was. It.

"Where are the rest of your clothes?" I asked. "This can't be everything."

"Most of it," Halli said. "I like to travel lightly."

"But . . . there has to be more." There was no way she could live her life, traveling all over the world, and have that closet—while I, who rarely leave the house, have the mess that's mine.

"There is a little more," Halli said. "Coats, outdoor gear—those are all up in Ginny's room. But for day to day, yes, this is it. I mostly just wear the same thing all the time—don't you?"

She had a point. And the very thought of my closet right now was starting to make me sick. Definitely my next project.

"I feel like eating kiwi," Halli said. "How does that sound?"

"You have kiwi? See what I'm saying? It's all the same here."

"What did you think it would be like?" Halli asked.

"I don't know, flying cars, six-legged animals, people with three eyes—I'm not really sure."

"And instead . . ." Halli sighed dramatically, ". . . you just get me. And Red."

He thumped his tail at the shout-out.

"Food," Halli said. "Right now. We'll figure out the universes later."

And if I thought our worlds were too similar, I was about to see how wrong I could be.

Hint: there was no Cap'n Crunch.

Twenty-one

"Come pick out what you'd like," Halli said. I followed her into the kitchen. But instead of stopping there, opening up some cupboards or a refrigerator (she didn't even have a fridge, as far as I could tell), Halli led me through a door at the side of the kitchen. We stepped out into a cold walkway with bare white walls and a plain stone floor, and stood outside another door.

It turns out Ginny hadn't left Halli just one house on that piece of property, she'd left her two. We were about to enter the second one.

"We leave our shoes here," Halli said, even though she was wearing just her fuzzy red socks. She slipped on a pair of black fabric clogs sitting at the side of the door. "You can wear those."

I took off my sneakers and stepped into the second pair of clogs, and realized they must have been Ginny's. Which felt a little weird. I've never worn a dead person's clothes before.

I told myself to pretend they were my Grandma Marion's shoes, but that didn't really help. She has some really gnarled up feet from wearing high heels too much when she was young. Every time I look at her feet I feel all the more attached to wearing flat shoes the rest of my life. I wasn't too psyched about wearing anything her human foot-claws might have been inside.

I know, I'm a really awful person.

Halli opened the door to the second house. And a wave of warm, moist, earthy air met me in the face.

It was a jungle. And an orchard. And a tomato patch and a vegetable garden and a farm, all contained in a two-story house the exact size of the one we'd just left.

What took a long time for my eyes to adjust to was the verticality of it all. Plants weren't just growing in pots and tubs and other containers sitting on the ground, they were also vining down and climbing up, and hanging from boxes and poles that went all the way to the second-floor ceiling. I had no idea how someone would harvest those pea pods I saw way, way up at the top, or how someone thought it would be safe to have bananas growing high above where we walked. It made me want to duck and hurry on.

"What is this place?" I asked.

"The greenhouse. Don't you have things like this?"

"Maybe some people do—I have no idea. I've never seen anything like this in my life."

Halli picked up a woven basket with a handle, and handed me another one just like it.

"Look around," she said. "Take whatever you like. We'll go back and cook it up or make juice or soup out of it or whatever you want."

I wasn't about to go through that fruit and vegetable megamart and just start picking things off their stems. I waited to see how Halli did it.

She went first to the peach tree in the far corner, picked a few of those, then kept on going down the fruit plants. Kiwi, apple, strawberries off their ground-hugging vines, then Halli pulled a cord above her and the column of plants above started moving. As soon as the bananas were within reach, she picked one of those.

"Want one?" she asked.

"Yeah." I couldn't believe what I was seeing. And for Halli it all seemed perfectly normal.

She threw me a banana and picked another, then sent the column back on its way.

"Vegetables?" she asked.

"Sure."

It was like being in the lunch line at school, only the food here actually had colors found in nature.

Halli gathered up big green leaves from a bunch of different plants—I only recognized the lettuce. Then she picked a tomato, a cucumber, some sweet peas (same trick with the cord, making the peas up at the ceiling come to her), and pulled two small carrots out of the dirt by their frilly green heads.

"It smells so good in here," I said.

Halli took a deep breath. "I know. I like to sleep in here sometimes."

"You do?"

She pointed to a pad, pillow, and blanket under one of the planting benches. "I don't do it very often. Red doesn't really like it in here—I think it's too warm for him. You notice he didn't follow us."

I looked around. She was right.

"But he'll sleep in here with you anyway?"

"Poor boy," Halli said, "he hates to be alone. Think we have enough here?"

I looked at the two baskets. Halli had piled a lot of the greens in mine since hers was so full of the fruit.

"I think so."

We were about to leave when finally something penetrated my attention: a sound, so soft I hadn't consciously noticed it until now.

"What is that?" I asked, pointing at the ceiling. Halli looked up to see which plant. "No, the sound—is it music?"

"A combination of music and timed oscillations," Halli said. "The plants really seem to love it."

"What's the music?" I asked. "I mean, does it have a name?"

"Something by Mozart," she said. "I'm not sure which one this is."

I grabbed her arm. "You have Mozart."

"Had," Halli said. "He's been dead a long time."

Now I was getting excited. "Shakespeare? Did you have him?"

"Yes."

"And . . . Beethoven?"

"Yes."

"What about . . . " My brain was freezing up in all the excitement—why weren't these names coming to me? "How about Isaac Newton?"

"I think so."

"And Albert Einstein?"

That one seemed a little harder. "I . . . think so," Halli said. "We can check the histories. After dinner."

But one more name, coming from the opposite direction. "Who's the President here right now?"

"Nye."

"What's he look like?" Maybe since Halli and I were the same person, just with different names, it was the same for the President of the United States. Then I could just work backwards and figure out when all the names started changing.

But Halli blew that theory away by answering, "She. It's Angela Nye. Tall, dark hair—"

"Wait a minute—your President is a woman?"

Halli gave me a strange look. "Of course."

"That's so cool! Is she the first one, or have there been others?"

"Can we talk about all this later?" Halli asked. "I have to eat something—now. I hiked down a mountain today."

"I know—you're right, I'm sorry—but just tell me: have there been others? How many female Presidents?"

"I don't know, three or four . . ."

"Three or four? Are you kidding me?"

Halli groaned and butted me lightly with her head. "No talk—EAT!"

Twenty-two

I learned two important things about my parallel self today: one, she gets very crabby when she's hungry. Two, she's an excellent cook.

I have eaten vegetables before. Not often, usually not voluntarily, but I have been known to do it. I prefer them nuked and covered with melted cheese—ideally as part of nachos. But I can honestly say that if I could have vegetables picked from Halli's greenhouse every day, prepared the way she prepared them tonight, I might be willing to give up microwaved or cheese-smothered veggies forevermore.

And then dessert: all those fruits cut up and arranged so their colors complemented each other, then topped with a granola-y kind of thing and lots of cinnamon.

"Do you eat like this all the time?"

"Sure," Halli said. "What's the point of eating otherwise?"

I gave up all thought for a while and just enjoyed the food. Forgot where I was—in a different state, in a different universe, in a house that my genetically-same but totally-different grandmother had left to my own genetically-same but different alternate self, eating heavenly food I had just seen hanging from the ceiling in a greenhouse that really was a house. With a big yellow dog lying near my feet snoring happily away because both of his girls were in the same room. If he really thought of us as two separate girls.

That's something I keep wondering about—how does Red see us? And smell us? Does he view us as two distinct entities, or are we like the split photons in that experiment I was telling Halli about? Maybe when Halli is alone she seems like one particle, but when we're together she just seems like the same particle split into two, and so that's why Red is always so happy to see me—another member of his pack, like Halli said. Or a new toy—his regular girl, times two. I have no idea. I wish dogs could talk in Halli's universe—it would make it all so much easier.

After we'd properly stuffed ourselves and carried our dishes to the sink, I noticed the silver boxes on her counter again.

"What are all those?" I asked.

She pointed to each one in turn. "Grinder, chopper, juicer, dehydrator, brewer, blender, heater, presser, mixer—"

"Do you use all of those?"

"Practically every day," Halli said.

There was a noise coming out of one of them—if I remembered right, it was the dehydrator. I asked her what she was making.

A mischievous smile lit up her face. "I've been waiting to tell you. Are you ready? Sit down."

Halli sat across the table from me and clasped her hands in front of her. "I have a surprise. Wait—" She jumped up again. "I'll be right back." Red followed her into the living room, then followed her back a few moments later.

Halli laid out a map in front of me on the table. It looked like it had already been on a trip or two—it was ripped at the edges and had been folded and refolded. Halli smoothed it down, then pointed to a spot a little to the right of the middle.

But before I could concentrate on that, my eyes strayed to the caption on the bottom of the map. *Alps.*

"See this?" Halli asked. "This is one of the greatest places in the world. I haven't been there in two years—last year Ginny and I went to India later than usual, and so we never had a chance to get up there."

"To the Alps."

"Yes," Halli said with a smile. "To this one specific hut. It's always been my favorite—wait a minute, I'll show you."

She ran back into the living room, lifted something off one of the bookshelves, and ran back to the kitchen.

"Here," she said. "Look."

The item in her hand looked like a flashlight, but the light that came out of it seemed to splash a bluish glow all over the map.

And suddenly the map came to life.

Not flat lines anymore, but mountains and trails and trees growing out of the paper in 3D—a holographic map that made everything look so real I was surprised I didn't hear the little streams flowing.

I gazed up at her in happy astonishment. "Can I borrow this for a second?"

She nodded and I scooped up the light. I held it out in front of me as I jogged through the living room, shining it on as many maps as I could reach. Some never changed, but a lot of them—maybe a third—leapt into form as soon as the light reached them. Mountains and cities I felt like I could reach out and touch.

Halli followed me in. "That's new," she said. "Maybe the last five or six years. They're called holomaps."

That explained why some of the older-looking ones stayed flat. What an amazing technology. It might even make me interested in geography.

"I love it here," I said.

Halli laughed. "I'm glad. Now can I show you? About the Alps?"

We returned to the kitchen and Red settled down once more. All this jumping up and room-changing—it interfered with a dog's sleep.

"So," Halli said, "usually by this time of year there's snow up in this region already, but I got a comm today—a weather report. They're having an unusually warm autumn this year, and they expect it to last another few weeks. So I'm going."

"To the Alps."

"Yes."

"When?" I dreaded hearing the answer.

"Tomorrow."

Tomorrow? I had just met her, and already she was going away! But she had no reason to change her plans just because I had shown up—I understood that. I couldn't be selfish. But still, tomorrow?

I smiled bravely. "I hope you have a great time."

Halli laughed. "Audie! What are you thinking? You can come with me!"

Poor Halli. She had no idea how things worked in the real world—in my real world.

"I can't go," I told her. "I have school, I have my mom—we could never afford it anyway—"

Halli just folded her arms and waited.

And then my brain caught up with hers.

"Ohhhhhh . . ." I smiled. "I can just meet you there."

"Exactly."

"But I can't," I still realized. "I have to go back to school tomorrow. I can't spend all day in meditation."

"You won't have to," Halli said. "They're eight hours later over there. Their day is our night."

I did a quick calculation. If I came right home from school, I'd be available by 3:30. Which would be 11:30 at night there. No good.

But—if I went to bed early and got a few hours sleep, then set my alarm for, say, 2:00 in the morning, that would be 10:00 AM there, which could be really nice. I'd have to start getting ready for school by 6:30. But that gave me four and a half solid hours of checking out the Alps with Halli. The *Alps*. I've never even dreamed I could go there.

As Halli and I discussed some of the logistics, it all sounded too easy. It wasn't possible that people could just pack up and go mountain climbing on a day's notice—mountain climbing in Europe. At least it wasn't possible for me—was it?

"But what if something happens?" I asked.

"Like what?" Halli said.

"I don't know, like what if I can't find you? What if it's too far away or something?"

"Then we'll figure something out."

"But what if I oversleep and I miss our connection?"

"Then we'll try again later," Halli said.

"Will there be other people there?"

"Probably a lot," Halli said. "The Alps are very popular."

"Well what if someone sees me just popping in? Or what if I disappear again accidentally?"

"We'll take precautions," Halli said.

"But what if—"

"Audie, stop! I'll take care of everything—I promise. Don't you want to come with me? Tell me the truth."

"Yes!" I said. "Of course! Are you crazy? I'd love it! I just don't see how it's all possible."

"Did you think traveling to another universe was possible?" Halli asked.

"Well, yeah—sort of. At least theoretically."

"And now you've done it," Halli said. "So trust me—traveling to the Alps is possible, too. Let's just try it. I promise you'll have fun."

We went back to discussing more details—times to meet, clothing, food—when another thought occurred to me.

"What will we tell people?" I asked.

"About what?"

"About who we are—I mean in relation to each other. Twins?"

"Oh, uh . . ." For some reason Halli seemed uncomfortable with that. "Maybe we should just say we're cousins."

"Cousins? Nobody's going to believe that—look at us! We're identical."

Except for my lank hair and sallow skin and weakling little body. But I didn't feel it necessary to point out the obvious.

"Why can't we just tell everyone we're twins?" I said.

Halli hesitated. "It might be . . . a little complicated. We'll just have to see."

I didn't understand the issue, but I didn't want to argue with her, either. I was happy she was even inviting me. She could tell people I was her cousin, her sister, her brother, whatever.

As we wrapped up our plans, I felt a twinge of guilt. "Poor Red. What are you going to do with him?"

"What do you mean?" Halli asked.

"I mean where will you put him while you're gone?"

"Nowhere. He's coming with us—aren't you, boy? I'd never leave you behind."

Red thumped his tail wildly. If I had one I would have thumped it, too.

"That's great! But how will you get him there?"

"We call them airplanes," Halli said, and not at all sarcastically. She probably thought I'd never heard of them.

How stupid of me. People took their pets on flights all the time. She could just put him in a kennel down with the baggage. Although I've heard dogs don't really like that.

"—a seat away from any cats," Halli was saying to Red. "I'll let you have the window."

I wasn't sure I heard that right. "You mean he gets . . . a seat? Like, right next to you?"

Now it was Halli's turn to be confused. "Where else would he be?"

I just couldn't picture it—dogs riding next to their owners, getting their own little bags of pretzels or peanuts. That's something I would have loved to see.

But not enough to get stuck on some long, tedious flight to Europe. If everything worked out, I'd be traveling much more quickly—straight from the comfort of my bedroom onto some slope in the middle of the Alps. If I could perfect that—figure out the physics exactly, and then teach it to other people—think about how famous I'd be! Instant flights to Europe—oh, and by the way, it's the Europe in the next universe over. Think of it!

The authors of that textbook were right: Physics *is* phun.

Frequently Asked Questions:

How does the Admissions Committee distinguish among candidates?

In the end our goal is to find the students who are the best fit for Columbia. Each year, there are many more qualified applicants than there are places in our class. With such an appealing pool of applicants, it is the job of the admissions committee to select those that we believe will take greatest advantage of the unique Columbia experience and will offer something meaningful in return to the community.

[*Yes, sir, Professor Hawkins, I'm coming.*]

Twenty-three

Early Decision at Columbia

If you are offered admission under the Early Decision plan, we expect that you will maintain a rigorous course load and a strong academic performance for the remainder of your senior year.

The sun was fully in my eyes before I even thought about waking up.

I looked at the clock.

"No! No no no no no . . ." I stumbled around my room, shoving books and homework into my backpack. And there was the camcorder, just sitting there on my desk waiting for me to play it back. Come on, couldn't I just—

No. I practically had to pry my brain away from even the thought of it. Because I knew once I started watching, even if I could fast-forward through any of the boring parts, if there really was something on there—like me, let's say, DISAPPEARING

OR SOMETHING—then I'd probably want to replay that sequence about a hundred million times, and then I'd never get to school. And I needed to get to school. I'd already slept through all of first period and half of second. I was in deep trouble.

And why did I oversleep? Because I'd been up all night talking to Halli. Because we had a trip to the Alps to plan, people. And because I'd been smart enough to turn off my alarm clock and silence my phone so there wouldn't be any annoying sounds to pull me back into this world. So smart, I am. Which is why now I was racing around like a loon.

It was a good thing I was already dressed—same jeans and flannel shirt I'd worn over there. Do a quick toothbrushing, roll on some deodorant, stick my hair in a ponytail, out the door.

As I grabbed my backpack, I took one last longing look at the camcorder. Couldn't I just bring it with me? Watch the film over lunch? Not have to sit there all day at school and torture myself wondering what it showed?

But my high school is a notorious den of scoundrels and thieves, and I couldn't risk it even a little bit. That camcorder held the only evidence anywhere of what might be happening as I bridge over into Halli's world. The idea that I might lose it somehow, or someone might rip it off? Not worth it. The camcorder stayed, I went.

I drove faster than I ever do, had to park down the street from school because the student lot was already full, and ran until my legs and lungs burned, just to come skidding into third period about a minute after the bell. I heard it go off while I sprinted.

Chest heaving, I took my seat behind Winslow Henry. He half-turned around to look at me.

"You're sweating," he said, as if I could do anything about it. Winslow is about half my size and looks like he'd break if you made him run as hard as I just had to.

"I know. What did I miss in Algebra?"

Winslow shrugged. "The usual."

Winslow's like me, still trying to make it through Algebra in his senior year. Neither of us is happy about it.

"Did she start talking about the new chapter yet?" I asked.

"Yep." And that was all he said.

I could have strangled him. "How far?" I whispered, because Mrs. Arnold was already writing on the board.

He sighed and held up two fingers.

"Two problems or two sections?" I asked.

He shrugged and pretended to listen very hard to our English teacher.

Brat.

While Mrs. Arnold went over some of the symbolism of Dostoyevsky's *The Idiot*—which, as far as I'm concerned, is all symbolism because I don't understand it at all—I let myself worry over how I'm going to handle the sleep problem in the coming two weeks. Because it really can be a problem. Waking up at odd hours, trying to stay awake so I can have as much fun as possible, then waking up again—or staying awake some more—so I can get to school on time—yow. Theoretical quantum physics is hard enough. *Actual* quantum physics is even harder.

Then there's the mother factor—my mother. The good part is once she's home again I can ask her to make sure I'm up in the mornings. The bad part? Oh, where do I begin:

Scenario #1: I am in deep meditation, which allows me to bilocate (if that's what I'm doing) to Halli's world. I'm up in the Alps with her and Red somewhere, having an absolutely fabulous time, and my mom remembers she meant to tell me something about whatever, and she knocks and comes into my room. Jolting me out of my meditation, ripping me away from the Alps, maybe right in front of people, or while I'm holding a rope or something that Halli is depending on for her survival. Too bad, that's how it is when you've split yourself between two universes.

Scenario #2: I am actually, fully, physically leaving this universe and traveling to Halli's. As in, here one minute, gone the next. So let's say my mother happens to walk into my room at exactly that moment. Sees me disappear, has a heart attack, dies.

Scenario #3: Same as above, without the seeing and dying. Instead she knocks on my door, knows she saw me go in there, but when she comes in, I'm gone. Where did I go? Is the window open? Did I run away? Is my mother losing her mind? Should she call the police?

Scenario #4—

"Audie?" Mrs. Arnold interrupted. "What do you think about the villagers?"

Every teacher knows when a student isn't paying attention. It's like their special power.

"Uhh . . ."

Winslow Henry turned halfway in his chair and snickered at me. Thanks, buddy.

"I think maybe *they* were the true idiots," I bluffed. "That's what Dostoyevsky was trying to say. We're all ignorant in our own ways—we just think it's the *other* person who's stupid."

That answer seemed to satisfy her—miraculously—because she moved on to some fresh victim.

Winslow whispered, "Skate."

I kicked the back of his chair.

I wasn't so lucky in World History, when Ms. Tavino called on me and I didn't have a clue. This is what happens when you go to another universe instead of doing your homework. Nobody talks about that in the science books—how your obsessions keep you from taking care of the mundane aspects of home. I'll bet physicists all over the world forget to pay their electric bills and end up sitting in the dark.

"What's wrong with you?" Lydia asked me at lunch. She must have noticed me looking at the clock every two seconds.

Could this day go any more slowly? All I kept thinking about was that camcorder sitting back on my desk.

"Nothing," I said, "just . . . antsy, I guess." It didn't help that Gemma was over there at her lunch table laughing her big British laugh, showing off as only Gemma can. Will has a different lunch period, so Gemma always seems perfectly fine flirting with every single guy around her. Makes me want to kick her, accidentally, really hard. Although maybe Will will get sick of that some day and dump her stupid British—

"You should have heard her," Lydia said.

"Huh? Heard what?"

Lydia must have noticed where I'd been looking.

"Gemma's 'lessons' for how to get a man." Lydia rolled her eyes. "My brother is an idiot. Or as Gemma would say, an 'id-jet.' According to her, all men are."

I groaned. "What does he see in her?" Then I wished I could suck the words right back into my mouth. Had I said too much? Given myself away?

But Lydia didn't seem to notice anything. Instead she shrugged. "Maybe all men are id-jets. Davey certainly was."

"Yeah, so whatever happened with—"

"When's your mom coming back?" Lydia asked, clearly dodging the subject. She bit into her apple and gave it an extra vigorous chew.

"Oh, um, tomorrow. I'm picking her up at the airport around four."

"You can come over for dinner tonight if you want," Lydia said. "I think we're having leftover spaghetti."

"No, thanks," I said. "Too much homework." Which was true, even though it was only half of the story. I did need to do my homework first this time. I couldn't have a repeat of today.

Gemma guffawed again. I swear, the sound of her voice could kill birds in flight.

"Come on," Lydia said, "I'm sure Hairball's coming over, too. Don't leave me with her. She thinks we're friends now."

I didn't say it, but it sort of seemed like that to me the other night, too.

"Can't," I said. "I'm sorry."

Gemma's high-pitched laughter pierced the noise of the lunchroom. I stuck my hands over my ears.

Someone needs to disappear *her* to another universe.

Twenty-four

"Excuse me, Mr. Dobosh, do you have a second?"

"Yes, Audie, of course."

I had waited until everyone else filed out of our physics class before approaching the teacher. Mr. Dobosh is a nice man—he's always been one of my favorites—and he said he's writing me a great recommendation for my Columbia application. He's not exactly cutting-edge when it comes to modern physics—I think he wishes the whole field had stopped with Einstein, and he'd never even heard of Bell's Theorem or M-theory or any of that—but he's been a good basic teacher for me, and I really appreciate how encouraging he's been, despite my horrendous situation with math.

"Have you ever heard of someone named Dr. Whitfield?" I asked. "Skip Whitfield?"

"Skip, Skip . . ." Mr. Dobosh tapped his chin. "Yes, I think maybe so—let me look over here."

He went to his bookshelf in the corner of the room and started skimming through the titles.

"He's a professor at someplace called Mountain State," I said, "in Colorado. If that helps."

"No, I'm thinking he was someone at Yale . . ."

"Yes, he was at Yale, too," I said.

Mr. Dobosh kept scanning his shelves. Then he reached in and pulled out a book.

"Here it is," he said, dusting the top of it before handing it over.

The book was called *Above and Beyond: Human Potential and Its Implications for Physics, Space Exploration, and Communication with Other Worlds*. By Walter "Skip" Whitfield, Ph.D.

"Have you read it?" I asked, turning it over to look at the back. There was a picture of Dr. Whitfield there—very young, with thick glasses and dark bushy hair.

"I might have gotten a few chapters in," Mr. Dobosh said. "I think someone gave that to me." He borrowed it back for a second and looked inside the front cover. "Ah, yes, gift from a student—very nice of him . . ." Mr. Dobosh seemed to drift off for a second, no doubt trying to call up the face of his pupil.

"May I borrow this?" I asked.

"Of course, of course! As you can see, I won't be needing it right away. Pretty fantastical stuff, if I remember right. But keep it if you'd like. I'm sure whoever that young man was who gave it to me won't mind. Nice of him, though, hmm?"

"Thank you," I said. "I really appreciate it."

And then I raced for my last class.

The good thing about Algebra Support is you can get away with reading or doing homework for another class, so long as you don't make any noise. That's all Mr. Kreiner cares about—noise. He even lets people play games on their phones as long as it keeps them quiet. I heard he has one more year until retirement. Apparently he's already ready.

I flipped to the front of Dr. Whitfield's book, to read what he wrote in the Preface. I didn't have to read very far before I got to this:

"Why should a physicist be interested in what the human mind, body, and senses are capable of? Aren't those really the concern of the surgeon, the medical doctor, the psychologist, the anatomist?

"We should be interested because human potential is the untapped resource in a physicist's lab, as useful as the microscope, the telescope, the particle accelerator. While some search 'out there' for the answers relating to our cosmos, others have begun to search 'in here'—within the human capability itself—to find out what is possible, and how that can be applied to some of the most compelling questions facing physics today, including whether other worlds and other entities exist, and if so, whether we can communicate with them in ways not involving the possibly useless practice of sending radio signals toward the stars.

"What follows are some of the current discoveries in quantum physics, cosmology, neurophysics, neuropsychology, parapsychology, and other rapidly-evolving fields. Readers are encouraged to approach these materials with an open mind and perhaps a spirit of wonder. We don't know everything. What you'll find in these pages is the humbling realization that we may know very little at all."

I gently closed the book. I knew I'd be reading the rest of it, cover to cover, probably all in one sitting if I could, but for now I just wanted to keep it closed and think.

What did it all mean? Why was a book like this growing dust on a physics teacher's shelf? Why was Professor Hawkins acting like Dr. Whitfield was a joke? He sounded like a smart, serious scientist to me—one with very exciting ideas.

I turned the book over again and looked at Dr. Whitfield's picture. He seemed like a pretty normal guy. Nice face. Friendly smile.

And then my eyes caught the edge of a sentence below—down where the publisher had reprinted flattering reviews from people recommending the book.

Underneath the ones from *Physics Today* and *Scientific American* was one from a very familiar name: Herbert Hawkins, Ph.D., author of *To the Ends of the Universe: A Physicist's*

Exploration of Life. Here's what the famous professor had to say:

"Skip Whitfield is one of the great visionaries of our field. *Above and Beyond* is one of the most eye-opening, thought-provoking treatises I have ever had the privilege to read. I look forward to great things from Dr. Whitfield."

Apparently sometime between writing that review and writing his own book about parallel universes—the one where he makes fun of Dr. Whitfield and treats him like a joke—Professor Hawkins had changed his mind. What happened in between?

I glanced at the clock again. Finally it was moving the way I wanted—just seven more minutes of school. I stowed the Whitfield book in my backpack and prepared to launch.

There was a video waiting for me at home.

Twenty-five

I plugged the camcorder into my computer and uploaded the file.

My hand shook as I clicked Play.

And there I was, sitting there in my big coat and jeans and headphones, waiting for the meditation to kick in.

And then, *blip*, there I wasn't.

I rewound and replayed the sequence about a dozen more times, because even though the evidence was right there in front of me, I still couldn't possibly believe it.

Now it wasn't just my hand shaking, it was my whole body. I felt like any minute the CIA was going to burst through my door and arrest me for violating the laws of nature. I wanted to hide the video, but I also wanted to make copies—a lot of copies—to protect myself. From what, I didn't know.

What if my mother ever found that? What if she were looking on my computer for something, and she wondered, "Hm, what's this file?" and she clicked on it and saw me disappear? How was that going to work?

Or what if hackers got into my computer, and that video went viral and everybody found out? What would people do to me? Would I have to go into hiding somehow, and maybe bring my mother? Would we have to go on the run? Would the military try to kidnap me and make me show them how I did it? Would people just think I was some trickster and I'd faked it somehow? Or would they think I was a witch or something?

Or what if I got some computer virus, and lost the whole hard drive, and I'd already erased the cartridge on the camcorder—

I sat there in a semi-stupor for a while, not knowing what to do. My brain was clearly running away with me. Crazy thoughts—*crazy*—like maybe I'd go live with my Grandma Marion, or I'd have to figure out how to stay in Halli's universe forever, or I'd destroy the video so no one knew it existed, and I'd never, ever tell anyone about it, ever.

But after a while, I started thinking just the opposite: I have to tell someone. But whom? My mother? No—she'd completely freak out. She'd scream if she saw it. She'd think it was incredibly dangerous, what I was doing, and she'd make me promise never, ever to do it again.

Okay, then, Lydia? And say what? "Hi, Lydia, you know how I'm always reading all those physics books? Well guess what? I figured out how to do something no one else knows how to do. It's so huge, everybody on this planet is going to want to know how I did it. Can I come over for spaghetti after all? I'm a little scared out of my mind right now, and—what's that? Gemma and Will are there? That's great. Talk to you later."

Could I tell Will? "Hi, Will, I love you. You're the only person in the world I wanted to share this with. Please come over. I want to show you something."

Yeah, right. And then he'd see me disappear and he'd look at me like I was a mutant from another planet, and he'd run from this place so fast, back into the arms of—blech. No. Forget it.

And finally I got around to a more reasonable answer: I should write to Professor Hawkins.

And say what, exactly?

"Dear Dr. Hawkins: Hi, you don't know me, but I'm hoping to join your fine institution next year. I'm currently putting together my application, and hope to be selected for early admission so that I know I will be coming there and can apply for financial aid and can begin living the dream I've had for so many years—the dream to study physics with you. I have read every one of your books many, many times, and I admire you more than any other physicist in the world.

"Anyway, Professor Hawkins, I wanted to tell you something. I have this video of me disappearing and going to another universe. Well, you can't see the other universe on the tape, but I can tell you all about that separately. For now the only thing I have proof of is me leaving. Here it is. I hope you're interested.

"Sincerely, Audie Masters."

Yeah, like that's going to fly. It wasn't until I started thinking it through that I realized I really don't have proof of anything. There's nothing at all to show where I went—nothing at all to prove that I've been anywhere but in another room after learning some cool magic trick that makes it look like I disappeared.

I left my computer and dropped flat back onto my bed. Hopeless. So amazing, so potentially universe-shaking, but I didn't have anything to prove it. That tape really meant nothing.

See, here's the problem:

There's a fine line between theory and crazy. There are a lot of outlandish theories physicists have come up with over the years, but as long as someone can back it up with math, people will go along.

But if you said you *knew* something, you *saw* something, they'd jump all over you. If you said you'd just completed an experiment where you saw that the universe is actually made up of tiny vibrating mice, the other physicists would laugh at you. Some would be really angry. And all of them would demand of you, "Prove it."

And if you couldn't prove it—if what you saw was just a one-time thing, or no one else could duplicate the experiment in their lab—then they'd brand you a liar and a lunatic.

And then your career would be over. The most you could ever do is practice physics in the privacy of your home. No university would ever hire you, no publisher would want your books, you'd starve if you tried to make a living at it.

You'd have to take up teaching backcountry skiing, or something.

I sat back up.

No. I couldn't. Should I?

Not by e-mail—I'd already thought that through, and there was no way to do it properly in print. I'd just end up looking like a crackpot. Spam filter. Delete.

I'd have to call. It was the only way. What time was it? Would he still be in his office?

How late do the professors work at Mountain State College?

Twenty-six

I got his voice mail.

It came on so fast, I didn't have time to react. I just started babbling.

"Hi . . . Dr. Whitfield. Um, you don't know me, but my name is Audie Masters and I'm a high school senior in Tucson, Arizona." (My mother's name is—my favorite color is—get on with it, Audie!)

"Um, so the reason I'm calling is I read your *Above and Beyond* book—I mean, the Preface so far, which I really love, but I guess why I'm really calling is . . ."

Just get it over with. If he thinks I'm a freak, he thinks it.

So I spat it out really fast. "You know that part of Professor Hawkins's new book where he talks about the lunch he had with you? I think it's on page 236 or something. And he said you had a theory about vibrations and how to travel over to another universe.

"Well, I just wanted to tell you that I did that, and you're right. I've done it four times now, and the other person has come over here once. I just wanted to tell you that. Okay, thanks, bye.

"Oh, and if you want to call me back, here's my cell phone."

I hung up and caught my breath. I felt all glisteny with sweat. Nice work, Audie, you sounded like a real professional. Physicist to physicist. "Uh, um, hey, and so call me back, bye!" Right. No way he was calling me back.

But my phone rang about two minutes later.

I checked the Caller ID. *MtnSt.*

"Can you do a video conference?" the voice wanted to know.

"Um, what? I mean, yes."

"Here's my contact information. I want to see your face."

Then he hung up.

Very abruptly. Rather rude. My heart was beating like a firecracker.

I signed onto my video chat account, and then searched for Dr. Whitfield. In a minute we were face to face.

"Audie?"

"Yes, sir." I cleared my throat. I felt incredibly nervous. He was a real live physics professor. Who kind of looked like a forest ranger.

"I wanted to see your face," Dr. Whitfield said. "I need to know whether you're lying. Did someone put you up to this?"

"No, I'm not lying, sir, I swear." I gulped in some air. "I . . . actually have some video."

"Of what?" he asked.

"Me, last night. When I left here and went to the other universe. You can't really see much—just me disappearing at one point—"

"You disappeared." I watched his face as he said it. He didn't seem that skeptical.

"Yes, sir. At first I thought maybe I was bilocating—do you know what that is?"

"Yes," he said.

"So I decided I'd better set up a camera and find out. So last night I did. And I think it means I went over there with my whole body. At least that's my hypothesis."

I was happy I'd thrown in a technical term like that. Made me sound more knowledgeable.

"Audie, I need you to tell me everything that's happened. Can you do that?"

"Yes, sir." Then I told him everything I knew.

I thought I'd be more afraid, talking to someone in an official capacity like that, but it ended up just being a conversation. Dr. Whitfield asked me questions as I went along, and it just seemed easy after a while to talk about it—in fact, it was a big relief. I thought it would be like talking to a teacher, but it wasn't like that at all. It felt more like talking to Halli.

When I had told him the whole story and brought him up to date, he said, "Can you send me that video?"

"Sure, you mean now?"

"Now would be good."

I sent him the file and waited while he watched. I could tell when he got to the critical part. He looked up at me, then back at the video. Then back at me.

"Holy—"

"Do you believe me?" I asked.

"I think I do," Dr. Whitfield said.

And much to my shock, I burst into tears.

Twenty-seven

"What should I do?" I asked Dr. Whitfield.

"I don't know."

"I mean, this is real, right? I know it is. I've been there a bunch of times. It's real."

"Let's say it's real," Dr. Whitfield answered.

"So what should I do?" I said. "I mean, do I need to tell someone? Besides you?"

"That's really up to you."

He seemed like a really nice guy. Kind of like Mr. Dobosh, but more, I don't know—authoritative. Like he knew more. But not pushy. Not arrogant. Just comfortable being smart.

"Can I ask you something?" I said. Maybe it was impertinent, but I still wanted to know.

"Go ahead."

"What happened between you and Professor Hawkins?"

Dr. Whitfield laughed. "Ah, the Hawk. An interesting man, don't you think?"

"I've read every one of his books," I said.

"So have I," Dr. Whitfield told me.

"I'm trying to get into Columbia. My application is due in 38 days. I was sort of hoping this project would do it."

"Do what?"

"Get me in," I said. "You know, convince the admissions people I'm worthy."

"Believe me, Audie, if anyone is worthy, you are."

"I suck at math."

"So do I," Dr. Whitfield said.

And that completely took me aback.

"You . . . what?"

"So did Michael Faraday," Dr. Whitfield said. "Ever heard of him?"

"Sure," I said. "Physicist, inventor, discovered electromagnetic fields—"

"Also discovered the chemical compound benzene," Dr. Whitfield added. "Faraday was one of the greatest experimentalists of all time. So we're in good company. Don't worry so much about the math."

It was like someone saying to a little kid, "Don't worry that your parents are both four-foot-eight! You can still be an NBA player!"

"Then you . . . think they'll let me in?"

"Oh, hell, no," Dr. Whitfield said. "Those people are automatons. They'll look at your test scores and bump you in the first round. It'll take a personal recommendation."

He paused, and I waited. Inside, my heart was this crushed, shriveled up little flower.

"Is that what you want?" Dr. Whitfield asked me.

"Want what?" I said.

"A personal recommendation. Is that why you called me?"

"No!" And it really wasn't—it hadn't even occurred to me. "I called you because it was your theory—I thought you'd want to know that it worked."

His tone was softer now. "I did want to know—thank you. But I have to tell you, Audie, I don't think you should do it anymore."

"Do what? You mean go over there? Why?"

"Because we don't know if it's dangerous."

"But it's not!" I said. "Look at me! I'm perfectly fine—I'm better than fine. I haven't felt one bad thing from going over there. I promise you—I'd tell you if I did."

"How old are you?" he asked.

"Seventeen."

Dr. Whitfield muttered something under his breath. "Look, I can't ask a minor to continue doing this experiment," Dr. Whitfield said. "There are too many unknowns—it would be unethical of me."

"You're not asking me!" I said. "You have nothing to do with it. You wouldn't even know about it if I hadn't called you." And now I was starting to get mad. Isn't it always this way? You tell some adult about something you think is cool, and next thing you know, they forbid it.

"I have to go, Dr. Whitfield."

"You're angry now."

"Whatever. I have to go."

"Are you going back there?" he asked. "Tonight?"

"I don't know." As if I were going to tell him.

"Audie? Look at me."

I stared straight at the screen.

"I'm asking you," Dr. Whitfield said. "I think this might be dangerous. I'm not saying it is, I'm just saying I don't know."

"Wouldn't *you* keep doing it if you could?"

Dr. Whitfield sighed. "Yes, Audie, I would."

Twenty-eight

Two o'clock in the morning. That's what Halli and I agreed. I went to bed early, around 10:00 PM, then was up with the first beep of the alarm. I reset it so I wouldn't oversleep for school again. This whole thing could work.

I knew Halli wouldn't be in the Alps yet. She was flying to Munich, Germany, and staying overnight in Ginny's apartment there—well, technically Halli's apartment now. Halli wanted to rest up before heading for the mountains. She knew she'd have jet lag.

Not me, sister. What a great way to travel. No lines at the airport, no trying to figure out what to pack, no trying to sleep while sitting up—just stick on the headphones, fluff up the pillows behind my back, and head across the ocean.

"Heya."

"Heya," I said back. The dog tackled me before I could catch my breath.

Ginny's apartment in Munich was so unlike the house in River Grove it could have been decorated by a completely different person. And maybe it was. Maybe she had people all over the world designing and furnishing houses and apartments for her. I was starting to get the idea that Ginny might have been rich.

Which sounds stupid—of course she was rich if she could afford six houses and who knows how many apartments around the world. But I mean RICH rich.

The place was blue and white. Nothing else. White walls, white floor, white furniture. Blue pillows, blue dishes, blue curtains, blue rugs. The only contrasting color was the yellow dog who now lay stretched out on the white couch, head on a bright blue pillow.

Halli handed me a cup of steaming hot coffee (blue mug). "I've already had about ten of these," she said. "It's the only thing that works with the time change."

Her coffee was so vastly superior to that tub-o-coffee stuff my mom buys at the warehouse store, there was really no comparison. I might want about ten cups of it myself.

Halli glanced at the clock. "So it's 2:10 in the morning back home."

It had taken me only ten minutes to get there this time. The two of us were getting better—more in sync. That was good. The kind of detail I should make a note of in the research notebook I was starting to keep.

Because talking to Dr. Whitfield and then reading through his book—forget the rest of my homework, all I wanted to read was that—really inspired me to go at this in a whole new way. Not just be so in awe of everything going on, but really take the time to be detailed and scientific about it. Not act like it was so weird anymore, but treat it just like any other experiment a trained physicist might do.

Because believe me, Dr. Whitfield has done his share of wacky experiments. A lot of things involving brain studies and parapsychology, as in ESP. Although he didn't call it that. He just called it "AB"—"Above-Beyond."

As in learning how to use our normal five senses in ways we aren't used to. My favorite example was this:

Dr. Whitfield worked a lot with a highly-respected neuropsychologist, Dr. Dale, who was very skilled at hypnotizing people. What the two scientists liked to do was just take volunteers off the street—students from the university (that would be Yale), or parents visiting campus for the day, or ordinary groundskeepers trimming the hedges outside the psychology building, and ask those people to come inside and try a little experiment.

Then Dr. Dale would hypnotize the whole group, and give them all one instruction: when he brought them out of their trance, they would no longer be able to see Dr. Whitfield. From then on, he would be invisible to them.

Then the hypnotist guy brought them all out of their trance, and the real experiment began.

Dr. Dale had a lot of little items in his pocket. And one by one, he'd go and stand in front of the research subjects, and pull these items out of his pocket. But the trick was, he'd always have Dr. Whitfield stand between Dr. Dale and the subject, blocking Dr. Dale from view.

"What am I holding in my hand?" Dr. Dale would ask the person.

"A keychain."

"What does the keychain look like?"

And the person would describe it—perfectly, accurately.

But do you understand? They shouldn't have been able to see anything in Dr. Dale's hand. Because Dr. Whitfield's whole body was standing in front of him! But the hypnotized people had been instructed that Dr. Whitfield was invisible, and so their senses just worked around that. They were able somehow to look right through Dr. Whitfield, and describe whatever was in Dr. Dale's hand.

Okay, so like that's not amazing? How about this:

Again, with just normal people off the street.

Dr. Whitfield would stay in a closed room with one of the subjects, while Dr. Dale would go off driving in his car. And at a set time—say twenty minutes later—Dr. Dale would stop his car, get out, and go look at something. Maybe a road sign or the front of a restaurant or somebody's house—wherever he ended up.

And at that same time, Dr. Whitfield had the person inside the room start drawing a picture of whatever Dr. Dale was seeing at that moment. The person also had to describe it out loud. And over and over again, the people were dead-on with their descriptions—they were actually able to see what Dr. Dale was seeing, even though these people had no special psychic skills whatsoever.

The book was full of things like that. And then all this stuff about the current research on parallel universes and other stuff physicists were just starting to really study back when Dr. Whitfield wrote the book.

And his point was this: maybe the human mind has capabilities beyond what any of us think. Maybe we just need to untie ourselves from whatever beliefs we have that hold us back. Because if it's possible that we can do all these trippy things like seeing through people's bodies and seeing what they're doing from afar, then maybe we're evolving into the kind of species that will one day be able to communicate with entities from more advanced civilizations.

In other words, it's up to us to keep developing these skills, like students learning our ABCs. As we use our brains more and learn new ways to extend our senses—above and beyond—maybe there's hope for us someday being able to see and hear and talk to creatures from other galaxies. It's a theory, at least.

And there I was sitting in a blue and white apartment in Munich, Germany, Universe Unknown, having a chat with a creature who looked exactly like me. And she was having the same experience back. Our two civilizations—whether you considered them advanced or not—had made communication with each other. As far as I knew, Halli and I were the first ones from our planets to do it. How cool is that?

I told Halli all of it—from my conversation with Dr. Whitfield to everything in his book.

Well, okay, I did leave out one part.

I decided not to tell her what he'd said—about how I shouldn't come over there anymore. I didn't think there was any real danger, and I didn't want Halli to worry.

Okay, maybe I thought there could be *some* danger, but I still didn't want Halli to worry. Mostly I didn't want her to agree with Dr. Whitfield and say we shouldn't try it anymore. The only way to discover more about something is to keep studying it and experimenting with it.

And I intend to keep studying and experimenting.

And not just because it's fun.

Number of days remaining to come up with some definitive proof of my huge discovery that will convince Columbia and Professor Hawkins to let me in, no matter what Dr. Whitfield says about my chances: 37

Twenty-nine

"Hi, sweetie."

"Hi, Mom." She gave me a big motherly hug and I took her carry-on from her. She looked whipped.

Apparently she thought the same about me.

"Are you okay? You look a little pale." She reached out and felt my cheek. "Are you sick?"

"No, I just didn't sleep very well last night. Lots of homework."

Memo to self: four hours of sleep is not enough. I barely stayed awake through any of my classes today. Tried to take a nap at lunch. Did take a nap during Algebra Support. Guess that's why they call it support.

"Honey, don't you think you're pushing yourself too hard? This whole business with Columbia—"

"I'm fine, Mom. How was your trip?"

I fell asleep during the drive home, which was okay since I wasn't driving, but it didn't help my credibility with my mother.

"Audie, you obviously need more sleep. How about if I order some takeout and we both put ourselves to bed a little early tonight?"

"Sounds great." Boy, did it. If I could get to bed by 8:00 or something, I could catch a full six hours of sleep before I had to meet Halli. I'd love even more sleep than that, but six was a good start.

I logged on when we got home, and there was a video chat message: call from Dr. Whitfield.

My mother was in her bedroom unpacking and checking her e-mail. Maybe I could chance a quick call.

"Hi, Dr. Whitfield." I kept my voice low. "I can't talk very long."

"Did you go over there last night?"

I knew he was going to ask. And I'd already decided not to lie.

"Yes. Everything was fine."

"Good. Because I've been thinking."

He laid out his theory for me:

"Do you know what psychokinesis is?" he asked.

"No . . . I don't think so."

"It's the ability of consciousness to affect physical matter—mind over matter. Have you heard of that?"

"I guess so."

"It has a very special application in quantum physics," he went on. "You know about the observer problem in physics—"

"Audie?" my mom called from the other room.

"Just a second!" I turned back to Dr. Whitfield. "It's my mom. You have to be quiet. I'll be back in just a minute—"

"You haven't told her what you're doing, have you?" Dr. Whitfield guessed.

"Honey?" my mother called.

"Coming!"

I raced out of my room, into the kitchen where my mother stood holding a fistful of menus. "Chinese, Vietnamese, or pizza?"

"Um, Vietnamese." I turned to race back.

"Almond milk tea?"

"Sure," I said.

"Tapioca balls?"

"Yeah," I said, "great."

Big conversation going on, Mom. Discussing the theory of the universe here. Can't really talk about tapioca balls.

She picked up the phone to dial it, so I was safe to run back.

"Sorry," I sat as I plopped back into my chair.

"I think you should tell her," Professor Whitfield said.

"Later," I said. "Now tell me what you were saying."

Dr. Whitfield gave his beard a scratch. "All right. You know about the observer problem in quantum physics?"

"Yes," I said. "Heisenberg's uncertainty principle—the fact that subatomic particles behave differently when they're being observed by scientists than when they're not."

"Correct," Dr. Whitfield said. "It's a minor application of psychokinesis, although no one wants to admit it. They'd rather call it the 'observer problem' and leave it at that. But what I think is—"

"Honey?" My mom opened my door. She had the phone to her ear. "Rice noodles or vermicelli?"

I shouldn't have tilted my screen away. That's what tipped her off. She got a funny sort of smile on her face. "What are you doing there?"

"Nothing. Vermicelli sounds great."

"Mrs. Masters?" came the voice from the screen.

"No," I mumbled. "Seriously."

"Mrs. Masters?" he said again.

I hate teachers sometimes.

My mother spoke into her phone. "I'll call you back." Then she gave me a warning look and stepped over in front of my computer.

What else could I do? I turned the screen to face her.

"Dr. Whitfield, this is my mother. Mom, Dr. Whitfield."

"Nice to meet you, Mrs. Masters."

My mother scowled. She really hates being called that. "Actually, it's Ms. Fletcher."

"Sorry," Dr. Whitfield said. "Nice to meet you."

My mother looked from him to me. "Would you like to tell me what this is about?"

"He's just this physics professor I've been talking to," I hurried to explain, before Dr. Whitfield could say anything himself. "We've been talking about this book he wrote—he has some really interesting theories, and I was hoping he could help me with the project I'm doing for my Columbia application. Right, Dr. Whitfield?"

"In . . . part," he answered.

"He knows Professor Hawkins," I added. "And I was hoping he'd give me a personal recommendation. I'm sorry I didn't ask you about that before, Dr. Whitfield. Will you?"

Dr. Whitfield was not amused. He shook his head.

My mother isn't stupid. "What's going on here?"

"Audie, you should explain your experiment to your mother," he said in a stern voice. I could tell he wasn't very happy with me. "I have to go. Nice meeting you, Ms. Fletcher. Audie, call me when you're ready to talk more about science—and less about Professor Hawkins."

And with that, he hung up.

"What was that all about?" my mother asked.

I shrugged. "Scientists are so touchy sometimes."

But she wasn't about to let me off the hook that easily. "What sort of experiment are you doing? What does he have to do with it? What are you doing calling someone like that—do you even know that man?"

I improvised. "Mr. Dobosh gave me his book to read." I pointed to where it lay over on my bed. "And Professor Hawkins talks about him in his parallel universe book. So I thought maybe if I contacted him, he might be willing to talk to me about some of the concepts in his book, and maybe write a special letter to Professor Hawkins or something."

"Honey, you know I'd be thrilled for you if you got into Columbia—it would really be wonderful. I'm not happy that you'd move so far away from me, but I know it's what you've wanted for a long time.

"But lately, this obsession! Look at you—so exhausted you can barely keep your head up. I'd rather see you go to a state school than wear yourself out like this. Are you sure it's really worth it to you?"

I slouched back in my chair. "Mom, it's *everything* to me. I don't care if I don't sleep until the November 1st deadline. I've got to have the most killer application I can come up with, or they're never going to let me in—you know that! Not with my math scores."

"What makes you think Dr. Whitfield can help you get in? He didn't seem very enthusiastic when you asked for the recommendation."

"I know. I think maybe he and Professor Hawkins hate each other. Maybe the whole thing was a mistake."

My mom went over to my bed and picked up Dr. Whitfield's book. She flipped through a few pages of it, then turned it over to look at the back cover.

"A lot younger," she said.

"Yeah. Look down below—see what Professor Hawkins said about him."

My mom read it. "Sounds like they were friends back then."

"I know. I wonder what happened."

Without her noticing it, I'd totally deflected the conversation away from ever talking about my experiment. It was my own little version of psychokinesis: mind over mother.

She glanced at her phone. "I guess I should call back for our food. Let's eat soon so we can head for bed. I'm beat."

"Me, too," I said. "I just have to finish some of my homework."

"Honey, I love you. I want you to be happy. Just don't push yourself so hard, all right? I worry about you."

"Thanks, Mom."

I am a horrible daughter.

But on the other hand, at least this way she won't worry.

So maybe I'm a good daughter after all.

How does the Committee review applicants?

We look at a variety of factors to help us inform our decision on a candidate including:

The character and personality of a candidate.

[*Can we talk about my math scores instead?*]

Thirty

Beautiful morning. Birds tweeting, sun gently caressing my eyes, drool collecting in a little pool under my lips. A perfect night, fully-rested, long, beautiful sleep—

I jerked awake and looked at the clock.

AAAAAAH!

I'd totally missed it! Slept right through and missed it. Ate my bún with vermicelli, slurped up the happy little tapioca balls at the bottom of my almond milk tea, dressed in warm clothes to go meet Halli on the train from Munich to the Alps, then sleepily tucked myself into bed.

And forgot to set a single alarm.

Stupid! Aaaaah! What must Halli think? She probably tried and tried to reach me last night, and I was too busy dreaming. What an idiot. What a useless excuse for a scientist. Can't even stay awake for an experiment of this magnitude? I don't deserve to go to Columbia. I might as well just stay in bed and watch cartoons all day. A lot of people do that, right? And they're happy, right?

Instead I brushed my teeth, took a shower, and felt massively sorry for myself. Idiot. Stupid. Loser.

Not that I deserved it, but the day did start looking up almost right away.

"Hey, Aud! Wait up."

Will jogged up to me in the hall before first period. He smelled like Dial soap. How do I know it was Dial? Because I made a project a while back of sniffing him, then going to the store and sniffing all the soaps until I could find the match. Then I bought it and I've been showering with Dial ever since, so I can smell like him. Yes, Dr. Whitfield, that's what I do with *my* AB "above-beyond" senses. What's that? Not what you had in mind?

"Hey, you going to the office this afternoon?" Will asked.

He knows Wednesdays and Fridays are my workdays.

"Yeah, why?"

"The new computers came in last night," Will said, "so I'm going to install them after school. Thought I'd give you a ride so you wouldn't have to take the bus."

I could have melted in a puddle at his feet. That guy is so *nice*. First to remember that my mom is back in town, which means she's using the car, and second to even think about what that might mean to me—having to take the bus and all.

"Yeah," I said, "I'd really love that! Thanks for offer—"

"Heeeey, Audie girl," came the silky voice from behind

him. Of course it was all too good to be true.

"Hey, Gemma." I didn't even look at her, but stayed focused on Will. "So then I'll . . . meet you?"

"Where we going?" British chick asked, just like I was afraid she would.

"Just work stuff," Will told her. "I need to hit the office after school."

Gemma tossed her hair and gave me a wink. Dang! She got me! I didn't even realized I'd looked over at her until it was too late.

"Hope you won't keep him for long," Gemma told me, as if I had anything to do with it. To the contrary, I hoped instead that the boxes were all missing critical parts, and Will would have to spend hours and hours searching for them and then calling tech support. We'd order in some Chinese food, sit around all night, I'd get to look at him and smell him to my heart's content—

Gemma curved her manicured fingers around the back of Will's neck, then leaned over and flicked her snaky tongue inside his mouth. Ugh. So disgusting. My school needs to do better about policing PDAs.

"So I'll see you," I told Will, already turning away. I was hoping I could get that last image out of my brain.

"Yeah, see you," Will said with a laugh, and when I looked back they were going at it again.

AAAAH! MY EYES!! MAKE IT STOP!

What can he possibly see in her?

And what can I do to be more like that?

Thirty-one

I raced home from work, got there by 5:15. If I could quickly do a few hours of homework, eat something fast, get to bed by 9:00, SET MY ALARM for 2:00—five hours sleep wasn't much, but it would have to do. I *had* to find Halli tonight.

It was hard to tear myself away. Will was still working on the computers when I left, but our mothers were both in the office, too, so I couldn't really just sit there all afternoon staring at him the way I wanted to. And besides, the bookkeeping always backs up when I don't stay on top of it, and it's close enough to the end of the month that I figured I might as well pay the bills.

"How are we doing this month?" Elena asked me when I brought her the checks to sign. My mom looked like she was busy catching up on her paperwork, so I decided not to bother her.

"Not too bad," I said. "Same base donations, and a lot of new people responding to the fall campaign." Every August and

September, *Build a Fund for Good* does a special donation drive to buy supplies for some of the low-income schools in our community. We should be able to write some pretty fat checks and make a lot of kids happy once all the deposits are in.

"How about consulting fees?" Elena asked.

I ran a quick report from our accounting program. "A lot better than over the summer—look at those two extra gigs in Houston."

Lately my mom has been making more of a push to get her consulting services out there. Other non-profit organizations around the country hire her to come in and assess the way they're running their businesses. My mom spends anywhere from a couple of days to a week, looking over their finances, reading the personnel files, talking to management about what goals they'd like to reach. Then she usually meets with the staff to do a kind of motivational/educational workshop that gets everybody fired up and ready to really move the organization forward.

I know it's very rewarding for my mom to see the changes she can help people make, but it's also pretty exhausting. And lately she's been taking those trips at least two or three times a month.

She let me take the car home and said she'd grab a ride from Elena. So I had the house to myself for a little while. Time to try Dr. Whitfield again.

He answered almost right away. He was wearing a lab coat this time. I wondered what kind of experiment he might have just been doing.

"I'm sorry about yesterday," I said.

"Did you tell her yet?" the professor asked.

"No, but I will. I promise."

"Audie—"

"Please, Dr. Whitfield, can we go back to what you were telling me? About the observer problem and psychokinesis. I really want to know."

He sighed in a grumpy way, but he obviously couldn't resist. "All right. This is just a theory I'm working on right now, but it seems to fit. Tell me what you think."

Hold up: *He* wanted to know what *I* thought about some physics theory of his. I almost blurted out, "*Really?*," but managed to play it cool.

"The observer problem," Dr. Whitfield continued, "tells us that elementary particles are affected by what we, as humans—as observers—do to them. Even just looking at them can change their velocity or position. In fact, some physicists say that particles such as electrons don't even exist until someone looks at them."

I'd read all of that in Professor Hawkins's various books, but it was still sort of hard to understand. Or maybe not so hard to understand, but just hard to picture. How could something not exist until you look at it? Some physicists have even gone so far as to say that the moon doesn't exist unless someone is looking at it. If everyone on Earth looked away at the same time, the moon would disappear from the sky. Not just no longer be visible, but no longer *exist*. Trippy.

"So in effect," Dr. Whitfield said, "consciousness—what our minds are doing when we observe something—is able to directly affect matter. If just looking at a particle can change its speed or position, or even bring it into existence in the first place, then that means consciousness has manipulated matter. Which is all psychokinesis is. Mind over matter. You with me so far?"

He waited and watched my face while I thought that through.

"Yes," I said. "I'm with you."

"Good. Now," Dr. Whitfield said, "let's bring this whole theory to bear on your situation."

I got a little chill.

"Quantum physics agrees that consciousness affects matter at the microscopic level—electrons, protons, and so forth. What you have shown, I believe, is that the same holds true at the *macroscopic* level—big things, like human beings.

"Can you see if I do it here?" Dr. Whitfield held up a pad of paper and wrote my name on it.

"I can see."

He drew a circle around "Audie."

"You, Audie, are the observer. Your consciousness is at work during your experiment. And what are you observing?" He wrote down my name a second time, and put a triangle around it. "Audie, the macroscopic entity. You could be a photon, a neutron, but you're not—you're a person. You with me?"

"With you," I said.

"Why shouldn't Audie the observer," he said, pointing to the circle, "affect Audie the object?" he finished, pointing to the triangle. "You set out to move your body from one universe to another using your consciousness alone—not some teleportation machine or other mechanical device. If consciousness alone can affect the universe at the subatomic level, then why not at the visible, human level?"

"Wait a minute, wait a minute," I said, the excitement building inside me. "You mean I thought myself over? Across the gap from my universe to hers?"

"What else could it be?" Dr. Whitfield said.

"But what about Halli's part in it?" I asked. "It didn't work until she started meditating again."

"I think it might be a resonance field," Dr. Whitfield said. "The two of you created sympathetic resonance with each other. It's like two pianos being in the same room: if you hit a middle C on one of them it causes that string in the piano to vibrate, and then the middle C string on the other piano will start vibrating, too."

"So it is vibration," I said.

"Yes, but it's more than that." Dr. Whitfield pointed at his drawing again. "It's psychokinesis, Audie. It's your mind moving your matter. That's my theory, at least. What do you think of it?"

I tipped my head back and whooped. I didn't know what else to do. It was so thrilling—so wonderful to talk to someone about it and hear such an elegant, complex quantum physics solution arising out of the puzzle. I felt like I was reading a textbook and *in* it at the same time. Me the observer, me the observed.

"Professor Whitfield, I think it's *brilliant*. Seriously wonderful and brilliant. Thank you so much—I can't believe you came up with that."

Dr. Whitfield smiled. "It's not me, Audie, it's you. I could have fiddled around with ideas like these for a long time and never had an actual demonstration of them. Thank you. What you've done is remarkable."

I would have loved to stay on the computer with him for another hour or more, but I heard my front door open. My mom was home.

"I have to go," I told the professor. "I'm really sorry. I wish we could keep talking about this. I'll call you tomorrow—"

"Is that your mother?" Dr. Whitfield asked. "You should tell her—I need you to tell her. If this theory is right, I may want to pub—"

I clicked off the call.

My mother stood in my doorway. "Hi, sweetie, how's the homework?"

"Not bad. I'm going to try to get to bed early again tonight."

My mother pushed her hair off of her face. "Sounds good to me. Pizza tonight?"

"Sounds great."

I looked at the clock. Almost 6:30. I still had at least a few hours of studying to do.

But the delay was so, so worth it. I sat there and replayed in my head the whole conversation with Dr. Whitfield. Wow. Not just microwow, but *macro*wow.

Was it really true? Had I really done all that he said? And what about the resonance field he talked about? We didn't discuss that nearly enough.

I scrubbed my hands over my face. Unbelievable. So huge and thrilling and totally unbelievable.

But someone believes. Not only believes, but understands, and can explain it.

I kept my voice down, but I had to squeal. I whispered a "Yaaaaay!"

"Pineapple and onion?" my mom shouted from the kitchen.

"Pineapple and onion sounds great!"

Thirty-two

I squinted. Not because the sun was so bright—it was actually this sort of golden light, much gentler than what I'm used to at home—but because my eyes weren't used to what I was seeing. Rock and rock and rock and rock. No trees, no shrubs, just rock.

And a deliriously happy dog. And Halli. Who grinned at me and offered her usual "Heya" before handing me a bundle of clothes.

We'd agreed that I'd show up wearing just the thick long underwear my mom bought me a few years ago when we decided to try sledding in the mountains above Tucson. That lasted half a day—we realized neither one of us likes being cold—but I still had the clothes, since I never seem to get rid of anything.

"This is good," I said of the private little nook Halli had found us off the trail. It was hidden enough that no one could see us from below or above.

"Hurry, though," Halli said. "People could come over that rise any minute. I'll keep a lookout."

"I'm so sorry about yesterday!" I said. "I overslept and then I had to go to school—"

"It's fine," Halli said. "Just hurry." She glanced above her up the trail. She was making me nervous.

"Did I miss anything important?" I asked. It's hard to dress when there's a dog constantly trying to lick you, but I sped it up as best I could.

"No, just the train ride and a night at the inn. Hurry—two hikers up above."

I finished pulling on the black hiking pants she'd brought me, then slipped the thick fleece shirt over my head and pulled it down. I hadn't bothered wearing shoes, since I didn't have anything appropriate anyway. I slipped on the brand new pair of hiking boots Halli handed me.

"Did you buy these?" I asked. "For me?"

"I didn't have an extra pair in your size. Ginny was a nine."

"Thank you," I said, almost ridiculously pleased. My first gift in another realm.

"You're welcome. But keep an eye out for blisters. Ideally I should have had you start wearing those a few weeks ago to break them in." Halli smiled. "But, then, I didn't know you a few weeks ago."

Which almost seems impossible. Has it really only been six days?

"Besides," Halli said, "I didn't know myself I'd be coming up here until a few days ago. I owe that entirely to you."

"To me?" I laced up the second boot even though Red's face kept blocking my view. "What did I do?"

"You woke me up," Halli said.

"How?"

She sighed and leaned back against the rock. "I've been so isolated this past year—on purpose. I haven't gone anywhere or done anything. Every adventure I've ever had has been with Ginny. I wasn't sure if I wanted to do it anymore without her.

"But then you showed up," Halli said, "and I saw how I used to be."

I stared at her in shock. "*I* remind you of how *you* used to be?" What, I thought—weak and pasty and scraggly-haired?

"Adventurous," Halli said. "Curious. Willing to go try new things and go new places just to see what the world is like."

She stood up and brushed off the back of her pants. "We should go. We have a lot of ground to cover today."

I was glad that she turned and started hiking, because I didn't know what to say to her. The idea that *she* found *me* inspirational in any way was just ludicrous. I mean, I understood her point about sort of giving up for a while after her grandmother died, but my experiment in meditation was nothing compared to all those maps I'd seen on Halli's walls. She's obviously lived a *much* bigger life than I've ever even imagined for myself.

To which I know she would have said, "But you traveled to another universe."

Yeah, but it almost feels accidental. Like I just stumbled on an idea that turned out to be right. A good idea—don't get me wrong—but a lucky one, nevertheless.

The people Halli had spotted up above caught up with us soon enough. When I saw them at a distance and noticed how fast they were hiking, I thought they must be really young and fit and burly.

No, turns out they were really old and fit and burly. At least as old as my Grandma Marion, if not older.

"*Grüs Gott*," the woman said to Halli.

"*Grüs Gott*," Halli answered back.

I just smiled and gave them a quick nod.

Then Halli and the two of them started talking in what I could only assume was German. While I stood there smiling like an idiot.

At one point the woman turned toward me and asked Halli a question.

"*Nein*," Halli answered. "*Das ist meine Cousine.*" Which, even though she pronounced it "coozeena," sounded an awful lot like "cousin." So I guess we were skipping the twin thing.

"Ah," the woman answered, smiling and nodding at me. I smiled and nodded back.

"*Auf Wiedersehen*," the woman eventually said, giving us a little wave as she hiked on.

"*Wiedersehen*," Halli responded.

The old man smiled at us and followed his companion.

As soon as the couple was far enough out of hearing, I said, "So I'm your cousin, right?"

"It just seems easier," Halli said.

"Fine with me. I don't know any of these people."

But that was the thing, as I was soon to find out.

They knew *her*.

Thirty-three

At first I thought people were just being friendly. I thought maybe that's how it was with everyone in the Alps.

Stopping to talk, to ask a few questions, to smile, and sometimes shake Halli's hand. I heard "coozeena" a lot. Apparently a lot of people had to be told I was her cousin.

At one point a few hours into the hike, two young men with long legs and big strides caught up to us and were ready to just pass us and keep on going, when one of them stopped and elbowed his friend. The two of them whispered. Then the one who'd been elbowed said in hesitant English, "Excuse—Halli Markham?"

"*Si*," Halli answered. "*Buon giorno*." Then they carried on the rest of the conversation in Italian. While I smiled stupidly because I couldn't understand. Although the words *mia cogina* did sound a little like *Cousine*, which meant Halli had to explain our similarity again.

The two guys were *really* into Halli. I mean really. They talked faster and faster, and one of them made hand motions like waves on the ocean, and the other one slapped his forehead at that and then talked *really* fast, and all the while Halli was . . . polite. That's the only word I could use to describe it. She certainly wasn't as animated as they were. She said "*Si, si,*" a lot and let the guys go on for quite a while. But finally you could see she was trying to wrap it up.

She said something more in Italian, made an "I'm sorry" shrug of her shoulders, and the young men each took a turn shaking her hand and kissing both of her cheeks. Then she waved goodbye to them and they finally trekked on, and once they were far enough ahead of us, Halli sagged down onto the trail.

"Sometimes they wear me out."

"Who, those guys?" I asked. "Do you know them?"

"No, just . . . admirers, I guess."

"Of you?" It came out sounding more surprised than I meant it to. Of course people would admire Halli. She was obviously cool.

Halli looked at the sky. "We only have another half hour or so before you have to wake up."

Seriously, I was *so* disappointed to remember that. I was just getting into the hiking. It was arduous in places, but it was also incredibly beautiful out there in the cold mountains above the treeline.

"I wish I could just pop back there, tell my mom to let me sleep in today—tell her I'm sick or something—and come back."

"Can you do that?" Halli asked.

I considered it. Went through a quick checklist of what I thought we'd be doing in each of my classes. Tried to decide if there was anything too important to miss.

I've never been a school ditcher. Never. It's just not in my nature. But maybe it's because I never had a better offer.

"Let me do this," I said. "I know if I tell my mom I'm sick, she'll fuss over me for a while, so I won't be able to come right back. Let me see if I can talk her into going to work at her normal time, then I'll come back as soon as I can."

"What time should I look for you?" Halli asked.

I did the calculation. "Let's make it 5:00 this evening, just to be safe. That's 9:00 AM my time. I'll tell her I just want to sleep, so I'm turning off the phone. She might come home for lunch to check on me, but we'll just have to take our chances."

That would give me from 5:00 at night to as late as 1:00 in the morning Halli's time, if my mom stayed at work all day. Not that I'd need to be in Halli's world that long. I was sure that after a long day of hiking, she'd want to go to bed pretty early.

We hiked a little bit further, then started looking for a convenient place from which I could disappear. We sat in the shadow of a small cliff and waited for my alarm to go off. No sense in leaving any sooner than I had to.

"I'll be looking for you," Halli said. "Five o'clock."

"Five o—"

Then the horrible, hideous beep from my clock.

I pushed out of bed and stumbled toward the kitchen, where my mother sat sipping her coffee and reading the paper.

I leaned against the doorway and groaned.

"Oh, Mom, I feel *soooo* sick."

Thirty-four

Halli said we'd be sleeping in a hut.

I had a perfect image of it in my mind. We'd crest some hill, and there it would be, this sweet, simple little wooden structure—a hermit's hut—where we could sleep for the night. No electricity, just lanterns or candles. Although Halli did say there would be food there. So maybe just cold bread and water.

And even though she hadn't brought sleeping bags and pads like she had with her at the campsite where I first met her and Red, she did bring something called a sleep sack for each of us, and said that would be enough. Apparently there were mattresses of some kind in the huts, and blankets, and you just sleep in your little sack like a cocoon, and layer the blankets over it.

But when Halli and I met up again in the bedroom of the hut, and she escorted me out into the hallway to show me around, all I could think was, hermit's hut?

Um, excuse me, it was a party.

As in *hordes* of people. Maybe a hundred? Young, old, men, women, Italians, Germans, Austrians, Swiss, and yes, even a few other Americans besides Halli and me.

"Why are all these people here?" I asked, slightly alarmed.

Halli laughed. "I'm not the only person who knows about the Alps."

She gave me a quick tour of the place—or at least the bottom floor. The building was more like a dorm than a hut. A big dining hall, several floors that she said held plenty of rooms and beds, community bathrooms (for each gender, of course—even in a parallel universe they understand the need for modesty), and special heated rooms where everyone could hang up and dry all their moist, stinky clothing and boots.

"Where's Red?"

She pointed her thumb behind us. "Dogs sleep in their own building." She leaned over and whispered, "Which is why this isn't my favorite place. Wait till you see where we're going tomorrow."

I missed my little buddy. Missed always being tackled first thing when I showed up in Halli's universe.

Maybe that's a sign. Maybe I need my own dog some day.

"Hungry?" Halli asked.

I was, but I wasn't sure for what. It was breakfast time to my body, but here it was dinner time. I could adapt.

Halli took me to the dining hall. Propped just outside the doors was a menu written on a chalkboard. The menu was in German. Halli translated it for me.

The main theme seemed to be potatoes. Which was fine with me. My preferred preparation is in the potato chip form, but I've also been known to dive face-first into a bowl of mashed. I'm not picky.

Halli pointed to the listing for the vegetable stew. "Mmm, that's my favorite here."

"Okay, I'll take that, too."

Halli placed our order—in German, of course—with the hut manager. She paid the manager, too, with a handful of some kind of coin I've never seen before. I couldn't even offer to pay my share, since (a) I wasn't sure the place took dollars, (b) I hadn't stuffed any cash into the waistband of my long underwear, and (c) I wasn't sure if doing that would have worked anyway. I had no idea if money traveled.

Once the hut manager turned away, I asked Halli if I could see one of her coins.

One side had an image of two intersecting circles. Pretty basic. The other side showed a man's face in profile. He looked sort of vaguely familiar, which kind of surprised me. But his name wasn't jumping out at me—not that it would have been his name over in Halli's world anyway. Still, it bugged me that I couldn't think who he reminded me of.

"What do you call these?" I asked Halli as I handed her back the coin.

"Icies."

"You mean, like . . . ice?"

"No, international currency. ICs."

"International?" I said. "Does that mean everybody uses the same money? In the whole world?"

"Of course," Halli said. "Don't you have that?"

Dollars, Euros, rupees, yuan, pesos—I couldn't even think of all the different kinds of money out there. It seemed sort of overcomplicated, now that Halli mentioned it.

"Let's go in," Halli said. "They'll bring us our food in a minute." Then she opened the door and led me into the noisy dining hall.

All of the tables were full. Or at least mostly full. We found two seats at a table near the front, and as soon as we approached I heard more than one person in the room shout, "Halli Markham!"

Halli gave them all a little wave, then sat down.

The young woman beside Halli pointed at me. I heard Halli give her usual introduction, "*Meine Cousine.*" Why did everyone care so much who I was? It was kind of getting annoying. But everyone smiled at me and I smiled back. Whatever.

Then for the rest of the evening the conversation swirled around me, all in languages I didn't understand. Halli was pretty good about translating for me as we went along, but sometimes the conversations went too fast. It's like those scenes you sometimes see in movies where the foreign character says something really, really long and complicated, with many parts, with lots of emotion, and when it comes time for the translator to translate, he says, "Mr. Kobenevsky says 'No, thank you.' "

"What language was that?" I asked after someone new had stopped by the table and conversed with Halli for a few minutes.

"Polish."

"How many languages do you speak?"

Halli laughed. "A little of a lot."

I ended up retreating to my own special world where it was just me and my delicious dinner. We understood each other perfectly. A big heaping bowl of vegetable stew made of potatoes, onions, carrots, and cabbage; tons of bread; some sort of fried dough with powdered sugar on it for dessert (unbe*liev*ably great).

By the time my belly was full, I was totally exhausted. Not just because I'd been hiking over rock and more rock for several hours earlier, but because being in the middle of a noisy crowd and not being able to understand people is really mentally tiring.

Plus, I'd already been up for hours, with very little sleep before that. So the whole thing was catching up to me.

Looked like it finally caught up to Halli, too. Shortly after dessert, she yawned deep and wide. She leaned over and patted my leg. "Let's go say goodnight to Red."

We headed back to our room to get our coats so we could take the dog out for a brief walk. As we made our way toward the far end of the long hallway, I noticed a lot of our dinner companions turned off and headed up the stairs to the next floor.

"Where are they all going?"

"To the *mattress lager*."

"What's that?"

"You'll find out tomorrow."

Very mysterious. And too mysterious for me to care. I just wanted to lie down and sleep.

But first, a certain furry companion.

We grabbed our coats and were just about to leave the room when Halli's screen rang. She gave out a sound between a groan and a growl.

"Better hide," Halli told me.

I crouched down behind one of the two beds, and Halli stood as far away from me as she could. Then she pressed the top of her screen and we watched her mother's head swirl into view.

"What," Halli said.

"Hello," her mother answered cheerfully. "Where are you?"

"You know where I am."

"Where, *specifically*?"

Halli told her the name of the hut—something long in German.

"Are you alone?" her mother asked.

"No, there are about a hundred people here. They're all my friends."

"Don't be sarcastic."

"I'm not. They know me up here. I've come often."

"How long are you staying?" her mother asked.

"A long time. Until the snow runs me out of here."

"Could you be more specific?"

"Why do you care, Regina?"

I heard a sniffling sound. I stole a look over the top of the bed. Halli's mother was wiping what might have been a fake tear. Halli rolled her eyes at me.

"I'm tired, Regina," Halli said. "I have to go to sleep now."

"Please be careful."

"I'm always careful," Halli said. "I wouldn't still be alive if I weren't."

With that, she punched some button on her screen and her mother's head disappeared. Halli growled in irritation, then stood there for a moment composing herself.

I didn't say anything. It wasn't my business.

"I need my dog," Halli said forcefully.

I wasn't going to argue.

"Hi, buddy! Did you miss us?" Halli asked as the dog jumped and whined with excitement. Other guests of the dogs' hut wagged their tails and yipped at us, obviously hoping for a little spillover love. I petted a few heads in the near vicinity, then Halli and Red and I took a walk.

There was a small lake in front of the main building, and the three of us strolled along one side. The night was clear and cold. Red pranced with his tail high, so happy to be with his girls.

"Does your mother do that to you?" Halli asked me after a while.

"Do what?"

"Make you want to throw something."

"No," I said with a laugh. "Hardly ever."

"It's gotten much worse since Ginny died," Halli said. "She never used to try to track me down before."

"Maybe she worries about you, or something."

Halli muttered, "Or something."

We wandered back toward the hut. By now I was so tired I wouldn't have minded taking a little nap in the dirt. But it was too cold for that, and I looked forward to that soft second bed I'd hidden behind back in Halli's room.

"Good night, boy," Halli said, pressing her forehead to Red's and scratching behind both his ears. "I'll come get you early tomorrow. Stay warm."

"He doesn't mind you leaving him?"

"No, he's been here before," Halli said. "He knows I'll always come back for him. Besides, he has some friends in there." She pointed to the Husky on one of the bunks in back, and a big fluffy mutt to the left. "Rodolfo and Moritz. Good company."

I gave Red a big hug around the neck and told him good night. "What time do you think it is?" I asked Halli.

She looked up at the sky. "Around 8:30, I'd say."

Amazing, I thought. "You can tell that from the stars?"

"No, from the sounds in the hut. Dining room is closed. Everyone's going to bed. Listen and you can hear it."

The night was so still, I could hear it. It's all in training yourself to find the noise. Maybe that's what Dr. Whitfield was talking about in his book—something as simple as this, listening for what you don't usually bother to hear, but your ears are perfectly capable of picking up.

"I should probably go," I said. "My mom might come home for lunch to check on me. I should be sick in bed."

"When are you coming back?" Halli asked.

"Tonight. I mean tomorrow morning, for you. Is 10:00 still okay?"

"I'll be on the trail," Halli said. "I'll find us a good spot and wait for you. But let me warn you: tomorrow's a big hiking day. So get your sleep and have a good meal. We have a lot of terrain to cover before we get to the next hut."

I felt this weird kind of tickle on the back of my neck. Or maybe it was on the back of my skull. I scratched there to make it go away.

"Are you coming back in?" Halli asked.

"No, I'd better not—" The tickle felt very uncomfortable now, very hard to ignore. "I think I should—"

My brain yanked at my body. Ripped it right out of Halli's world back into my own. I must have landed back on my bed in the splittest second before my mother opened the door.

"How you feeling, honey?"

Groggy and disoriented and WEIRD.

"I'm . . . fine, Mom."

Something had just happened. Something out of my control, and yet it felt fully part of me. Not like when my phone rang that first morning, and the sound of it summoned me back to my world. Not when Red did the same to Halli.

This was something more subtle, more internal, and kind of made me a little sick to my stomach. There hadn't been any sound that I was aware of. It was just a *feeling*, and that feeling was enough to instantly bring me back.

While my mom made us soup for lunch, I quickly logged on and checked Professor Whitfield's class schedule for Thursdays. It looked like he was done by 1:45. I checked my clock—a little more than an hour to wait. As soon as my mom went back to work I had to find him. Because this was definitely weird. And I thought if anyone might have insight, it would be him.

I think it's possible I just had my first psychic experience.

Thirty-five

"Not psychic," Dr. Whitfield corrected me. "Remote sensing."

"Okay, remote sensing," I said. "What's the difference?"

"Calling something psychic implies that only someone with special abilities can do it. Remote sensing is something we're all capable of—we just need to train our brains to pick up on the signals."

Kind of what Halli described last night—or this morning, really—when we were listening outside the hut.

"But what was it?" I asked. "It made me feel . . . itchy."

"Describe to me again the experiences you and Halli had when you heard noises back home."

I went through the two scenarios again.

"Interesting . . ." He scratched at his beard. I was starting to get used to the gesture.

"Professor?" I was also starting to get used to that. I liked calling him "Professor" instead of "Dr. Whitfield" all the time. It felt more informal, and he didn't seem to mind. "Do you want to hear my theory?"

"Yes, of course," he answered immediately. Like there was no question I might have some good ideas.

"I've been thinking more about the observer problem. One thing Professor Haw—" Maybe it wasn't so good to keep talking about him all the time—especially in front of Professor Whitfield. "One thing I've read in various books," I began again, "is that the observer problem might also affect whether something is a wave or a particle. When we're looking at it, it's a particle. When we look away, it goes back to being a wave."

"That's one of the theories," Professor Whitfield said. "Go on."

"So what I was thinking was that maybe that's what's happening to me. Maybe when I'm over there I'm a particle because I'm focused on myself and what I'm doing, but there's still an aspect of me that's a wave, and maybe it leaves like a kind of vapor trail, you know? Like when an airplane goes through the sky."

"A vapor trail . . ." The professor scratched his beard. "Some sort of signature wave that you can follow back?"

"Right," I said. "And maybe the wave version of me is aware of things going on back here that the particle version of me could never know."

"So it signals you—"

"And then the wave whooshes me back. That's what it felt like, anyway."

"Fascinating," the professor said. "So you think it was in response to whatever stimulus was associated with your mother coming home? Because you didn't consciously hear anything this time, right? Not like when you heard the phone ringing."

"Right," I said. "It must have been subconscious. My wave form knew I would get into trouble and so it called me back."

He shook his head. "This is all so—"

"I know," I said. "Bizarre."

Professor Whitfield chuckled. "That's one word for it."

It was such a relief to be able to have a conversation like this—an intelligent, complicated discussion with someone who actually knows enough quantum physics to understand how bizarre it really is. I've been craving that for so long. It was just the kind of conversation I once dreamed of having with Professor Hawkins.

Professor Whitfield smiled. "Audie Masters . . ."

"Yes?"

Then he simply clapped. "Excellent work today. You should be very proud of yourself."

I beamed. "Thank you, sir. So do you think I'm right?"

"I don't know, but I can appreciate some fine analysis when I see it. I'm going to think it over tonight. Let's talk again tomorrow."

Thirty-six

Halli wasn't kidding about the day's hiking being hard. The trail went straight up in some places—there were even thick cables along the side of the cliff faces so you could pull yourself along and not fall off.

"Sorry I'm so slow," I said to Halli.

"Don't worry about it. You're doing fine."

But I wasn't really doing fine. I could tell I was holding her back. My genetic double and I are *not* genetic doubles when it comes to physical strength. Clearly Halli could have gone twice as fast if I weren't there. I really have to start working out.

Plus I didn't want her to know, but she'd been right about the boots: they were giving me blisters—big, fat, honking ones. I just had to keep hiking, and hope the boots would break in at some point.

The trail we were on wasn't just steep, it was also slick in places where the rocks were in shadow and never quite dried. I was walking like an old woman, making extra, extra sure of my balance and footing. Meanwhile Halli seemed to be made of mountain goat genes—the slippery rock didn't bother her at all.

I might have been walking like my own version of an old woman, but the real old women—the burly-looking Austrian woman who passed us, the two German ladies who looked like they could have fully kicked my behind, and proved it by sprinting past both Halli and me while we picked our way up the trail—those were the women I want to grow up to be some day.

I mentioned it to Halli, and she agreed.

"I always look at women like that," she said, "and wonder what they were doing at my age. I like to backtrack and think, 'To be her at 90, I have to do this at 17.' "

"Like what?" I asked, thinking maybe I should start doing those things, too. Although really the question was, to be Halli at 17, what do I need to start doing right away?

"I try to eat the way they eat," Halli said, "get out and hike as much as they do—do you realize a lot of these older people have been hiking these mountains all their lives? 'Oh, look, it's Thursday, I think I'll go climb a peak.' So I try to be like that. This whole past year Red and I have gone out every day—hiking and backpacking in the summer, skiing or snowshoeing in the winter."

I thought about my own life and my own schedule—there was no way I could do something like that every day. Maybe go for a walk or do some sort of workout, but hike or snowshoe all day? No way.

And finally something occurred to me that I must have known, but hadn't really considered before. "You don't go to school."

"No," Halli said. "Ginny taught me everything herself."

"And that was . . . okay? I mean, with your parents?"

I should have known better than to ask that. Halli scowled. "They didn't have anything to do with it."

I needed to go back to a safer topic.

"So is that what Ginny was like?" I asked. "These old women we keep seeing up here?"

It worked. Halli smiled. "No—much, much tougher. Ginny could have out-hiked even those Italian guys we saw yesterday. She was amazing."

Sometimes it seems like Halli doesn't want to talk too much about her grandmother, but this time she did.

"The last time I was up here with Ginny," she said, "I was fifteen. We stayed about three weeks, just hiking around, never wanting to leave." Halli turned around to check on me. "Keep your hand on the cable. Good. That's good. Try to keep your eyes forward—don't always look at your feet. It'll make you dizzy."

She was right about that. I was becoming a little rock-blind—that's the only thing I'd been looking at for hours.

"This hut we're going to today," Halli continued, "it was Ginny's and my favorite. We tried to come back here every year."

"Is that all the two of you did?" I asked. "Travel around? India for a month, the Alps—where else?"

"Lots of places. That was my education. Ginny taught me by showing me."

"Is that why you know so many languages?"

"Yes," Halli said. "It's from living with people and having to learn to understand them. Ginny hardly ever translated for me. She wanted me to learn."

I hoped Halli wasn't going to throw me into the deep end of the pool by refusing to translate for me anymore. I already felt isolated enough during dinner last night. If Halli hadn't occasionally said things like, "He says he's been hiking for a week, and finally the weather is perfect," or "She wants to know if this is your first time here." (When I smiled at the woman and nodded, she asked Halli a flurry of other questions. I saw Halli grow more and more uncomfortable. She said, "*nein*" a lot, meaning "no," and finally shrugged and gave a short, almost stiff response. The woman shrugged, too, and gave me an odd look. The whole thing was weird.)

The sky was that golden yellow again. I loved the sun here. I almost didn't need to wear the sunglasses Halli had brought me. It felt good to lean back sometimes and feel the sun on my face—especially whenever we came out of one of those dark, slippery patches where I kept imagining losing my footing and careening down the mountain.

Around noon Alps time, Halli and Red and I found a warm patch of flat rock where we could sit and have our lunch.

Halli unpacked a whole container of peaches. Not ripe, heavy peaches like I'd seen back in her greenhouse, but sliced peaches that she'd been dehydrating that night at her house while we discussed the details of our trip. First she dehydrated them to take all the water out so they'd weigh nothing for most of her travels, then she rehydrated them with water she had poured over them this morning. They plumped right up and tasted sweet and fresh. She threw a few to a very grateful Red.

But that wasn't all. She also unpacked a loaf of bread with sunflower seeds all over the outside, like a crust. And a fresh cucumber that she cut slices off with her camping knife, and a kind of savory spread that she said she also made fresh at home, then dehydrated, then rehydrated again today.

Lots of process, but it was so worth it. That lunch was better than anything I ever have at home or at school. Which might not be saying much, since I'm usually going straight for the Doritos and dessert at the cafeteria, but still, it was an impressive feast for how few resources she had out there on a mountain.

After we'd eaten, Halli took a few minutes to herself to lean back against the rock and close her eyes and feel the golden sunshine on her face. And looking at her doing that, it occurred to me what the real difference is between the two of us.

We're like those side-by-side experiments scientists do sometimes to see what's best for a plant. I'm the one getting too little water and not enough sunlight, and Halli's the one being fed all the best nutrients, getting the best spot in the sun, and having Mozart played to her twenty-four hours a day.

Our hair is only part of it, but maybe it's the best evidence of all. Hers is so thick and shiny, mine is like a limp, tattered rag. Now expand that to my whole body, all the way down to the cellular level, and that's probably how I compare to Halli. It's certainly how I feel when I'm around her.

"Do you think I could ever be like you?" I asked. Then I was sort of horrified, because I didn't realize I'd actually said that thought out loud.

"You *are* me," Halli said. "Isn't that the whole point?"

Might as well keep going. "No, I mean, yes, we're genetically the same, but look at you. Look at me. I'm like you if you'd lain sick in bed for half a year."

Halli tilted her head a little more forward and squinted at me. "You know what Ginny would say?"

"No, but I'd like to hear."

" 'Get off your butt!' " Halli shouted in her old-lady voice. " 'Stop your whining! You think this mountain is gonna climb itself? You think this river is gonna flow backwards just so you can rest for awhile? Get up! Quit yer griping and your suffering. No one but the birds and the beasts is gonna hear it.' " Halli coughed and returned to her regular voice. "Or something like that."

I had to laugh. "Was she really like that?"

"Sometimes. She was really funny. And really tough. And I really, really miss her."

The sudden look of sadness on Halli's face told me maybe I'd gone too far.

"So what do you say?" she asked, slapping her palms against her thighs. "Better get going. This mountain isn't going to climb itself."

Just then we heard a shout. Or more like a cross between a shout and a curse and a cry of pain. It came from just around the bend, from that slippery section of trail we'd maneuvered right before looking for a sunny spot to take a break.

Red's hackles went up. "Easy, boy," Halli said. "Let's go see." The two of them went off to investigate. I followed more slowly, extra-mindful now of the treacherous footing that lay ahead.

When I rounded the bend, I found Halli kneeling in front of a guy whose leg was outstretched. He sucked in his breath every time Halli touched his ankle. I saw him shake his head at some question, then grimace as Halli tried to rotate the joint.

There were two other people with him—another guy around his same age—around Halli's and my age, actually—and a young woman with long blond hair. All three of them were talking to Halli, and none of them seemed to notice me.

But then Halli looked up as I approached, and the girl turned around to look, too.

And oh, great masters of physics, please say no. Please say it isn't possible.

The girl? Was Gemma.

Thirty-seven

I stared at her in shock. She smiled a strange smile, then said something to Halli. I heard Halli answer something about "cousins."

My first thought was that Gemma had somehow figured out a way to follow me over.

But then I realized no, Hairball wasn't even a fraction that smart. And then my brain started doing the processing for me, now that it was over its initial horror.

Gemma had her own version over here in this universe, just like I did. But honestly, did I *have* to run into her? What were the physics of that?

But then my heart immediately lifted. Because if she was here, did that mean Will was, too? I looked at both of the guys, hoping it were true.

The one on the ground—the one in pain—had short, blondish-brownish hair and a strong, athletic-looking build. Definitely not Will.

The other guy—the one with his back to me—had dark brown hair, but not as dark as Will's. Unless over here the sun had lightened it. I cleared my throat, hoping to get him to turn around.

He did, and said in a British accent, "Hello there."

Not Will.

"Change in plans," Halli told me. "We're going to have to help Daniel here onto some dry ground, then I need to wrap his ankle."

"What happened?" I asked.

Gemma gave the guy on the ground a gentle shove. "My brother is an ahse, that's what."

He completed the trio of British accents by answering, "I'm afraid so. Sorry, everyone."

Halli told him not to worry, then organized the rest of us to help support him the last hundred feet or so from the shady patch into the sun. "We'll have more room there," Halli explained, "and none of us will have to freeze."

As soon as I was close enough, Gemma held out her hand and said, "Sarah. This is my brother Daniel. And that lot is Martin."

I did my dork wave. "Hi. I'm Audie."

"Halli Markham's cousin," Gemma—or Sarah—said.

"Yes."

"The resemblance is remarkable."

"People say that all the time," I said.

"I didn't know Halli Markham had a cousin," Gemma/Sarah said. "Nobody's ever mentioned you."

What did she mean, nobody had ever mentioned me? What business was it of hers whether Halli had fifty cousins or none? Gemma was just as annoying here as she was back home.

"Which side?" the guy called Martin asked.

"Excuse me?" I said.

"Cousin on which side—mother or father?"

Halli gave me the subtlest of head shakes. "We should start moving him," she told everyone. "That ankle's already starting to swell."

That diverted their attention, for which I was grateful. But I still didn't understand why I was being questioned by these total strangers. Why did they even care?

It took a while to help Daniel hobble and hop from the slick to the dry, the cold to the warm. But totally worth it. My fingers were frozen by the time we got back to our lunch spot. It didn't take long to get chilled in the shade.

We helped Daniel recline again, his back up against a rock, and then Halli went to work. She gently unlaced and removed his boot, while he winced and cursed and sucked in his breath.

His ankle looked like someone had stuck a pump to it and inflated it. It was already turning a grayish sort of purple. No wonder Daniel didn't like it when anyone touched it.

While Halli dug into her pack to get the first aid kit, Gemma/Sarah and her friend Martin went back to questioning me.

"The reason I asked that," Martin said, "was I wondered if Virginia Markham was your grandmother, too."

"Oh." I glanced at Halli for guidance. Again she subtly shook her head.

"No, we're cousins on my father's side."

"Who's your father?" Gemma/Sarah asked.

Now look here! I wanted to say. *Butt your big face out.* But again Halli stepped in.

"Our families don't really get along," she said. "It's a shame, really, because Audie and I have only just rediscovered each other. I think the last time we were together was when we were babies."

Daniel grimaced as Halli started wrapping his ankle in white tape. "Will we be reading about the two of you now with all your adventures?" he asked, looking like he wanted to distract himself with any sort of inane chat.

"Hope so," Halli answered, smiling at me.

I smiled so hard back at her I had to look away before I embarrassed myself. But seriously, that might be nicest thing I've ever heard.

"Pity you missed the Atlantic," Daniel said to me. Then he leaned back and closed his eyes and gave up talking for a while as Halli really got in there and wrapped.

I tried to play along. "Yeah, I'm sorry I missed it, too."

"How old were you when you did that?" Gemma/Sarah asked Halli.

"Twelve."

"Right!" Gemma/Sarah said. "Unbelievable!" She ticked off the accomplishments on her fingers. "The only grandmother-granddaughter rowing team ever to race across the Atlantic, the eldest and youngest competitors ever to race, and the eldest and youngest ever to successfully finish." Gemma/Sarah shook her head. "Brilliant."

"Thank you," Halli said, not looking up from Daniel's ankle. I tried to catch her eye—to get any sort of clue—but she stayed focused on her tape job.

"What did you think of that, Audie?" Gemma asked. (I had to start thinking of her as Sarah. *Sarah*.)

"Uhhh . . . I thought it was great!" I said. "Really great. Very proud."

I saw Halli smile. Not smile with pride, but almost like she was enjoying watching me try to improvise.

While I, on the other hand, was not enjoying hearing about this from Hairball instead of my own alternate me. Didn't she think I would have loved details like this? Rowing across the Atlantic? Are you kidding me? Why had she been holding back?

"Don't you wish you'd been out there," Sarah continued, "battling the waves and the sharks?"

"Umm... that's really more Halli's thing than mine."

"Maybe the two of you will race together now," Sarah said. "Now that Virginia's—"

"How's that feel?" Halli asked Daniel a little bit more loudly than she needed to. She smoothed her hands over the taped-up joint.

Daniel reached down and felt the ankle, too. "Remarkably well," he answered. "Thank you."

"Can he walk?" his friend Martin asked.

"No," Halli said. "We'll all still have to help him. The more he tries to walk on it, the longer it's going to take to heal."

"How long will it take?" Sarah asked.

"Could be a week," Halli said. "Everyone's different."

"A week?" Sarah said. "But that's nearly our entire holiday!"

"I'm really sorry," Daniel told his companions.

"Let's just shoot him and leave," Martin suggested.

"Love to, but my mum would be mad," Sarah answered. She sighed dramatically. "All right, we'll let you live, you git." To Halli she said, "How far to the next hut?"

"You don't want to know," Halli said. She glanced up at the sky. "We should get started. We don't want to get caught out here at dark."

I wasn't sure about my own time limit anymore. How long ago had we stopped for lunch? I went through the calculations again—noon here was 4:00 in the morning at home. Six-thirty, when my alarm would go off, was 2:30 in the afternoon here. Which it might be close to.

The math was making my brain hurt.

I went over to Halli and whispered, "Time?"

She nodded. "Might be a problem."

She looked around us, then pulled me toward the shaded section of trail. "We'll be right back," she told the others. "Sorry. Just wait right there. Audie needs to check something."

"How are you going to explain it?" I asked as we both hurried out of sight. "That I'm just gone?"

"I don't know," Halli said. "This is bad. Obviously I wasn't expecting these people."

I looked up and around us. "Is there any place you could say I went?"

"No. There's nothing around here except the next hut."

We both crouched on the cold trail and thought.

"I'll say you took a shortcut," Halli invented. "Those people don't know this trail. I'll tell them you went a different, harder way to get things ready at the next hut."

"You think they'll believe that?"

"I wouldn't," Halli said, "but they might."

I knew I had to go, but first I needed to get this off my chest.

"Halli, why didn't you tell me? About rowing the Atlantic? What else don't I know?"

Halli sighed. "I don't know—a lot, I suppose. Can we talk about it later?"

"But then will you tell me?" I asked. "Everything? I mean seriously, starting from the beginning. I don't feel like I know you at all."

"Will you tell me everything from the beginning, too?" she asked.

"Yeah, right," I said. "Like I've done anything nearly as important."

"I want to know," Halli said. She stuck out her hand. "Deal?"

I rolled my eyes and shook her hand. "Deal. But mine's boring."

"How do you know mine isn't?" Halli said.

"I don't know, somehow anything that starts with, 'There I was, rowing across the Atlantic,' seems like it would be a pretty good story."

"There I was," Halli countered, "living in an alternate world . . ."

"You'll see," I told her. "Boring."

But undeniably getting more interesting with each passing day.

Thirty-eight

"What is with you lately?" Lydia asked me at lunch. "You look like you never sleep anymore."

Oh, I sleep. For a few hours. Then I hike the Alps the rest of the night and sometimes help rescue injured young Englishmen. And still make it to school by first period.

I lifted my head off the cafeteria table, grunted something unintelligible, and went back to trying to sleep, which was hard to do with Gemma hyena-ing to her buddies over at the far table.

"I could teach you a special yoga pose," Lydia offered. "Twenty minutes of it is like taking a two-hour nap."

That got my attention. "Really?"

She crumpled up her lunch sack. "Let's go to the library. They have carpeting. I'll show you."

Since this was the first time I'd ever agreed to even try a yoga pose, she was pretty excited.

She showed me how to sit back on my knees, then curl forward, my arms loose at my sides, while I settled my forehead (excuse me—"third eye") flat against the floor.

"Now breathe deeply," she said, although I found that kind of hard while I was curled over that way. It must take some getting used to.

By the time I was in position there were only ten minutes left of lunch, but if ten minutes equaled one hour of sleeping? I'd take it.

And I needed it. Because as much as I would have loved to go straight home after school and grab a nap, it was Friday, and I had to work.

"Just got another consulting request," my mother told me when I came in. "Philadelphia next week. Is that all right? I know I just got back."

"It's *great*, Mom," and I meant it. What a relief. Maybe while she's out of town I can ditch another day or two of school and both get more sleep and spend more time with Halli. I've never really looked forward to my mother's trips before. Now I'm all for them.

I started entering the data for all the new donations that had come in, but my heart wasn't in it. What I really wanted to do was go home and get some sleep. But first call Professor Whitfield and report in to him—tell him about the whole Gemma/Sarah thing. I wondered what he'd say about that.

"What do you think of the new computers?" Elena asked me. She'd caught me looking at the clock again instead of entering data.

"Oh, I love them," I said. "They're so much faster than the old ones. Will really did a great job finding these for us."

"And so cheap," my mother said.

"Will's great," I said. It's the kind of thing I like to say as often as possible, whenever I have a good excuse. Because Will is great. Will is great. Sounds like one of my old juvenile poems. Except I would have thrown in a few rhymes here and there. "Will is great. Wish he'd ask me on a date. Then I'd celebrate. One day he'll be my mate. Our love is fate."

And so on to a barfalicious extent.

A little before 5:00 I started wrapping it up. Usually I don't care at all if I work overtime, but tonight I had better things to do.

My mom seemed to notice my antsiness. "Honey, can you give me about another half hour?"

"Oh, um . . ." I glanced at the clock for the two hundredth time. "Sure, I guess, but . . . could you maybe get a ride with Elena? Then I could take the car."

"What's your hurry?" she rightfully asked.

"No hurry, it's just . . . I have some things to do for the Columbia app. I wanted to check some statistics I heard about. Supposedly there's this graph on the Web about how many people they take from western high schools versus eastern ones."

Totally made up, total lie. And not a particularly creative one.

My mom looked a little put out. "Just half an hour—"

"Mom, really, if you wouldn't mind—"

"Fine," she said, holding the keys out to me. She didn't sound very fine, but I took them anyway. I really wanted to talk to Professor Whitfield before she came home.

"Thanks, Mom. Really. I appreciate it."

But she'd already gone back to reading an article on her computer. I'd have to make it up to her later. I was feeling pretty guilty.

But still, it had worked. I raced home and quickly logged on and contacted Professor Whitfield.

I told him the whole thing—how out of all the universes, Gemma had to show up in my life both places. And how Halli apparently had this whole big mysterious adventure-racing childhood that I knew nothing about.

I was only about fifteen minutes into the phone call, and just at the part where Professor Whitfield and I were laughing about the fact that if either of us could do math we could calculate the probability of someone like Gemma existing in every possible universe—when suddenly the door to my bedroom flew open, and there stood my mother.

She'd obviously sneaked into the house. I never heard her come in. I was better at detecting her with my vapor trail than I was with my regular ears.

"What is going on?" she demanded, striding purposefully over to my computer. She glared at the face on my screen. "Do you know my daughter is only in high school?"

"Mom!"

"Hello, Mrs.—Ms. Fletcher," Professor Whitfield said.

"Answer me!" she said. "What is this all about? What do you two have to be laughing about in such a chummy way? Why is my daughter sneaking home to talk to you?"

"I wasn't sneaking home—"

"Audie," Professor Whitfield said, "don't you think you should tell—"

"Bye," I said, and clicked off the call.

My mother planted her hands on her hips and glowered at me. Obviously I was in bigger trouble than I thought.

"Mom, he's just helping me. It's for the Columbia application."

"Don't give me that!" she said. "I can see there's something going on."

"Like what?" I asked, worried that she might have overheard some of what we'd said.

"He's obviously very attractive—"

"What? Eww!"

"Do you have a crush on this man?" she asked.

"No, Mom! Seriously! That's disgusting."

She folded her arms over her chest and kept glaring at me. "Audie . . ."

"Mom—" I almost had to laugh. Of all the things for her to suspect. "I *swear* to you, I have no interest in Professor Whitfield except as a teacher. How could you even think that?"

Her shoulders relaxed a little. "Sometimes teachers—"

"Ew. Stop. I promise you, Professor Whitfield is not that kind of person. He's just a regular, nice guy. He's helping me figure out some really hard science so I can impress the Admissions Committee. He's being *nice* to me—that's all."

My mother pursed her lips. It was her version of Professor Whitfield scratching his beard.

"You could tell me, you know. If there were anything wrong—"

"I know, Mom. I do. Of course. But there's nothing creepy going on."

Now she really relaxed. She sat on the edge of my bed and patted the spot next to her. I got up from my desk and joined her.

"Sweetie, I worry about you sometimes."

"Obviously," I said. "But you don't have to worry in this particular category. There's nobody. There's never been anybody." Except Will. In my heart.

She put her arm around my shoulder. "You're pushing yourself too hard. This Columbia thing is too much."

"It's due in a little over a month," I said. "I just have to do it right. If I get in, then I can relax the whole rest of the school year. But it's worth it to me to work extra hard right now and try to make it happen."

She leaned her head against mine. "I understand that, honey, but I think you have to be realistic. You're putting all your eggs in one basket."

"For now," I said, wishing she'd have a little more faith. "If I make Early Decision, I'll know by mid-December. Otherwise I have to wait until March or April. So it's worth it to me to know—to start working on the finances of it, too. But mostly just to know. You know, for my future."

My mother let go of me and sat up straight again. "So this professor—he's really going to help you?"

"I think so. He already is in some ways. He knows a lot about physics."

"Where does he teach?" she asked.

"A school in Colorado. Some college up in the mountains."

"I don't mean to be insulting to him," my mom said, "but why isn't he teaching at one of the better schools? Like Columbia?"

"I'm not really sure," I admitted. "I didn't think it was polite to ask."

"But you think he has enough clout to help you get into Columbia?"

"I don't know," I said. "I hope so."

My mom got up and went to the door. She paused and turned back.

"Honey, I don't want to hurt your feelings, but I really think you need to consider some alternatives. If this Columbia situation doesn't work out—"

"I know, Mom. But I just need to concentrate on that for now. Just until I get the application in. Then all I can do is wait."

"I love you, sweetie. I just don't want to see you disappointed."

"I know, Mom. It's okay."

But it wasn't okay. As soon as she left I sank back against my bed. If your own mother doesn't believe in you—

It was time to stop fooling around. I needed to start putting some of this experiment onto paper, in a form that would completely blow Professor Hawkins's hat off. He needed to give it just one glance to know that I am the star pupil he's been waiting for, and that the next big discoveries in quantum physics and cosmology are obviously coming from me.

I got up, went to my computer, opened up a new document on my screen.

EXPLORATIONS IN PARALLEL UNIVERSES, by Audie Masters.

Then I gave it a catchy subtitle: THE HIDDEN SECRETS REVEALED.

I pictured it in book form one day, my own photograph on the back. And down beneath that, the review from Professor Hawkins:

"Audie Masters is one of the greatest cosmological explorers and experimental physicists of our time. I knew from the moment I laid eyes on her research that she was destined to become one of the greatest students I'd ever have. *Explorations in Parallel Universes* is one of the most eye-opening, thought-provoking treatises I have ever had the privilege to read. I look forward to great things from Dr. Masters."

I started typing the introduction: "I've always been an admirer of Dr. Hawkins . . ."

I knew somewhere in there I'd need to mention Professor Whitfield, too. Give him a really big part. Clearly he deserves it.

Wonder what Professor Hawkins will think about that?

Thirty-nine

I'd already told Halli that since it was Friday night I could meet her a little earlier and then sleep in later. I never knew how much I could love a weekend until I started messing with my sleep this way.

So instead of setting my alarm for the middle of the night, I just stayed up until I knew my mom was asleep. I told Halli that would probably be around 10:00 my time—6:00 AM hers—and I wasn't far off.

I changed into my long underwear and made the journey. Soon to be tackled by a big yellow dog.

"Good boy, Red, hello!" It took a few minutes to wrestle him off me, and by then I was covered in fur. Not that I minded at all.

"Where are we?" I asked Halli.

"Paradise," she said.

Close enough.

Green, green, green. After all those miles of nothing but rock, this place was like an oasis. Green trees, green grass, even green paint on the wooden beams above the rustic stone hut.

There was fog rising from the ground. And some weird, eerie sound coming from the forest around us.

"*Hirsch*," Halli explained. "Red deer. They're bugling to each other."

Once I knew what it was, I thought the sound was beautiful. Not weird or eerie at all. Just . . . nature. Part of being outdoors. Part of a life I've never even been interested in before. But now I can see why people do this. It's a lot more interesting than just watching nature shows on TV.

I was happy to change into the clothes Halli handed me—this place was cold. I wondered if we were higher up.

As I pulled on the warm pants and shirt, I looked around some more.

We were hidden at the side of a small white building that looked more like the hermit's hut I'd imagined. But off in the distance, across a meadow of high grass, I could see the real hut—the stone one with the green beams.

There were several long wooden tables set out in front of it, and I could see a bunch of people sitting at them, drinking coffee and eating their breakfasts. This place was much more primitive—and pretty—than where we'd spent the night before—or was that two nights ago? I've completely lost count. The main hut was maybe only a quarter as big, too. Instead of the place holding hundreds of people, it looked like there were maybe only thirty or forty.

But enough of admiring the scenery. I had a parallel version of me to cross-examine.

"Start talking," I told Halli as I laced up my boots.

"About what?"

"You know about what. All of your adventures. All the things you apparently weren't going to tell me, and I had to find out from strangers."

"Audie, it's really not—"

"No. No excuses. Tell me everything. Start with rowing across the Atlantic." I added, "Please."

Halli sighed. "We only rowed it once."

"Ha! Only once! No wonder you didn't tell me."

"Audie, you don't understand . . ."

"Then tell me," I said. "I want to understand."

Halli drew up her knees and wrapped her arms around them, and rested her chin on top.

"What no one seems to understand," she said, "is that it was Ginny, not me. She was the adventurer. Once I showed up as a little baby, she just kept on going and brought me along."

"Kept on going where, for instance?" I asked.

"The North Pole—"

"North Pole," I repeated.

"Antarctica—"

"Of course."

"Some South American rivers—"

"Oh, like the Amazon?" I asked.

"Yes."

"So you traveled down the Amazon."

"Yes," Halli said.

"And you didn't think I'd want to know that?"

"I'm sure there are lots of things I don't know about you," Halli said.

"There's no comparison!" I said. "I've hardly left my house."

Halli shrugged. "Like I said, those were really Ginny's adventures."

"A twelve-year-old girl rowing with her grandmother across the Atlantic? I'd call that *your* adventure, too."

"All right," Halli said, smiling reluctantly. "I guess it was."

But then her expression changed. "You have to understand, Audie. All of that feels like a different life to me now." She motioned toward the crowd in front of the hut. "All these people up here who recognize me? Who think I'm famous? I'm only famous because of Ginny. We were a pair. And now she's gone. I don't know what I'm supposed to do anymore."

"But you came here," I said. "Alone. I mean, except for me every now and then, but obviously I'm not doing anything but following along. You did this by yourself."

"Yes, but so what?" Halli said. "With Ginny everything was . . . different. She was so brave. So confident we could do anything together. And she made me believe it, too."

I didn't say any of the obvious, like, "But you're brave, too. You can still do these things on your own." I could tell she didn't want to hear it. Maybe she didn't believe it. It wasn't my place to try to talk her out of her feelings. I had no idea what it had been like to be her before, or to be her now, without Ginny.

But I did know this:

"Halli, if what you told me before is true—if your grandmother really did try to keep you from following her the day she died, so you wouldn't see it happen—then don't you think it's because she wanted you to go on? Wouldn't she be sad to think you'd stopped all this?"

Halli shrugged. "I've had a whole year to think about what she might want. But you know what? She should have told me. She shouldn't have just sneaked away like that. I don't know if I'm supposed to continue like this alone, or completely change my life and do something different.

"I like maps," she said, looking at me with an intensity I wasn't used to. "Ginny and I lived by our maps. Why didn't she leave me something? A note, a sign—anything?"

"I don't know," I answered quietly. I petted the thick neck fur of the dog lying beside me. "I'm sorry. I really don't know what to say."

"I don't, either," Halli said. "Which is why I don't talk about it much. It always ends up in the same place—not knowing."

She reached over and scratched her dog's ear. "Ready to start the day?" she asked me. "How much time do we have?"

"Until I'm too tired to stand up any longer."

"Good," she said. "Then let's start by sitting down."

Forty

Breakfast was already over, and some of the hikers were heading down the trail to wherever their next destination was, when Halli and I finally came out of hiding. As we approached the hut, I could see Gemma/Sarah sitting at one of the tables next to the guy called Martin. I didn't see the injured Daniel anywhere.

Sarah called to us and waved us over.

I groaned. Then I realized I'd completely forgotten to tell Halli who Sarah was.

"There's this guy," I said, "back in my world." I hesitated before saying the next part, but then figured I might as well. I couldn't accuse Halli of holding back information from me if I wouldn't share my own.

"This guy I'm completely in love with," I went on, my heart pounding because I never, ever say that out loud. Halli's eyes got wide. She smiled at me.

I waved her off. "No. Forget it—he doesn't like me. It's hopeless. Anyway, Sarah is his girlfriend, but her name is Gemma there. And she's the most annoying person I've ever met. I kind of hate her guts."

Halli nodded toward Sarah. "But she doesn't seem that bad."

"Wait till you get to know her," I said. "I'll bet she's horrible."

But I was forgetting my physics. Forgetting what I'd already discovered about parallel universes. Halli wasn't exactly like me, so why did Sarah have to be like Gemma?

Still, it was hard for me to look at that girl's face, no matter how friendly she was acting.

And she was acting very friendly.

She insisted that I sit next to her, with Martin on her other side. Then she scooped up my hand in hers and pressed it firmly against her cheek.

"I'll pay you a million icies," she said, "to stay with my brother so Martin and I can run away."

"Uhhh . . ." I wasn't quite sure if she was joking.

"Two million," she bargained. "You don't even have to feed him. Just watch over him, give him water when he moans, and I promise we'll come back for him after we've had our fun. Right, Martin?"

"Right, love."

Sarah turned to Halli. "Or I'll pay *you* two million if you heal him today so we can continue with our holiday."

"Can't," Halli said. "Sorry, it doesn't work that way. I looked at his ankle this morning—he's not going anywhere today."

Sarah collapsed her head onto the table. She knocked her forehead twice against the wood. Then she went back to wooing me.

"Beautiful Audie, I can see that you're a generous soul. My brother is a wicked, hateful person, but I do love him, and he did pay for this trip for me, so I can't really abandon him, can I?"

I was starting to catch on. "No."

"But you see, Martin and I—" She leaned over and kissed his cheek. "You see that?"

"Yes."

"And so you see why the two of us need to run away together *immedjetly* so we can be free of our escort and see if we really are compatible."

I smiled. "I see." No matter how much I didn't want to like her, I was having trouble sticking to that plan.

She picked up a limp clump of my hair. "May I cut this?"

"Excuse me?" I said.

She picked up even more of my hair and sort of bounced it in her hands. "Right about . . . there." She pinched the hair between her fingers a little bit above my shoulders. "This is where the stalk starts thinning. You should let me cut it. I'm an expert, aren't I, Martin?"

"If you say so," he answered.

"Are you a hair stylist?" I asked.

I glanced across the table at Halli, who seemed to be greatly enjoying the whole exhibition.

"Not by profession, but by inclination," Sarah answered. "I see beautiful things and I need to—"

"Cut them, obviously," Martin finished for her.

"Make them even more beautiful," Sarah corrected, sending him a withering look. "So please let me cut it. Or really, just think of it as pruning."

It was weird how she almost read my thoughts from the previous day—about me being the weaker plant, and Halli the strong one. Maybe some pruning was exactly what I needed.

"What about my hair?" Halli asked, bringing her long ponytail in front her shoulder for inspection.

Sarah held her hand to her heart. "Never! Put that back—back! Don't touch it—ever. But you—" she said, turning back to me. She wasn't going to let it go. "Martin, do you still have that knife?"

He shook his head and laughed, but still fished it out of one of his pockets.

"Is it sharp?" Sarah asked.

"Sharp enough for hair," Martin said.

"We should go to the grass," Sarah said. "People won't want clippings in their tea."

After a few more minutes of Sarah's charm and cajoling, I had to give in. I mean, why not? Maybe she really could make it look better. Plus I was starting to get into the spirit of this whole thing being an adventure. If Halli could go to the North Pole and down the Amazon, I could let some strange Englishwoman who looked like my most hated nemesis chop a few inches off my hair.

Although it was more than a few inches. When I saw big clumps of brown hair falling into the grass, Sarah sang, "No worries! I do this all the time."

"Where?"

"At school," she said. "We all cut each other's hair. Practically every week."

Whoever cut hers did a pretty good job. I only hoped Sarah had the same skills.

After a while, she said, "Feel it."

I reached back, nervous to find out exactly how short it was. But it wasn't that short—a little below my shoulders. What mattered more, and was obviously the cause of the huge smile on Sarah's face, was the fact that when I touched my hair now, it felt thick and fresh. Not limp and sad.

"How does it look?" I asked.

"Brilliant."

I couldn't take my hands off it. It felt thick and heavy and . . . Halli-ish.

Thank you," I said. "So much. I really appreciate it."

Sarah waved away any gratitude and folded up Martin's knife. "If we really have to stay here a whole week because of Daniel, I may have to cut it again just to fill the time. I may cut everyone's hair. Or else run away with Martin."

"How long have you been dating?" Not that it was any of my business, but I liked the way the two of them were together. SO different from how Gemma is with Will.

"Oh, we're not dating," she said. "We only met a few days ago. He's a chum of Daniel's from school."

"But, I thought . . . I mean, the way you were acting . . ."

Sarah laughed. "I go to an all-girls' school. Forgive me if I'm a bit invigorated being around someone of the opposite sex for a change. My parents would prefer I didn't even know they existed. Luckily Dan has always been male and tends to have friends who are, too."

I had to laugh. I couldn't believe it—I actually *liked* this girl. As in, would have liked to have been friends with her. Here, though—not ever at home.

If only I could have told her! *"You wouldn't believe how horrible you are in my universe."* Somehow I think Sarah would have really enjoyed hearing about Gemma's antics. Compared to how smooth Sarah was with her flirting, Gemma is obviously an amateur.

But I couldn't tell Sarah, could I? I couldn't tell any of these people the truth. I didn't want to be responsible for blowing some stranger's mind. Some scientific discoveries are meant to be broken to the public in a gentle way. Not by suddenly announcing, "Hey, I'm from another universe, and there's another one of you over there, too."

As we came tromping back through the grass, Red ran out to greet us, wagging and acting like I'd been gone for hours. Sarah patted him on the head and then called out to the group, "What do you think?"

First Martin applauded, then Halli and Daniel—who was now at the table with them—joined in. Some of the people at the other tables looked up and offered some light applause, too, even though they probably didn't know what they were clapping for.

Sarah paused to take a bow. I, on the other hand, felt completely shy. I was used to being more invisible than this. And I didn't have my usual curtain of long hair to hide behind.

"So, the invalid awakes?" Sarah said to her brother as we rejoined the group. Daniel sat on the bench next to Halli, his leg outstretched between them. Sarah and I joined Martin on the other side of the table. Sarah flung her arm around his shoulder and offered him her cheek, which he kissed. Then she dropped that same arm under the table, and the two of them joined hands. It was very sweet, and actually made me feel a little lonely. Not achy, angry-lonely like I do when I see Gemma and Will together. Just plain . . . alone.

"I've been awake," Daniel answered his sister. "I was sitting inside, watching from the window."

"Always watching, our Daniel," said Sarah. "Very mysterious. Is he like this at school?" she asked Martin.

"We call him The Professor," Martin answered. "Always studying and thinking."

Sarah sighed. "So different, we are. No wonder our parents prefer me."

I had to laugh at that.

Martin pulled up their joined hands and kissed Sarah's knuckles.

"Don't fall for her, mate," Daniel warned.

"Too late," Sarah told him. She turned toward me and ran her free hand through the ends of my hair. "What do you think, Dan, isn't she beautiful?"

Across the table Daniel smiled at me and nodded. He had nice eyes. This sort of light brown, like oak furniture. He had a nice face, too, with a little bit of light stubble going. And a nice smile—actually, a really nice smile.

But then he had to go and ruin it.

"So, Audie, where were you last night?"

Forty-one

"Oh," I said, snapping out of my analysis of his face. "Umm..."

Halli stepped in. "She got a little lost on that other route. By the time she showed up there wasn't any more room in the *mattress lager*. They had to put her up in one of the outbuildings."

"What outbuilding?" Daniel asked in a friendly enough way.

"There." Halli pointed to the little hermit's hut off in the distance. "How was it in there, Audie?"

"Nice," I said. "Very comfortable."

I'm not really good at lying. I was glad Halli took the lead.

"And this morning?" Daniel said to me. "I didn't see you at breakfast."

Halli answered again. "Audie loves to get up before dawn and go watch the sunrise. How was it today?"

"Beautiful," I said. "Stunning."

Daniel smiled at me again. "I see."

I found Halli's leg under the table and lightly kicked it. She kicked me back.

"So," Halli said to Sarah, "what are your plans for the day?"

"Martin and I are climbing," Sarah pointed to a rocky peak in the distance, "that."

"Are you?" Daniel said.

"Are we?" Martin asked.

"This is my holiday," Sarah declared, "and I came to be a mountain climber. I'm not leaving until I thoroughly am one. I don't think yesterday qualifies, since carrying the wounded is not exactly the road to valor and fame, is it, Halli Markham?"

"Well—" Halli started, but then Daniel broke in.

"Jealous?" he asked his sister.

"Of Halli Markham?" Sarah said. "Terribly! And look at her—she's gorgeous beyond belief. Everything about her makes me boil."

Sarah said it in such a friendly, off-hand way, it made Halli laugh.

I could tell Halli thought Sarah was as much of a kick as I did. There was something so careless and casual about her, but also confident and spirited. She was the kind of person who'd be great at parties. Not like Gemma at all, sticking her hand down the back of a certain person's pants and making everyone uncomfortable.

"So what do you say, Martin?" Sarah asked. "Shall we conquer the peak today?"

He propped his legs up on the bench across from him. "Or we could stay here and keep Daniel company."

"Oh, yes," Sarah scoffed. "Poor dear has hardly gotten any attention at all. How many women tut-tutted over you at dinner last night, Dan? A dozen? More?"

"That's right," he answered, "I botched my ankle for attention."

"See?" Sarah said.

"I still think a day off wouldn't be a bad idea," Martin said. "Let our legs catch up with us."

Sarah sat up straighter. "Do *not* try to deter me, sir. Halli Markham, you are a woman of adventure. If the men will not be men, I appeal to you. Would you care to be my guide up that mountain?"

"I would, but . . ." Halli turned her gaze to me. "It depends on my cousin. Audie, can I talk to you for a moment?"

"Sure." I got up and followed her away from the group.

"Do you want to go with us?" Halli asked. "It might be fun."

I did, but I didn't. The blisters on my heels had gotten worse. And even though I'd made it through the hiking so far, I wasn't sure how I'd feel climbing nonstop up that huge mountain Sarah had pointed to.

And then there was the confidence problem. As in, I had no confidence that I could actually keep up with Halli and Sarah. I could tell that when Halli was with me she held herself back from hiking as hard and fast as she could have alone. And looking at Sarah, I was sure she was in better shape than I was, too. It was embarrassing. I didn't want to be the weakest one in the trio.

And last, there was the disappearance issue. What if hiking that peak took all day? There would come a point, I knew, when my body would *have* to get its sleep. The longest I've ever stayed up studying for a test was 4:00 in the morning. That would be noon Halli's time. I'd planned on leaving some time before then—finding some private place to just disappear from, and heading back to my bed. What was Halli supposed to tell Sarah when I suddenly wasn't there anymore?

And since that was the least humiliating, that was the excuse I went with.

"Then I'll stay, too," Halli said. "I'm not going to leave you."

"Why? No, you should go—it sounds like fun. I'll be fine. At least Daniel and Martin speak English—it won't be like that last place."

"Are you sure?" Halli asked.

"I came here to have an interesting time, and I will—I am. Just being here is a thousand times more interesting than being home. I'll stay for a little while longer, then head home. I could use the sleep. Then I'll see you tomorrow and you can tell me all about it."

Halli and I rejoined the group, where Sarah was happy to announce, "It worked. Martin's coming, too."

"Now that she's upbraided my manhood," he said.

"Will you still go?" Sarah asked Halli.

"Sure," she said.

"That way if either of us breaks something," Sarah said, "we know you can get us back down."

"Let's rather not," Martin said.

"Agreed," Halli said.

While the three of them gathered up their gear and packed their lunches, Daniel waited. He waited while they said their goodbyes. Waited while I went inside the main hut to get us both cups of hot, dark coffee. Waited while I brought them back out and sat across from him, ready to begin a polite hour or so of making simple, courteous conversation.

But Daniel had a different idea.

He leaned across the table, looked me straight in the eye and said, "Halli Markham doesn't have any cousins. Or any siblings. So tell me, Audie, who are you really?"

Forty-two

There are times in your life when you feel like you've just reached the top of the roller coaster, and suddenly the track falls out from underneath you.

"Wh-what?" I'm sure my face went either completely white or completely red. Either way he had to know he'd caught me.

Daniel didn't bother repeating his question. He knew I'd heard it. He just waited and watched me die.

"Uhhh, like Halli said—our families don't really get along."

"Which families?" he asked.

"You know, her . . ." I had to think fast. She'd told the three of them that I wasn't related through Ginny's side. That meant Halli and I had to have a common grandparent on . . . my father's side? I couldn't think it through as completely as I wanted to. Daniel was still watching, waiting for my answer.

"Halli's father hates my father. They're brothers." That would make Halli and me cousins, right? Without Ginny being our same grandmother. I felt pretty good about the quick answer under pressure.

"What are their names?" Daniel asked.

"Whose names?" Obviously I was stalling. I started to feel sick to my stomach.

"The two brothers'," Daniel said patiently.

"Oh, uh . . ." It was worse than being called on by Mrs. Arnold. Worse than being called on in any class, because usually even if I haven't done the reading I can still fake my way through. But here, I really didn't have a clue.

Had Halli ever said her father's name? I searched my brain. If she did tell me, I had no memory of it.

And what name should I say for my father? Should I go with his real name, or make up something?

I went with the real. Because there was no time and I just couldn't think of anything else.

"John."

"John what?" Daniel asked.

I knew this answer was going to be wrong, but I didn't have a choice. I couldn't think of any name that would have been better, so I went ahead and told the truth. "Masters. I'm Audie Masters."

Daniel nodded, his gaze still fixed on me. Did I say before that his eyes were nice? They weren't. They were hideously mud-colored and piercing and annoying.

"So you took your father's surname?"

"Of course," I said without thinking.

"I see. And his brother's name is?"

I was lost and I knew it. "Uhh . . ."

And then I came to my senses. Why was I killing myself for this guy? I didn't owe him a thing—not an answer, not an explanation, not even courtesy. I could just get up from the table and walk away. It's not like he could follow me with that sprained ankle—at least not very fast.

I glanced around at the other tables to see if anyone else was listening. I wouldn't want someone else chasing after me saying, "Yeah—who are you? Tell us!" in whatever language they spoke.

But in the time Daniel and I had been sitting there, everyone else had packed up and left. Either to go on some sort of day-jaunt like Halli and Sarah and Martin, or off to some other hut for the night.

I looked back at Daniel. Who still waited for my answer.

"Would you like some help?" Daniel asked. A kind sort of smile teased around his lips.

My shoulders slumped. "Yes, please."

He reached inside his coat and pulled out a screen. It was thin like the one Halli had, but smaller—more the size of a paperback book.

Daniel pressed the surface of it a couple of times, then read to me.

" 'Halli Markham, explorer. Daughter of Regina Markham and Jameson Bellows—' "

Jameson. I never would have guessed that. And certainly wouldn't have come up with Bellows.

" '—Granddaughter of Virginia Markham, explorer.' "

Audie Masters, granddaughter of Marion Fletcher, shopper.

Daniel pressed the screen once more, and read again. "'Jameson Bellows, creator of osmotic power technologies, President and CEO of Osmotic Power Systems . . .' " Daniel looked up from the screen. "We'll skip ahead to Jameson Bellows's family, shall we? 'Parents: deceased. Siblings: none.' "

Daniel and I stared at each other. So I wasn't Halli's cousin on our fathers' sides. But I wasn't out of options yet.

"Okay, so I lied. My father is Halli's mother's brother." I said it quickly, hoping maybe that would confuse him.

It didn't. Daniel poked his little screen. " 'Regina Markham . . . et cetera, et cetera . . . parents deceased, siblings none.' "

"That's not true!" I said, thinking of my uncle Mike. He might not get along with my mother, but he does exist. "There's a brother."

Daniel poked again, and came up with the answer. "'Virginia Markham, et cetera. Children Regina Markham, et cetera, and Claude Markham, deceased.' "

"Deceased?" I asked. "How?"

Daniel consulted his screen. " 'Died age five. Kidney failure.' "

Poor Uncle Mike! Poor Ginny, losing her little boy like that.

Daniel looked up at me again. "So, Audie, the question remains: who are you?"

I felt exhausted by the whole thing. Not only by the genealogy test I'd just flunked, but also by all the effort I'd put into lying.

"I'm who I said—Audie Masters. That's all I can tell you."

Apparently Daniel wasn't expecting an answer like that. "Why?" He didn't seem irritated, just genuinely curious.

"Because it's very, very complicated."

Daniel pointed to his outstretched leg. "I have nothing but time. I would be grateful if you'd explain it to me."

I looked at him. Considered him. He had a nice open face. Looked like a calm enough guy. Hadn't he proven that yesterday, joking around when he was obviously in pain? And despite what I said, he actually did have a nice smile and kind-looking eyes. He seemed . . . decent. Even though he'd obviously and cruelly tricked me into confessing I wasn't who Halli and I said I was, he wasn't all, "Ah-hah! Liar! Seize her!" about it. He just wanted me to know that he knew. I might have done the same thing.

Although I probably wouldn't have been able to carry it out as slowly and methodically as he had. That was actually kind of impressive.

So, taking all that into consideration, I had to wonder what it might be like to try out my story on a total stranger—not just any stranger, but this one. Would he believe me? Would it freak him out? Would he pass it all off as fantasy?

And what are the rules about this whole thing? I know with time travel you're not supposed to let yourself see yourself—it affects the space-time continuum and can seriously fry your brain. And I think you're not supposed to reveal to other people that you've come from the future or the past—it might alter their choices, and you're not supposed to meddle with that.

But if you've traveled from one parallel universe to another, and you don't know anything about that other universe's future or past (which was obvious, based on the test I'd just flunked), and you don't have any secret information that might mess up the direction of someone's life—do you have an ethical duty to keep silent? Or is it all right to share?

And if it was all right to tell someone, was this guy the right one? I didn't know Daniel Whoever-He-Was any more than I knew any of the other people Halli and I had come across in the Alps. Why hadn't I told that Austrian woman a few days ago, "Hey, I'm from another Earth!"? Or break that news to the two Italian guys—just to see how they'd take it?

Meanwhile Daniel the injured Brit was still waiting patiently, gazing at me with those warm brown eyes.

"I'm not sure I'm supposed to—"

But it wouldn't have mattered if I was supposed to tell him or not. Because some things are out of your control.

An itch. A tingle. Right at the base of my skull.

And then a yank, a rip, a whoosh.

Leaving Daniel, I was sure, with nothing to look at but an empty pile of clothes.

Forty-three

I love my mother, but I'm looking forward to her leaving on her next trip.

"Oh, I'm sorry," she said as she poked her head in and saw me stir—or really, thud back onto my bed. "Did I wake you?"

"Um . . . not really." My skin felt moist. Like maybe the vapor trail had left a layer of dew all over me. Or maybe I started sweating mid-air.

She came in and sat on the edge of my bed. "I'm sorry about earlier," she said.

I had to search my brain to remember what she was talking about. Half of me was still back in the Alps.

"I want you to know I trust you," she said. "You're a smart, honest girl, and I never should have suspected you of sneaking around behind my back."

Oh, *that*. The Professor Whitfield thing. "It's okay," I said, knowing very well that while I wasn't lying to her about what she thought I was lying to her about, there was this whole other thing.

"Well, I should let you get back to sleep." She patted my leg, but she didn't leave.

When she sat there another minute more, I finally thought to ask, "Is something wrong?"

My mom sighed. "Just this Philadelphia situation. I woke up thinking about it and haven't been able to get back to sleep."

"Why, what's wrong?"

"Their board wants to fire the whole executive staff," my mother said. "That's why they're flying me in so last-minute. They're hoping I can save them. But I was reading over some of the materials they sent me, and the company really is in a mess."

She patted my leg again, but this time she got up. "But, I don't need to keep you up, too. I just wanted to check in on you—old habit."

"Do you . . . do that a lot?" I asked. I never would have cared before, but now the information seemed pretty critical.

"Not so much anymore," she said. "Not like when you were little. You'll understand one day when you have children. Sometimes you just like to watch them sleep. It's very, I don't know, calming."

Not for me! Opposite of calming for me.

"That's nice, Mom, but . . ."

She laughed. "I know. Silly at your age—you're almost a grown woman. But soon you'll be going off to college, so maybe I have to store away as much of you as I can."

She leaned over and kissed my forehead.

Then she squinted at me in the dark. "Did you do something to your hair?"

I'd totally forgotten. My hand flew to the ends.

My mom reached over and turned on the lamp beside my bed. "Audie! You cut your hair."

"Oh . . . yeah," I said. "Does it look bad?"

"No, it looks very nice," she said. "But when did you do that?"

"Um, I don't know—before I went to bed."

"I would have cut it for you, honey. I didn't know you wanted it shorter."

"I didn't know, either," I said. "It was sort of a whim."

"Well, it looks nice," she said again. She ran her fingers through a section of it. "You did a really good job. I should have you cut mine someday."

"I don't know, I'm sort of just a beginner—"

"Well, I should let you get back to sleep," she said. "I didn't mean to wake you up and chat with you all night. I know how tired you've been lately."

"It's okay," I said. "But yeah, I'm kind of tired."

She turned off my lamp. "Then I'll see you in the morning. Good night, sweetie."

"'Night, Mom."

She quietly closed the door behind her. I waited until I heard her go back to her bedroom.

Then I turned on my light again and jumped out of bed. I stood in front of the mirror behind my door.

My hair. If I needed proof, this was it. It had gone over one way, come back another. I really was traveling to another universe with my full body. And what happened to my body over there stayed with me once I came back. That was an incredible piece of news. I couldn't wait to tell the professor.

But the other thing is, I was starting to look like Halli.

Not strong and muscular like her, but the hair was definitely a big step. It didn't look sad and scraggly anymore—it looked rich and strong and thick. I twisted my head back and forth to make the hair swing. It felt full and silky. I loved it. I loved Sarah for making it that way.

I really had to stare at myself for a long time. Was Halli inside me somehow? I mean, not her personally, but the potential of Halli? Could I ever look—or even better—*be* like her? It was a pretty staggering thought. All brought up by a little beauty parlor session out in the grass of the Alps.

I turned off the light and went back to bed. And thought about something else: Daniel saying he thought I looked beautiful. Well, he didn't exactly say it, but he agreed when Sarah asked him. So how nice was that?

But then of course that brought up all the other thoughts about Daniel, like how I'd probably blown a circuit in his brain.

What did he think when I just disappeared? Did he think he was dreaming? Did he think he'd lost his mind? Did he look for me? Where—under the table? But then he would have found my clothes, and then what did he think? Do they have magic over there? Maybe he thinks I'm a magician.

There was nothing I could do about it for a whole day. Halli was off hiking with Sarah and Martin, and wouldn't be looking for me again until tomorrow. So Daniel would just have to spend the next however many hours trying to figure it out for himself.

All I could think about was that last look on his face, as he patiently waited for me to answer his question about who I am. Telling me he had nothing but time. Telling me he'd be "grateful" if I'd explain what was going on.

Well, he probably wasn't feeling grateful toward me anymore. I could pretty much guarantee that.

Forty-four

I slept in, after who knows when I finally fell asleep. I woke up to the sound of the phone. I checked the clock: 9:15. I wondered how early I could talk to the professor on a Saturday morning.

But I was going to have to wait a little while anyway. Usually my mom goes into the office on weekends, at least for a few hours, so all I had to do was wait for that. Then I could call the professor and video chat with him in private.

I padded out into the kitchen. My mom was still on the phone. "That would be nice," she was saying. "I'll see you in a little while."

She hung up and said, "Sweetie, I love your hair!"

"Thanks," I said with a yawn. "Who was that?"

"Elena. She's at the office, but I told her I'm going to work from home today. I just need to go by and pick up some files first."

"Why . . . are you working from home?"

"I feel like I've been gone an awful lot lately, and it might be nice to just stay put for the weekend."

"Oh, you don't have to do that because of me—"

"It's not because of you," she said. "I'm just plain exhausted. I want to sit around in my sweatpants and do my reading here. I don't need to go to the office for that."

"But—"

My mom gave me a quizzical look. "Don't you want me here?"

"Of course! Absolutely! I just thought . . . but no, you're right. That would be great. You should relax."

I headed for the bathroom to splash my face and brush my teeth. And mostly to keep from babbling. She was going to get suspicious if I kept it up.

"Oh, and Elena invited us over for dinner tonight," my mom called after me. "I'd said we'd go—I assume that's all right?"

"Yeah, sure." Actually, it sounded really nice. Maybe that's what I needed: a good dose of Will. It had been days since I'd been able to breathe in the scent of him—ever since our all-too-short drive from school to the office on Wednesday.

And who knows? Maybe he'd take a second look at me now that I had Halli hair. Was that so wrong to hope?

Around 10:00 my mom left to go pick up some paperwork at the office. I wasn't sure how long she'd be away, but I figured I had at least half an hour.

I quickly contacted the professor. He was already in his office.

"Look at my hair," I said right away.

"Oh. Yes, it's very nice, Audie . . ."

"No, look at it! Sarah cut it yesterday. Or last night—whenever. But she cut it over *there*. And it came back with me looking like this." I paused. "Do you understand? Don't you think that's amazing?"

Professor Whitfield laughed. "Yes, Audie, I do think that's amazing—you're absolutely right. I'm sorry I didn't react right away. I'm still taking it all in."

I also told him about the vapor trail, or whatever it is, yanking me back last night. And about poor Daniel being left there to try to deal with it.

"What would you think if that had happened to you?" I asked. "If you were talking to someone and they just suddenly disappeared?"

"I'd think it was quantum tunneling or something like that," the professor said. "Have you considered that, by the way?"

"Quantum tunneling?" I said. "Not really."

"Well, I think we have to add that to the list of possibilities," the professor said. "If an electron can disappear on one side of a barrier and reappear on the other, maybe it's the same explanation for you.

"Listen," he said. "I've been thinking about something. Right now all we have are theories, but I'd like to start gathering some practical data. That hair of yours is a pretty significant step, but we'll need a lot more to do a thorough analysis of what's going on. Do you think you'd be up for some testing?"

"What do you mean?" I asked.

"This is something you'd have to clear with your mom—you've told her about it now, haven't you?"

"Oh . . . yeah. I told her everything yesterday after she came in while I was talking to you."

I was shocked at how easily the lie came out. But I was too interested in what the professor was going to say to let the whole thing about my mother stand in the way.

"How'd she take it?" Professor Whitfield asked.

"Not great," I improvised. "She was pretty upset at first. But after a while, she realized what an opportunity this is for me."

"Really?" the professor said. "She didn't . . . seem more concerned than that?"

"Oh, yeah, she was at first—definitely," I said. "But she seems okay with it now. It was a *long* talk."

"Hm. I'm surprised she didn't want to talk to me, too."

"Oh, she did," I continued lying. "But I told her you'd just say the same things, and we probably shouldn't bother you."

I wondered if he could see the sweat that had broken out on my face. Maybe his computer resolution was too weak.

"So anyway," I said. "What were you saying about the testing?"

"What I'd like is for you and your mother to come up here to the college," he said. "I have a lab with a lot of pretty sophisticated equipment. I'd like to set up a few experiments so we can monitor you while you're having the experience—see if we can really figure out what's going on. What would you say to that?"

"That's a great idea!" Except for the part about my mom coming, too. "You mean you'd hook me up to machines, or something?"

"Something like that," he said. "I'd like to test your brain waves, your physiological responses, some other aspects—make sure everything is safe."

That sounded like an excellent idea. And it might be just the thing I need for my mother.

Because as I was lying to the professor about having already told her, I realized that day is going to come at some point, whether I like it or not. And it's probably going to come pretty soon, since I plan on putting all this in my Columbia application. I can't very well reveal it to the admissions committee and not to my own mother. She's going to find out one way or the other, and I suppose it had better come from me. Soon.

But wouldn't it be so much better if I could tell her *after* I've proved it's safe? Be able to hand her some test results of some kind and assure her that what I'm doing isn't dangerous?

And I suppose if it is dangerous, I should probably know that, too. That will give the professor and me a chance to correct my methods so it really will be safe.

A total win-win.

Even though I'm going to have to tell some of the biggest lies of my life to get there.

"So, when were you thinking?" I asked. "Like, sometime soon?"

"The sooner the better," Professor Whitfield said. "I'd like to get to the bottom of this."

I'd already been staring at the calendar on my desk. I knew what I was about to do, but it still felt so . . . wrong. But I had to remember that the goal was ultimately to reassure my mom.

"How about next week?" I said. "Like on Friday? We could come up for the weekend."

Not mentioning the fact that my mother will still be in Philadelphia over the weekend. No need to mention that.

"Friday would be fine," the professor said.

But then I realized a major hurdle. "Um, how would we pay for it?" It was one thing to be a liar—I wasn't also going to be a thief by charging up my mother's credit card.

"Don't worry about that," Professor Whitfield said. "There's a travel budget written into all my grants. I'll pay for your plane tickets and a hotel. I can make the arrangements today."

It was all happening so fast. And so easily. I know I should have felt more guilty. But I just kept thinking about my mom.

And okay, about me.

"Do you need to check with your mother first?" the professor asked.

"No, I'm sure she'll say yes. It's just a weekend—it won't be a problem. And she's really been wanting to meet you."

"All right, good." He had me give him my mother's and my full names, our birthdates—everything he needed for the reservations.

I heard the front door open.

"Okay, so I have to go," I said, "but it sounds like a plan."

"And you'll keep me posted until then?" Professor Whitfield said. "I want to hear about anything unusual."

I heard my mom drop her keys in the front basket.

"Yep, sounds great," I said. "Talk to you soon!" And I clicked off just in time.

My mom stuck her head in my doorway. "Did you have breakfast? I brought back bagels."

My mom and I may not cook, but it doesn't mean we don't eat.

"Sounds great," I told her. Everything sounds great.

I'm going to Colorado.

Alone.

I wonder how this whole thing will work?

Forty-five

I took my time getting ready for tonight. I was in a good mood, ready to hang out with Will. I washed my newly-cut hair and picked out the kind of clothes I thought Halli might wear for an evening out: clean jeans and a long-sleeved red T-shirt. I checked myself in the mirror. I really did look different.

I was feeling so good I thought maybe even Gemma wouldn't bother me for once. Of course she ruined that idea right away.

"Audie, girl," she said as soon as we walked in, "what did you do to your hair?" She laughed and winked and tossed her own hair. "It's so— "

"Thanks." I didn't wait to hear what it was "so." Because I realized that as much as I hated Gemma before? Now seeing how she *could* be, as Sarah, made how she *is* so very worse.

Do you know that you're actually fun? And nice? And a pleasure to be around? And you don't constantly wink or flip your hair or press your boobs against your boyfriend's arm? Do you know you have some freakin' dignity over there?

Will bit into a tortilla chip. "I think it looks good."

I'm sure my face beamed. "Thank you, Will." I had to resist the urge to really dork it out by adding, "Do you really like it? Do you? Oh my gosh, I'm so happy! You like it!"

Lydia was still teaching her yoga class, so it was just the two moms and the happy couple and me for a while. I tried to focus on Will alone, but Gemma kept interjecting herself, draping herself over him, jabbering away about some "ball" her family was going to be throwing in a few weeks.

I didn't want to get involved, but I couldn't resist. She was so stupid and irritating.

"You mean you're renting a ballroom," I said. "We don't actually call them 'balls' here—they're just parties."

"No, it's a ball," she insisted. "Like we have in England."

Whatever. I couldn't believe I even let myself get drawn in. Now she was going to keep talking about it.

"Why are you throwing a ball?" my mother wanted to know.

"It's for Daddy's 50th," Gemma said. "He can't get away to go back to England, so Mummy has invited everyone to come here to celebrate. It's a surprise for him. People will be flying in from all over the world. Everybody loves Daddy—it should be quite the event."

I turned away and rolled my eyes. It was better than punching her in the face.

My mother caught my eye. She winked. I've grown to hate the wink, now that Gemma has ruined it for me, but this time I had to smile. My mother could see the girl was driving me crazy. At least someone was on my side.

"Will your brother be coming?" Elena asked Gemma, probably just to be polite. But suddenly I was paying attention.

"Oh, yes, Colin will be here for a week or so. He had to get permission from the headmaster, but everyone understands Daddy's 50th takes priority."

"Your brother's name is Colin?" I asked. "Is that your only brother? How old is he? What does he look like?"

Gemma shot me a suspicious look. I never ask questions, and here I'd given her four in a row. But I couldn't help myself—finally she had some information for me that I was actually interested in.

"He's eighteen," she said, choosing to answer just one. "He's very successful—top marks at his school. He'll be at Oxford next year, with Daddy."

Gemma's father is a professor at Oxford. The only reason Gemma is here making my life miserable right now is that her father accepted an invitation to teach at our university for a few years. He's going back at the end of the school year—just long enough for Gemma to keep interfering with Will all the way up to our graduation.

"So when is this ball, did you say?" I asked.

Gemma seemed strangely reluctant to answer. "October 20th," she sort of mumbled, then she looked around the room. "And, um, of course you're all invited . . ."

Oh. No, of course we weren't. She'd forgotten that polite little detail.

"I'll just let Mummy know to add—" She glanced around the room again. Apparently math is even harder for her than it is for me. "—three. Or I suppose four, if you think Lydia will want to come."

"Thank you," Elena said. "That's very nice of you. I'm not sure we'll be able to—"

"I will," I said immediately. Are you kidding? A chance to see Daniel's duplicate in the flesh? Wait until Professor Whitfield heard about that. If the Sarah-Gemma differences were any indication, I bet this Colin guy would be nothing like Daniel. It was too juicy to pass up. Of course I had to meet him.

This dinner wasn't so bad after all. Science can pop up when you least expect it.

I was in a much better mood by the time Elena served up her fabulous enchilada pie and three-bean salad, and didn't even mind so much that Gemma never stopped talking and primping and winking. I was hungry for whatever she might say about her brother. How weird to think I would see him here, in my own universe, in just a few weeks. I couldn't wait to see if he looked exactly like Daniel, or if there were subtle differences like between Halli and me.

Eventually Lydia came home and nuked up her leftovers, and then Gemma started filling her in on the ball. Apparently now that she'd felt pressured into it, Gemma was going to start acting like inviting all of us was her idea.

"Hey, Aud," Will whispered from behind me while the two of them carried on. "Can you come talk to me for a sec?"

"Of course. Great. Sure." I tried not to leap up like a little kid just told there was a pony waiting for her in the yard.

Will led me down the hall. He looked back to make sure we weren't followed. Then he opened the door to his bedroom.

I hardly ever get to go into Will's bedroom anymore. Maybe the last time was a few years ago, when he had some book he wanted to lend me.

Looking around his room now, I could see the décor had changed quite a bit. No more posters from his favorite movies and TV shows. Now the walls were bare, painted a sort of dark beige, and there were shelves and narrow tables everywhere to accommodate all his computers. I counted four different monitors, two laptops, a bunch of hard drives, stacks and stacks of computer manuals—it was like walking into a computer store that slightly smelled of socks.

Will reached behind me. "Let's close the door."

A thrill went through me. This dinner just kept getting better and better. Will pulled down the top of his bedspread, and dug his hand under his pillow.

He came out holding a box. A small, velvet-covered, burgundy box. The kind you see in movies. The kind that hold engagement rings.

I felt a little dizzy. And not because I'd suddenly lost my mind and thought Will was going to propose—at least not to me. I'm not stupid. I was starting to feel sick.

Will flipped open the box.

A ring. A beautiful gold ring with two tiny diamonds on either side of a light blue heart-shaped gem. Not a classic-looking engagement ring, but a ring nonetheless.

I didn't say anything. I could feel a clammy sweat breaking out on my face.

"Do you think it's too much?" he asked.

He was expecting me to speak.

"Um, no—not at all." My voice crackled. "It's really pretty. Nice."

Will let out a breath. "Great. Okay, thanks." He flipped the box closed and stowed it back under his pillow.

"So that's for . . . Gemma?" Might as well crumble my heart all the way.

"Yeah," Will said. "She's been sort of hinting around—"

I bet she has.

"I got a good deal on it," he said. "One forty-nine ninety-nine."

"Oh. Yeah. Great." He could have said, "I paid for it by selling my spleen," and I doubt I would have heard him any better. My ears were already shutting down. This was the opposite of Professor Whitfield's above-beyond senses: mine were going down and off.

"So," I said, "I'm going to go now . . ."

"Aud?" Will said. "You okay?"

"Oh, yeah! Yeah. I just think I should probably . . . go."

"Can I just show you one more thing?" he asked.

Because when you've already got someone on the torture rack, why not crank it a little more?

"Sure."

Will shifted around some of the papers on one of his desks and came up with a jewelry catalogue. He flipped to a page he'd already marked.

"What do you think?" he asked. "I thought about this one, too." He pointed to the same ring I'd just seen in the box, but this one had a red heart-shaped stone instead of a blue one. Still for the fabulous sale price of $149.99.

"No, the one you got her is great," I said. "Stick with that."

"You think so?" Will considered the pictures in the catalog. "Because I know she likes blue, but you know Gemma . . ."

I laughed. And to my ears it sounded like the laugh of a crazy person about to be executed. "Yeah, that Gemma. Hey, I really need to go." I yawned and stretched out my arms, just like a character in a cartoon. "So tired. Better get my mom and head home."

"Oh, sure." Will hid the catalog back among the papers. No doubt when he and Gemma were back in there tonight, he didn't want her snooping and ruining her surprise.

"So when are you going to give it to her?" I asked as I reached for the door. Even though technically I was beyond all caring. But it was like a disaster film—I just had to keep watching.

"At the ball," Will said. "It's just a few days before our one-year anniversary. I thought the timing was pretty perfect."

"Yeah, perfect," I snapped, yanking open his door.

And there was the hideous Gemma. Eavesdropping. Although she jumped back and pretended she wasn't.

"There you are!" she said, winking at Will. "What are you and Miss Audie up to, then?"

"Computer question," Will replied. I nodded. I didn't care anymore. I didn't care if she'd heard us, if Will gave her a ring, if she loved it, if she popped it in her mouth and choked on it—I didn't care.

I went back into the living room and caught my mom's eye. I motioned that it was time to go.

We said our goodbyes and got into the car. As my mom looked behind her to back out onto the street, she must have caught sight of my miserable face. I turned toward my window, but it was too late.

"Honey, are you crying?"

After all the lies I'd already today, one more seemed like one too many.

"Yes."

"Why?" she asked.

"I don't know. My life just *sucks*."

You make the biggest discovery in quantum physics history, and you *still* can't get the guy.

Forty-six

When we got home my mom went straight to her bedroom and dragged out our favorite quilt. It's one my mother's grandmother made out of scraps of my mom's old playdresses, like the one with the little cowgirl on it. I've always loved that quilt. It's seen me through some rough times.

My mom invited me over to the couch and fluffed up a pillow for my head. "Lie down."

I did. Then she propped up my feet on her lap and covered us both with the quilt and started rubbing my sad little feet. I draped my arm over my eyes. And waited for the whole world to go away.

My mother can be very patient when she has to. She just rubbed my feet for a while and waited. And finally I told her what was on my mind.

"How do you know who's right for you?" I asked.

I could tell she wasn't expecting that. And in a way, it wasn't a fair question to ask her. I know very well how unhappy she was when my father left us. My mother did not want the divorce at all. But it was just one of those things—at least that's what she's always said. "People fall out of love—it's just one of those things."

But I'd started down that road, and now I was stuck. So I just kept going.

"I mean, I'm not really talking about you and Dad—"

My mom laughed nervously. "Well, that's good."

Especially since we just found out a few weeks ago that he has a new girlfriend, and she's only eight years older than I am, which I think is gross, since she wouldn't have even been able to babysit me when I was little. I only hope she doesn't stick around long enough that I'll actually have to meet her.

"Is it Will?" my mom asked.

I nodded.

She bent my toes back and then bent them forward. I could hear some of the joints crack. "Will is a very nice boy."

I sighed. "Whatever. It's pointless. He likes Gemma," I said bravely, "and that's that."

My mother didn't try to argue. And I guess I respect her for that. No need for her to lie to her child.

"You're both very young," she said, as if that answered anything.

I shrugged. "Really, I don't care anymore. Tonight I was kind of surprised by something he said, but I'm over it now. Really."

That wasn't the truth, but I really wanted it to be. I mean, how many years can you give to a person or a cause or a pursuit before you realize it's just not going to happen for you? Isn't thirteen years enough? Shouldn't it be?

My mother had a different take on it. "You can tell a lot about a person by the choices he makes. You know I love Will—I think he's a very nice young man. But if that girl Gemma is the kind of girl he likes, then I'd say Will isn't the right boy for you. Not even close."

I laughed a little at that, in a kind of snotty way. That cry I'd had in the car was still lingering in my sinuses.

My mother squeezed my foot. "Audie, you're a wonderful girl. There's not a daughter in the world I'd rather have than you. And some day, someone is going to feel that way about you romantically. But I'd hold out for the right boy."

The right boy. The right guy. And who might that be? See any other prospects hanging around, Mother? It's not like I have my pick.

My mom glanced down at her fingernails. I know that gesture well. It means she has something to tell me that she doesn't want to tell me. She looked at her nails the night she broke it to me my father was leaving. She looks at her nails every time she has to discuss the budget with me, and we have to decide what to scrimp on this particular month because she wasn't able to pay herself out of the business, or my father's check is late, or the car ate up hundreds of dollars in repairs, or that cavity I had filled cost as much as two week's worth of groceries—it's varied over the years. But I know that gesture.

"What?" I said.

"Columbia," she said.

Now what. "What about it?"

My mother patted my leg for me to sit up. This wasn't the time for foot massages—we were about to have a serious discussion. A discussion about my future.

"Audie, I really believe you're one of the smartest girls in the world—"

Here it came—

"—and a university like Columbia would be so lucky to have you. I think you'd do great things there—*will* do great things, no matter where you go."

"But . . ." I said.

"But I know you were counting on that Dr. Whitfield to give you a recommendation—"

"Well, not really." She didn't know I'd just said that as a cover for why I was talking to him so much. But I still didn't understand why she was bringing this all up.

My mother hesitated, but then she got up from the couch. "Wait here a minute."

She went into her bedroom and came out holding a stack of papers.

"I decided to do some checking on him yesterday, after I saw the two of you talking."

"Mom—"

She held up her hand. "I'm not saying I don't trust you, Audie, but I think it's wise that we understand who he really is."

Now she was making me mad. "Who he *is* happens to be a really brilliant physicist. I'd be lucky if I could get a recommendation from him." I didn't realize it until I said it, but now I could see that was true.

"I'm afraid not everyone thinks as highly of him as you do," my mother said.

"What are you talking about?"

She handed me the stack of articles. "I just think you should read up on him a little more—really see what his standing is in the community."

"I don't need to read those," I said, pushing them away. "I know who he is. Why are you trying to attack him?"

"It's not him I care about," she said, "it's you. Audie, I'm so proud of you—you have no idea how much. And I want to see you succeed in the ways I know are important to you. But it's just a fact of life that some people can help you, and some people can hurt you. I'm afraid any association with Dr. Whitfield might hurt you—and your chances of getting into Columbia or anywhere else you might want to go.

"Just read them," she said. "That's all I ask."

She left me alone then, with just the quilt and a handful of articles. All about Professor Walter "Skip" Whitfield.

I started reading. Because what else could go wrong tonight?

Forty-seven

I read somewhere that when a scientist presents a new idea that's just a little over people's heads, everyone gets inspired. If he presents an idea that's a little *more* over people's heads, they all fall asleep. If it's yet another step above their heads, people get angry. And if it's too complex or challenging, then everyone wants to destroy him.

What I was reading was destruction.

I gave up after the third article. It was too sad and depressing. Poor Professor Whitfield. Obviously people felt threatened.

I took them back to my mother's room. She was already in bed, reading.

"Mom, I appreciate this—I know you want me to know—but I can tell you, all these other scientists are just jealous."

"Audie—"

"I know what you're going to say. You think I'm just defending him. But I've talked to him. I've read his book. I know how advanced his ideas are. People don't like to hear them—it's like Copernicus back in his day. It's dangerous to be too smart."

My mother set down her book. "Honey, I know you mean well, but you have to admit you get these . . . academic crushes."

"What? Mom, I told you—"

"I'm not saying you have a crush on Dr. Whitfield," she went on. "Not like that. But you have to admit that for years now it's been, 'Professor Hawkins this,' and 'Professor Hawkins said that,' and now it's obvious you've found another professor you like better."

I'm sure I was blushing hard. It's so embarrassing to have your mother call you out like that. Plus it wasn't true.

"I still respect Professor Hawkins," I said. "Totally. Can't I respect Professor Whitfield, too? He's already helped me a lot—he explained some really hard physics problems to me that I know Mr. Dobosh wouldn't understand at all."

"I'm sure he's very smart," my mother said. "All I'm saying is that not everyone in the scientific community seems to agree that Dr. Whitfield is worth . . . admiring."

It was so frustrating. How do you fight against gossip and pettiness? That's all it was—those articles were a joke.

Just like what Professor Hawkins had said in his book about Dr. Whitfield—meanness, complete unnecessary meanness.

I laid the stack of papers at the foot of my mother's bed. "Thanks, but I don't need to read these. I know what I know.

And Professor Whitfield is one of the best quantum physicists out there right now—I have no doubt about that."

"All right," my mother said. "I was just trying to—"

"I know, Mom. I get it. Thanks. I'm going to bed."

I shut the door to her room and went into my own. This day was done. Over. I couldn't take anymore. I didn't even feel like staying up and seeing Halli, I was in that bad of a mood. All I wanted was some sleep. I just wanted to go to bed and forget everything that had happened in the last four or five hours.

What a silly idea that was. There was still a *lot* more to come.

Forty-eight

"Heya," Halli said quickly. She glanced over her shoulder. "We don't have much time—"

"What? How? I didn't meditate tonight! I wasn't even trying! How did you do this? Wasn't I just asleep?"

"Put these on," Halli answered, shoving the clothes at me. I wore just my sleep shirt and boxers. I hadn't seen a reason to throw on the long underwear.

And Halli was right: we didn't have much time at all. I could already see Martin helping Daniel hobble toward us across the grass.

Red must have sensed how hyped up Halli and I were. It made him especially playful—which in this case meant tugging at the pants I was trying to put on.

The *hirsch* were bugling again. That odd, beautiful sound. And over the top of that, I heard Daniel calling out, "Audie?"

"Can you give us a minute?" Halli shouted.

"Only if you promise what I said," Daniel called back.

"What did you promise? Red, give me those!"

Halli sighed. "That guy is *persistent*. I couldn't get rid of him last night."

Of course. Last night. The night when he'd been talking to some girl earlier in the day about her family lineage and where she was from, and then suddenly—*zip!*—magico disappearo. I'd sort of forgotten about that.

"What did you tell him?" I asked. "Did you hear what happened?"

"Oh, I heard," Halli said. She fisted both hands, then made a whooshing noise as she exploded them open and let them drift apart. "Gone. Vanished."

"Did he have a heart attack?"

"No, but I almost did," Halli said. "He'd been standing at the trailhead so long, waiting for me to come down the mountain and answer him, his ankle swelled to about the size of a melon. I had to ice it and compress it and rewrap it. I don't think I've ever seen a sprain look so bad. So what happened to you? Why did you go back?"

"It's a long, horrible story," I said. "I'll tell you later."

Because our time was almost up. Martin and Daniel had almost reached the hermit's hut.

"What did you tell him?" I whispered to Halli.

"That you'd explain everything."

"Thanks a lot!" I said.

"Well, what else was I supposed to—"

"Audie," Daniel said, "may I speak to you?"

He was standing with his back to the sun, which meant I had to squint and couldn't really see his face. But his voice sounded pretty tight.

"Sure, um, let me just finish putting on my boots—"

"Take your time," Daniel said, awkwardly lowering himself to the ground. "I'm staying."

"Need anything else, mate?" Martin asked.

"Yes. Would you please escort Halli Markham back with you?"

Halli must have seen the look on my face, because she said, "No . . . I think I'll stay."   For which I was grateful.

Daniel turned to her. "You said I should speak to your cousin. I would like the courtesy of doing that alone. You gave me your word."

Halli looked at me. I looked at Daniel. Now that he was down on the ground with me, I could see that he didn't exactly look homicidal. Or even particularly upset. Just . . . determined.

"How about this?" I said. "Halli can go, but Red stays." Having seen the beast in action when I first popped onto the scene, I knew he could be ferocious if I needed him to be.

"Agreed," Daniel said.

Halli gave me an "Are you sure?" look, and I nodded. Then she and Martin headed back toward the outdoor tables.

Daniel hadn't taken his eyes off me for at least the last minute. It made me uncomfortable enough that I instinctively leaned forward to let my hair curtain my face. But it only did half the job. I reached up to feel it. And still loved it. Sarah really knew what she was doing.

"Well?" Daniel said.

I went back to tying my boot.

Daniel reached out and clasped my wrist.

"Ow!"

"Sorry." He let go. "I wanted to make sure you're real." Then he asked what seemed like a reasonable question. "What *are* you?"

I guess I should be used to that by now.

"I'm human, just like you."

"You can't be," he said. He reached out again for my wrist, but this time held it a lot more gently. Then he reached down and spread my fingers against his other, open hand.

"Your skin is warm."

"Y-yes." It didn't feel that warm to me. More like icy and a little clammy.

Daniel looked into my eyes, shifting his gaze from one to the other. Like he was checking for wires or computer hardware behind them.

I pulled my hand back. "I'm human. I'm normal. I'm just not from here."

Daniel swallowed. "Then where are you from?"

I squeezed my eyes shut, then let them open again. "Do you know much about science?"

"A bit."

"Do you really want me to tell you this? It might be hard to accept."

"Audie, seeing you disappear in front of my eyes yesterday was hard to accept. If you have an explanation, I'd be grateful. Please, I'm asking you."

He was so polite. And so . . . ready, I thought. He'd obviously had a whole day and night to think about it, and now he actually seemed to be in some kind of pain, wanting to know so badly. And I could explain. So why would I withhold the truth from someone who wanted it so badly?

I drew two lines in the dirt.

"This is my universe," I began. "This is yours."

Forty-nine

It's good to have a dog with you in times of stress.

Because I noticed that both Daniel and I needed to pet Red—a lot—to get through our conversation. Which was fine with Red. He even rolled onto his back at one point to make sure someone rubbed his belly. Maybe Halli's right and he doesn't like that many people, but he does like me, and now, it seems, Daniel.

"What are you two doing?" Sarah called to us about midway through the conversation. Daniel ignored her.

"Do I need to send Martin?"

"No!" Daniel and I both shouted back.

Because he got it. Even faster than Halli did. Which might not be a fair comparison, since the explanation I gave Daniel also incorporated the information Professor Whitfield and I have worked out together. String theory, three-branes, psychokinesis, the observer problem—Daniel seemed to understand all of it.

Not that it made it any easier to accept.

"So you're here," he said. "But only temporarily. You still always return to your own universe."

"Yes."

"Pity," he said, with an easy kind of smile. "I was starting to enjoy this."

I wasn't totally sure, but I thought it was probably a compliment.

But then I went back to the subject at hand. "You know, you said you only know a little bit about science, but I think you know a lot."

"Not this kind," Daniel said. "I assure you."

"But can I just say? You took this really well."

Daniel smiled. "I'd rather know there's an explanation behind someone disappearing in front my eyes. Even if the explanation is unfathomable. At least I know I haven't lost my mind."

"Well, thanks," I said.

"For what?"

"I don't know . . . being so nice about it."

Daniel laughed. "As opposed to what?"

I shrugged. "I don't know. Being . . . weird. Being angry. I thought maybe you were mad at me before."

"No," Daniel said, "I was alarmed. When Halli wouldn't tell me what had happened, I spent the rest of the night imagining all sorts of scenarios."

"Like what?"

"Most of them involved me having to turn myself over to the neurosurgeons for an adjustment. It wasn't a pleasant night."

I winced. "I'm really sorry."

Daniel shrugged. "No harm done. You're a visitor from another universe. Perfectly reasonable explanation—I wish I'd thought of it myself."

I laughed. Daniel smiled and picked at the grass near our feet. He's a pretty nice guy, I have to say. Smart, too. And pretty cute, if I have to tell the whole truth.

"Audie! Dan!" Sarah called. "I'm coming, so make yourselves decent!"

"My sister gets bored easily," Daniel said.

"I like your sister."

"I do, too," he admitted.

I helped him to his feet. Then I suppose it was natural that he draped his arm over my shoulder, like he had with Martin when they hobbled toward me.

But I don't think Daniel said anything like this to Martin: "I've never met anyone like you."

I laughed. Because I was sure that was true. People probably didn't pop in from other universes all that often in his world.

"Audie, I mean it. I feel very fortunate to have met you."

"Oh. Okay." I laughed a little again because I wasn't sure what else to do.

"Finished, are you?" Sarah said to her brother. "Audie, I've come to rescue you. I can't imagine what Daniel's been saying to bore you all this time."

"He hasn't bored me." In fact, the last thing he'd just said to me might have been the least boring thing I'd heard in a long time.

"Where did you go yesterday?" Sarah asked me. She transferred Daniel's weight onto her shoulders, freeing me. I stepped a little away, and the three of us and the dog headed back.

"You weren't there for the triumphant return of the mountain climbers," Sarah said. "Did Halli tell you how she saved that handsome young pilot from certain death and now he's obviously smitten with her?"

"What are you talking about?" I asked.

"Karl, the very muscular German pilot," Sarah answered. "Every girl should have one—I certainly want one."

"What about Martin?" Daniel asked.

"He should change his name, bulk up, and get a pilot's license," Sarah said. "Do you never listen to me?"

"Hardly ever," Daniel confirmed.

Just then, Halli and her very handsome escort came into view.

"Here, take him," Sarah told me, handing off her brother to me. "I want to go speak to Halli Markham."

"She means speak to Karl the pilot," Daniel said as she ran off. But he seemed good-natured about it.

I let him rest his weight against me again and he hobbled the rest of the way. I didn't particularly mind it.

"When will you be disappearing again?" Daniel asked me.

"I honestly don't know."

"Shall we share some tea until you do?"

Fifty

"You're sure you don't mind me leaving again so soon?" my mother asked me four days ago, on Monday. Her bag was already packed. It's not like she was going to change her mind.

"Mom, I'm glad you're going. Really. It's so good for the business."

Not to mention for me.

She pulled me over and kissed my head. "I'll make it up to you. We'll spend a lot of time together when I get back next week. Maybe go to a few movies?"

"Sounds great."

Monday to Monday. Eight days of solitude. Perfect. And it couldn't have been better timing, because as of Monday, Halli changed her hours on me.

It was supposed to be just a weekend thing, me staying up late instead of going to bed and waking up later, but Halli decided she liked me coming over at 6:00 AM her time, which is 10:00 PM mine.

I've been doing it that way all week. Going over for a few hours, coming back and grabbing a little sleep before school, and then relying a lot on that yoga pose Lydia taught me. I'm not sure if twenty minutes in it really does equal a two-hour nap, but so far I'm holding up pretty well. I haven't fallen asleep in class once. Except that one time in Algebra Support, which doesn't really count.

So why did Halli ask me to change our meeting time? Five words: Karl the muscular German pilot. Sarah was right—he's *hot*. Twenty years old, dark hair, blue eyes, obviously wild about Halli—

Plus he's a much better outdoor companion for her, so I don't mind at all the fact that she keeps ditching me to go off on various adventures with him.

Plus it gives me more time with Daniel. Shut up.

"What is it today?" I asked Halli as she and I sat behind the hermit's hut while I put on all my clothes.

"Rock climbing and rappelling," Halli said, a smile lighting her face. "Yesterday we hiked up to that peak and back." She pointed to it in the distance. "Took us about nine hours."

"Sounds fun," I said, my tone suggesting I thought the exact opposite.

"It was," Halli said with a sigh. "I haven't hiked that hard in a year."

Her cheeks had a ruddy glow in the early morning breeze, and her eyes looked bright and lively. I realized the only other time I'd seen her so invigorated was when she was bouncing around her house showing me the map and talking about our trip to the Alps.

I don't think it's just because of Karl, although she clearly seems to like him. I think it's because Halli is finally back to doing what she does best and what she obviously really loves. After all this time spent grieving for Ginny, Halli is finally coming back to life.

"I hate to rush off—" Halli said.

"Why?" I answered. "Go. You guys have fun. You, too, Red." I flapped up his ears as I scratched underneath them. "Oh, just one thing—" I added as she helped me to my feet. "Remember I go to Colorado this afternoon. I don't get in till kind of late, so we'll probably have to skip tonight. But I'm sure Professor Whitfield will want me to come here tomorrow morning. I mean your, you know, night."

"That's great," Halli said. "You can finally come for dinner and spend some time with us in the evening. I'm sure Daniel will love that."

"Shut up . . ." I mumbled.

The two of us rounded the front of the hermit's hut and headed across the grass.

"He likes you, you know."

"No, he doesn't," I said.

"Audie, you know he does!" she said with a laugh, and bumped me with her shoulder.

"Seriously, I don't want to talk about it," I said. "You're making me shy."

Halli shook her head. "You're a funny girl . . ."

"So anyway," I said, drawing her back to the subject, "let's plan on meeting around . . . 5:00 your time? That will be 9:00 in the morning on Saturday. I'm sure we'll have gotten started with the testing by then."

"Are you nervous?" Halli asked.

"Not really," I said. "At least, not about the testing. About everything else? Yeah."

Everything else being the lying, the traveling by myself, the more lying—I was going to have a weekend full of it.

I have traveled alone before. My mom has stuck me on a plane at least once a year to go visit my dad in California. But I've never had to figure out any of the logistics before. For a while I was young enough that some flight attendant would escort me to my next gate when I switched planes, and once I got older I could handle that much on my own, but somehow this feels different.

It probably is the lying.

I don't know how criminals can stand the stress. You have to think of so many details: forwarding the phone to your cell; making up an excuse to tell your friends so they won't stop by or expect to see you (not that Lydia would stop by, probably, but she might call to invite me over for dinner); telling your boss (Elena) why you won't be there on Friday (after school project), and hope she doesn't do anything to check up on it; forging a note from your mother to the school principal to miss half a day of school; asking your neighbor to pick up the mail and newspaper ("Going out of town with my mom. Be back Sunday night."); printing out the boarding passes, even though you know one of them won't be used; deciding whether to drive your car to the airport and leave it there, or take a shuttle (shuttle); and last, forging your mother's name to a special note for the professor. I felt particularly guilty about that.

But at least I could cheer myself up with the packing.

I decided for this trip, I'm going to try to be like Halli. Throw just a few items of clothing in a small bag, and not make a big deal out of it. Usually when I go to my dad's I bring at least two pieces of luggage—one of them mostly for books. But if Halli can get by for a few weeks in the Alps with just a backpack, and if half the clothes in there are the ones she's been carrying around for me, then I should be able to go to Bear Creek, Colorado for a couple of days and not have to bring a lot of stuff.

Halli and I could see Karl waiting off in the distance.

"You'd better go," I said.

Halli gave me a big hug. "I think it's wonderful, what you're doing with the professor. Very brave."

I had to laugh. "What's brave about letting someone hook a few sensors to my head? You're the one who's out there climbing cliffs."

"That feels normal to me," Halli said. "Being tested in a laboratory doesn't. Don't let them ruin anything about you. I don't want you to come back any different."

I almost got a little choked up at that. "Thanks," I told her. "I'll try."

She gave me another quick hug, then jogged off to meet Karl. He'd already packed their lunches for the day and was waiting near the base of one of the trails. Red ran after his girl. I watched the three of them head toward another mountain, and kept watching until I couldn't see them anymore.

And something just felt . . . off. I couldn't figure out what. Maybe I was just feeling sentimental because of what she said. Or maybe it was watching her go off with a guy she liked, and thinking about what she'd told me about Daniel. Or maybe it really was the nerves, and I was thinking that the next time I saw her I'd be in some strange place where someone was watching me and monitoring my brain while I tried to relax and go see Halli.

But somehow I didn't think it was any of that. I just felt strangely uneasy. I couldn't put my finger on it.

I snapped myself out of it and headed toward the outdoor tables. Where a certain Englishman waited for me.

Fifty-one

"Hi," I said, taking a seat next to Daniel on the bench. He passed me a steaming cup of coffee. It's become our habit.

"What's wrong?" he asked.

I shrugged. "Just a feeling. I guess I'm kind of nervous about tomorrow."

The morning was colder than it has been. I wrapped my fingers around the mug to warm them, but I still couldn't stop a little shiver.

"Cold?" Daniel asked. He took one of my hands off the mug and stuck it into the pocket of his coat. He kept his own hand inside there on top of it.

It may have seemed casual to anyone watching—it may have even seemed casual to Daniel—but it wasn't to me. That was the first time he'd ever done something like that. I'd had his arm wrapped around my shoulder before while I helped him hobble, but this was different. This was personal.

I tried to be cool about it. Even though inside I was all *Yesssss.*

I took another sip of my coffee, but I still felt cold. I scooted closer to Daniel. You know, for warmth.

He did what I secretly hoped he would. He took his hand out of the pocket and wrapped that arm around my shoulders. I leaned into him and rested my head against him.

"About time," said a voice from behind us. "Glaciers move more expeditiously than you two."

I sat up straight, embarrassed. But Daniel kept his arm where it was. Sarah planted herself on the other side of me and squished me even closer to her brother. She took a sip from her own cup of hot tea. "Brrrr—why is it so cold?"

"See," Daniel said, "the earth turns on its axis, and there are these phenomena called seasons—"

"Git," she said. To me she said, "Where's Halli Markham off to today?"

"Rock climbing. Can I ask you something?" I said. "Why do you always call her by her full name?"

"I don't know," Sarah answered, "suppose it's habit. It's how you always hear of her, isn't it? 'Halli Markham crosses the Gobi.' 'Halli Markham in the fight of her life.' "

"Which one was that?" I asked, mildly alarmed.

"Piranhas in the Amazon—very exciting to a young girl."

"I'm sure that was exciting for her."

"No," Sarah said, "I meant me! I used to write school reports about her as I was growing up—well, we all did, didn't we?"

"You did?"

Daniel shifted his arm off my shoulder and instead went back to holding my hand. I think he sensed there might be a problem coming up. He wanted to have a subtle way to signal me.

"Well, of course!" Sarah said. "She's the most famous young explorer in the world. And even more exciting, she's always been my same age. I used to think how unjust it was that Halli Markham was off having adventures while I was stuck reading about them in class. I think my first report about her was when I was seven. That was when Halli Markham and her grandmother first trekked to the North Pole."

"When she was seven? Wow."

Sarah gave me a funny look. "But you must know that."

Daniel squeezed my hand.

"Oh, well . . . see, I didn't really follow . . . our parents didn't get along—" I tried to think of the story Halli had told Sarah and Daniel when we first met. "We never really saw each other after we were babies—not until now."

"But you must have learned about her in school," Sarah persisted. "We all did."

"Yeah, um . . . my parents home schooled me—you know, taught me at home themselves. They never really talked about Halli."

"But surely you've come across her in the histories?" Sarah asked.

Obviously she wasn't going to let it go.

"No, not really," I said.

"Hmp!" Sarah said with obvious disapproval. "I'd say your parents kept you quite in the dark."

No kidding. They didn't even know there was another universe where someone like Halli might exist.

"Dan, hand me your tab." Sarah reached behind me and poked her brother and waited while he pulled his portable screen from a pocket inside his jacket.

"It might not have enough power," Daniel told her. "Yesterday was cloudy."

Sarah looked at the sky. "Today, too. We'll see what we can do."

She swept her finger over the screen several times and then pressed in a few places. Soon lights started swirling above the surface. Sarah set the tablet on the table. "Here," she said to me. "Watch."

It was a mini-movie. In 3D. A sort of holographic highlight film, chronicling Halli's life.

The figures were about six inches tall—a comfortable size to watch from close up. Much smaller than the nearly life-size head of Halli's mom when she called her on the comm.

"Oh, I love this one!" Sarah was saying as the figures began to move.

There we were, a very young version of me, riding what looked like a Mongolian pony with my grandmother. Although I'm pretty sure my Grandma Marion would have been screaming her head off, and I doubt I would have had the coordination back then—was Halli only four or five? Looked like it—to sit astride a galloping horse and stay on, even with a burly old woman perched behind me.

Cut to the next scene. Halli a little bit older, bravely leaning into a howling wind while she and Ginny trekked across snow and ice, both of them pulling sleds behind them loaded with supplies.

"So that's the North Pole?" I asked.

"Yes!" Sarah answered. She looked as delighted as she must have been when she first saw it as a child.

Scene after scene: Halli in the desert. Halli in the jungle. Halli rafting down crazy-scary rivers and yes, rowing across the ocean. Always with Ginny at her side, the old woman with either a grim, determined look on her face or laughing like she couldn't imagine doing anything more fun.

I got it, finally. No wonder strangers shouted out Halli's name whenever they recognized her—this footage was amazing.

She must have inspired a whole generation of children and even adults. She would have inspired me.

And then, I don't know what it was, but this horrible feeling started descending on me. This heaviness, this sort of self-loathing—the kind of thing you wish you could scrape off yourself like sludge.

"That's great," I said to Sarah, pushing the screen in her direction. "Thanks for showing me." I hoped she would take the hint. I hoped she would turn it off.

There must have been something in my voice, because Daniel sensed something was wrong. "Where's Martin?" he asked Sarah. "I'm surprised you've left him alone for this long."

She tossed her hair behind her shoulders—the first time I'd seen her do anything even vaguely Gemma-ish.

"He went off to the springs for a bath. None too soon, I assure you."

"Care to take a walk?" Daniel asked me, carefully maneuvering himself up from the table. "Halli said I should put more weight on my ankle today—it needs to be well by Sunday."

"Sunday?" I said.

"We're leaving," Sarah said. "Day after tomorrow. Back to London, back to school. It's horrid."

It was horrid. Just two more days together, all of us, and I was going to miss a major portion of it while I flew to Colorado. It wasn't fair.

I stood up and waited for Daniel to steady himself against my shoulder, but he was going to try it on his own. Sarah sat there at the table for a moment, eyeing us both.

"I'll stay here," she said. "I can see I'm not needed." Then she *winked* at me. She was turning into Gemma before my eyes.

No, I take that back—totally unfair. I'm sure statistically it was bound to happen that two iterations of the same person might every now and then use the same gestures. I suppose people might sometimes mistake me for Halli. Although I sincerely doubt it.

"Can you leave your tab, Dan?" she asked. "I'll watch some more histories while I wait for Martin."

"Actually," Daniel said, "I thought I'd take it with us. Audie might want to see more."

"All right," Sarah answered, slightly pouting. "But it's very boring here, you know. No Halli Markham, no Karl the handsome pilot, no Martin, no amateur young lovers such as yourselves to spy upon—what shall I do?"

"You'll find something," Daniel said, leading me away. "Try sitting quietly, for a change."

"Try kissing your girlfriend, for a change!" she shot back. "You haven't got all year, you know. Try acting like a normal bloke for once . . ."

Fifty-two

It was crazy, of course.

Worse than meeting a guy on vacation, having a little fling, and then saying, "Goodbye, I promise I'll write."

We couldn't write. We would never see each other. He lived in England, Halli lived in Colorado—when would we ever see each other again?

I suppose we could conduct some sort of holo-relationship where I phoned him using Halli's comm, and we could at least see each other that way—swirling lights turning into each other's heads above the screen—but it's not like we would ever be around each other again, unless he decided to come where Halli was or she went to him. He was in school. He had a life. Halli did, too.

Hopeless. No question about that.

"Champion idea," Daniel said as soon as we'd made it to the hermit's hut. He backed me against the wall and laid such a kiss on me I thought my own ankles would buckle underneath me. He held my face between his hands, then wove his fingers through my hair, and I swear, if he hadn't been holding me up while he kept on kissing me, I would have just liquified right into the dirt. Man, that guy can kiss. Why didn't we start doing that days ago?

It took me a little while to regain speech. When I did, the best I could say was, "Whaaa . . ." And then I gave up on making sense, and went back to kissing him. Sarah was right: not much time. Forget spending it talking.

Eventually a person has to breathe. And sit. And let the swirling lights in her head settle down.

We slid down with our backs against the wall, holding hands and looking out at the woods. The *hirsch* didn't have too much to say this time of morning. Just as well—I was already on sensory overload.

"Why were you upset back there?" Daniel asked.

"Hm?" My head felt foggy. My lips felt puffy and warm.

"When we were watching the holo of Halli," he said

It seemed so long ago, but somehow I could vaguely remember.

"Oh, just the usual," I said. "Feeling like such a loser compared to her. It happens all the time."

Daniel laughed. "Why?"

"Because I haven't done a single interesting thing in my life," I said. "Never."

Daniel nudged me. "Where are you right now?"

I sighed. I knew what he was trying to do. I wasn't buying it.

"Yes, I know—Halli says that, too. But you know what I mean."

"No," Daniel said, "I don't."

"This—" I waved my arms around us. "This is obviously fantastic. I'm not saying it isn't. But this is basically an accident. I couldn't have done it if Halli weren't meditating on a rock in the mountains that day. I just would have kept trying and trying, and nothing would have happened."

"It happened," Daniel said, "precisely because you kept trying and trying. How many other people would do that?"

"Daniel—"

He lifted my hand up to his lips and kissed it. My brain floated right out of my skull.

"You fail to see what I see," Daniel said.

"Huh?" I had to shake my head to clear it.

"You," Daniel said. "We're speaking of you."

"Look," I said, "I know you're trying to be nice. Thank you. But I think we can both admit that Halli Markham is the most amazing person either of us has ever met. And yes, there are times when I can't help but feel completely useless by comparison."

"You're seventeen," Daniel said.

"Yes. But so is Halli—"

"And I am eighteen," he interrupted. "Ask me what I've done in my eighteen years."

"I'm not talking about—"

"Me?" Daniel finished. "But I am." He released my hand and pulled his tablet out of his pocket. He poked and pressed at the screen.

"Here," he said, tilting the tablet so I could see it. "This is me."

It was him. There was his picture. Not a hologram, just a picture. He pressed a space underneath it.

It wasn't a bad biography. Details about his parents (his mother was an archaeologist, his father something called a "history producer"), his schooling, his sibling (one, Sarah), his victories at something called "yorking." He had participated in several science exhibitions in the past few years, and even won a prize for building something called a "crescograph."

"What's a crescograph?" I asked. "You never told me about that. You never said anything about being in a science competition—you said you only know a bit."

"A bit about plants," he said. "Not physics. Now let's look for someone else."

Daniel pressed and swept at the screen, then held it out for me again. "His name is Raad Rabiah. Same age as I am. Read."

Yeah, okay, I could see where a guy like that might make a person insecure. Honors in biology, chemistry, physics. Honors in translation of ancient texts. Admission to Oxford at age fifteen. Author of three books. Honorary professor of—

"Seen enough?" Daniel asked, gently taking the screen back. He pressed it on the edge and it went black.

"Do you know him?" I asked.

"We all know him. Every boy's parents know him. Every teacher knows him. Our ears are full of him."

"So you don't like him."

"I admire him, certainly," Daniel said. "But do I aspire to be him? No. Do I feel the lack of not being him? No. I recognize that there are Raad Rabiahs, and there are Daniel Everetts. I cannot help but be the latter."

"It's different for me," I said softly. "I really could be Halli. That's the whole point."

"*Could* you be her?" Daniel challenged. "Did you have a grandmother like Virginia Markham then?"

"No, not exactly."

"Have you spent your life traveling across the world with a woman known for attempting what others might never do—particularly with a young child in their care?"

"No, but—"

"Are your parents exactly, in every way, like Regina Markham and Jameson Bellows?"

"I mean, I'm sure they look the same—"

"Audie, unless you can duplicate the conditions of your environment, your heritage, your upbringing, and your experiences to within a millionth of a millionth of variation from those of Halli Markham's, you have absolutely no basis for comparing yourself unfavorably or otherwise in regards to your accomplishments or your qualities. Do you understand?"

The truth was, no. He'd said it so quickly and eloquently and with such authority, my overloaded mind was still trying to register the meaning. Plus I was wishing he'd kiss me again. But whatever he'd just said, I was pretty sure I'd be foolish to argue with him.

"Can you at least understand me?" I asked. "I look at Halli—"

"And you see yourself," Daniel finished. "And all the things you are not. And how do you know Halli Markham doesn't feel the same when she looks at you?"

I made a snorting sound. Very attractive of me, I'm sure.

"We only see ourselves and our inadequacies," Daniel said. "Everyone is the same."

"You think Raad Rabiah would be jealous of you?" I asked.

"Absolutely," Daniel said. "He has never won at yorking."

"What is york—"

My alarm sounded at home. My body flew back.

AAAAAARRRRGGGGG!!!

I lay there in my bed for a moment, trying to reorient myself. I was home. It was half past midnight. I'd set my alarm for even earlier than usual so I could get more of a full night's sleep before I went to Colorado. I figured it would be better to show up there alert than to spend another hour or two hanging out with Daniel and Sarah and Martin.

Of course, that was before I knew Daniel might spend the hours kissing me. What a stupid choice I'd made.

And now I was stuck. Halli wouldn't be looking for me until tomorrow morning—her Saturday night. There was no way I could go back, even if I wanted to. And I desperately wanted to.

I rolled over and groaned into my pillow. Why had I wasted so much of Daniel's and my time together tonight talking about my insecurities? He's leaving the day after tomorrow. No matter how much we might decide we like each other, it doesn't matter—it's about to be over.

This is why you don't get involved with guys from another universe. This is why you never let yourself fall for someone you're probably never going to see again. It hurts too much. The ache was palpable. I could feel it on my lips and in my chest.

How can I keep making this mistake, no matter what universe I'm in? Why do I keep falling for guys I can't have?

Fifty-three

Professor Whitfield met me at the airport. He was wearing jeans and hiking boots and a dark gray hoodie that said Mountain State. There was no mistaking who he was. I gave him a little wave. He looked confused. Let the lying begin.

"Where's your mother?"

I handed him the note. "She said she's so, so sorry, but she had to go on this last-minute emergency trip to Philadelphia for her work. She said to go ahead and do all our testing—she'll want to hear about all of it afterward."

Professor Whitfield read the note. I looked around the airport and tried to act casual. He folded up the note and looked at me. Looked at me a little longer than I was comfortable with.

"Oh, well," he finally said. "I'm sorry I won't get to meet her."

"You will, one day, I'm sure," I said cheerfully. I wondered if he could see how relieved I was.

He took my bag from me and led me out to the parking lot, to his white Ford Explorer. Surprisingly tidy inside.

Except for the enormous mass of fur in the back seat.

"What is that?" I asked. "A Saint Bernard?" The dog was at least twice the size of Red.

"No, she's a Bernese Mountain Dog," Professor Whitfield said. "Say hello, Bess."

She lifted her paw and let me shake it. I so want a dog.

"Hungry?" the professor asked me.

"Starving."

Over plates of fajitas and refried beans, the two of us discussed our strategy.

"I have you for a day and a half, basically," Professor Whitfield said. "But I know some of that time it will be night over where Halli is, so we'll try to adjust our schedule to get the most out of your interaction. How does that sound?"

I told him I'd planned on meeting her at 5:00 tomorrow night her time, 9:00 AM ours.

"Good," he said. "Perfect. I'll pick you up early and give you a little tour of the facility first, then we'll get to work."

I nodded and ate another tortilla chip.

The professor studied me from across the booth. "Nervous?"

"Not really," I said. "Just . . . ready. And curious."

"Curious is an excellent place to be," the professor said.

Okay, and yes, I was nervous—pretty seriously nervous, as a matter of fact—but I didn't want the professor to know that. It's just that sitting there with him, in person, after half a day of travel, suddenly made the whole thing seem very real. I wasn't sure if I was totally ready.

"So . . . what are you going to do?" I asked.

The professor filled me in on some of the specifics. "We'll be monitoring your heart rate, temperature, brain waves, oxygen level, room temperature, sound waves—"

"What do you mean?" I said. "Why room temperature and sound waves?"

"Because you might be creating a kind of . . . for lack of a better phrase, 'energy field,' " Professor Whitfield said. "We don't really know what goes on in your environment when you and Halli connect. I'm going to try to capture as much data as we can in these few days."

Now I was really getting nervous. It was a long way from a simple experiment in my own bedroom.

Professor Whitfield signaled for the check. "I'd like you to get plenty of sleep tonight, Audie. We have a lot to do tomorrow, and it's all going to depend on you. I'm sorry," he said, lowering his hand. "Did you want dessert?"

Maybe I did before, but now I'd pretty much lost my appetite.

The professor dropped me off at a hotel near the campus and said he'd be back to pick me up at 7:30 in the morning. I reached around to the back seat and gave Bess a pat before I got out. I think I'd like a life where I could take my dog with me everywhere.

"Need anything else?" Professor Whitfield asked after he'd helped me check in.

"No, I don't think so. Thanks." I glanced at the clock in the hotel lobby: only 9:45. I could have met Halli tonight after all. More important, I could have seen Daniel. But there was nothing I could do about it now—Halli wouldn't be looking for me again until tomorrow.

"Seven-thirty," the professor repeated. "Get some sleep."

"I will."

I took the elevator up to my room and opened the door to go inside. It felt weird standing there all alone, just a big empty hotel room and me. Different from being home alone. Everything looked clean and new, but it also felt a little cold. Impersonal. Like it didn't care whether it was me sleeping in one of the beds or some anonymous businessman on a trip.

Is this what it's been like for Halli, now that Ginny isn't around anymore? Sitting in her campsite, walking into some empty apartment in Munich, no one to talk to except Red? Until I show up, at least. Maybe Halli wasn't just being nice when she told me that one time she was happy for the company. I can see how maybe a person could go crazy spending too much time alone.

But I can also see the adventurous part of it. Because I have to say you do feel pretty bold and independent being in some strange city by yourself.

As long as you can still check in with your mom.

"Hello?" She sounded groggy. I forgot all about the time difference. It must have been around midnight where she was.

"Oh, sorry, Mom. I just wanted to say goodnight."

"Goodnight, sweetie. Did you have a good day?"

"Yeah, it was fine." I took two planes, sneaked off to another state, and right now I'm supposed to be getting a good night's sleep in a hotel room so tomorrow some professor you don't trust can run a bunch of tests to see whether it's okay for me to keep traveling to another universe to hang out with my parallel self. All totally normal.

We talked a little more, but I could tell she was barely awake.

"I'll let you go back to sleep," I told her. "I just wanted to say hi."

"I always love to hear your voice," she said. "Goodnight, sweetie. Have a good day tomorrow."

"You, too, Mom."

As soon as I hung up the phone I knew: I have to tell her soon. I can't keep lying to her like this. That's not what our relationship is about. My dad lied to her and she's never gotten over it. I can't be the second person in our three-person family to do that to her. It just isn't fair.

So I will tell her. Right after I get back. I'll figure out what to say and I'll say it.

And what if she freaks out and says I can never do it again? I can never see Halli or Daniel or any of them?

I'll just have to make sure that doesn't happen. Professor Whitfield and I have to prove it's safe. That's what this whole weekend's about: proof.

Because if one thing's clear to me, it's that I'm not going to give up the best thing that's ever happened in my life.

I'm just tired of lying to my mother to keep it.

Fifty-four

"What do you think?" Professor Whitfield asked me, standing on a little hilltop overlooking the campus.

"It's nice," I said. "Really nice."

And it was. Red brick buildings, lots of grass, lots of pine trees—like a little college carved out of the forest. Only about a fraction as big as Columbia University, if you look at the pictures, but cozy and sort of homey if that's what you're looking for. Not the sort of place you'd expect to go if you were someone with big ambitions.

"These are the labs," Professor Whitfield said, leading me toward one of the long buildings closest to the parking lot. He opened the outside door, and his dog Bess came in with us, too. Probably another thing that's different from Columbia— somehow I doubt Professor Hawkins lets you bring a dog into his lab space.

"We'll start at the botany wing," the professor said. "Work our way to mine."

He opened a door off of the hallway, and we went inside.

The air was humid in there, moist—a lot like Halli's greenhouse. And there was an easy explanation for that, since the whole place was filled with plants: rows of shelves along every wall, all of them holding plants with wires coming out of them.

"What are those?" I asked, pointing to the wires.

"Some of them are hooked up to polygraph machines, some to other kinds of sensors—it varies."

"Polygraph machines," I repeated. "As in lie detectors?"

"That's right," Professor Whitfield said.

"You're testing to see if they're lying," I said.

"No, not exactly—here," the professor said, indicating a young woman in a lab coat who was making notes on her laptop. "Hannah, why don't you explain."

"Sure, Dr. Whitfield." She got up from her desk and came over to introduce herself. "Hannah Trong," she said, shaking my hand.

"Hannah's a grad student," the professor said. "Did her undergrad here, too, didn't you?"

"Part of it," Hannah said. "I transferred in from Princeton. Here," she told me. "Let me show you what we're doing."

She led the professor and Bess and me down one of the rows of plants, back to the corner where some philodendrons sat in pots near the windows. The leaves of the plants had small electrodes attached to them. The electrodes led to computerized monitors that recorded what was going on with the plants.

"Have you ever heard of Cleve Backster?" Hannah asked me. I shook my head. "He was a specialist in lie detectors—he taught people in the FBI and CIA how to use them. One day back in the 1960s he got the strange idea to hook a polygraph up to the plant in his office. Then he tried a little experiment."

"I don't know if you know," Hannah said, "but polygraphs don't really test for lies, they test for fluctuations in stress levels—it's an indication of human emotions. So Backster wondered if he might be able to test for the same kind of thing in his plant."

"But plants don't have emotions," I said, "do they?"

"Well," Hannah said, "you tell me. First Backster gave the plant some water, and the needle on the polygraph moved. But it moved downward, like it was relaxing—not stressed."

"Really?" I said.

"Really," Hannah answered. "Then he decided to try dipping one of the leaves in the cup of hot coffee he had in his hand. Nothing."

"No stress?" I asked.

"None. But then," Hannah said, "the most incredible thing happened. Backster just had the *thought*—he didn't say it out loud, he didn't take any kind of action toward it—but he just had the *thought*, 'I wonder what would happen if I burned one of the leaves.' And right then, the needle on the polygraph went wild."

"You're kidding," I said.

"Not kidding," she answered.

"Wait a minute," I said. "Are you saying the plant *read his mind*?"

"Seemed that way," Hannah answered. "So then a lot of other scientists who heard about that experiment decided to start coming up with some of their own. I think my favorite one is the botanist in California who handed out sealed envelopes to all of his lab assistants, and in one of the envelopes was the note, 'You are the killer.' The scientist didn't know which person got that envelope, and none of the other lab assistants did, either.

"So the instructions were that whoever got that note should sneak back into the plant lab that night, leave all the lights out, and take one of the plants off the shelf. The person should smash it to the ground, step on it—really brutally murder the thing."

"That's awful!" I said.

"I know," Hannah agreed, "but totally fascinating."

"So what happened?" I asked.

I noticed Professor Whitfield was greatly enjoying this whole story.

"So the next day," Hannah said, "the scientist had each of the lab assistants walk one at a time through the plant lab, while he watched the sensors hooked up to the plants. And one by one the people came in, and the plants didn't react. But as soon as the *killer* walked in—" Hannah swung her hand up and down through the air. "*Huge* spikes in the sensors. The plants were going nuts. It's like you could almost hear them screaming."

"So they recognized the killer?" I asked.

"Recognized him," Hannah said, "remembered him, and could pick him out of a lineup. Better than some human witnesses to a crime."

"That's . . . incredible," I said.

"I know!" Hannah said. "Do you see why I got interested in botany?"

She looked at Professor Whitfield. "Of course, when I first heard about those stories while I was at Princeton, the professor who told us thought it was all a big laugh. 'This is what some so-called scientists are doing out there,' he said, and everyone acted like it was a big joke.

"But I didn't think it was funny," Hannah said. "I thought I'd finally figured out what I wanted to do with my life. When I told my professor—well, let's just say he wasn't very encouraging. I believe his words were something like 'career suicide.' But I didn't care. I found a place that would let me do it." She swept her hand across the lab. "Stayed here ever since."

"Thank you for the recruiting lecture," Professor Whitfield said with a smile.

"Are you thinking of going here?" Hannah asked me.

"No, um . . . I'm applying to Columbia."

"Oh," Hannah said. "Well, I'm sure that will be nice, too. Good luck with it." She sounded sincere.

The small monitor hooked up to the philodendron made a little beeping noise. "Hey," Hannah said to us, "you want to look? Last five minutes of results."

She changed the display on the monitor to show a graph of recent activity. For a while the line was steady, then it suddenly shot up into spikes.

"What happened?" I asked.

Hannah pointed at the dog. "Most of the plants in here already know Bess, but this philodendron is new. That's why I wanted to show it to you—I figured it would have a problem."

"Why?" I asked.

"We've found house plants in general get stressed around cats and dogs," she said. "Although they seem to hate cats worse."

"Why's that?" I asked.

Hannah leaned over and whispered. "Cats tend to chew on them and pee on them a lot more."

"Thank you, Hannah," Professor Whitfield said with a laugh. "I think we'd better let you get back to work."

"Sure," she said. "Nice meeting you." Then she went back to fiddling with the monitor.

As we neared the door, Hannah called out to me.

"You might want to rethink Columbia," she said. "Those big schools aren't always what you think."

"Okay . . . thanks," I said, and followed the professor into the hall.

"All of that can't be true," I said to the professor, "can it? About the plants?"

"Of course it's true," he answered.

"They have . . . emotion?"

"Of a type," he said. "Backster called it 'primary perception.' There've been a lot of studies since then—you should talk to Hannah some more if we have time. As you can see, she loves telling the stories."

I glanced back at the door to her lab. What a cool life. If I were interested in plants at all, I'd definitely want to go to school here and do what she's doing all day.

"Ready to see more?" Professor Whitfield asked.

"Definitely," I said.

Fifty-five

Columbia University—Department of Physics
Department Information

Research is an extremely important component of the Columbia physics experience. Because the department has a very small student-to-faculty ratio, essentially all physics majors engage in experimental, computational, or theoretical research under the close supervision of a faculty member during part, if not all, of their time at Columbia. There is nothing more exciting than the opportunity to engage in cutting-edge research as an undergraduate.

[*You're telling me.*]

As we walked down the corridor I thought about what Hannah had said about her experience at Princeton. I'm sure there are different teachers everywhere—you can find good ones and bad ones at every school. I felt sorry for her about what her professor had said, but it all worked out in the end. She's obviously happy where she is now. The same way I know I'll be happy at Columbia, studying under Professor Hawkins. You just have to find the right mentor.

Although I will confess, I had a moment there.

Okay, so let's just get it out of my system. Sometimes I like to do "what ifs." What if I decided *not* to apply for early decision at Columbia. The thing about early decision is that if you get in, you have to commit to going there, and it becomes like a contract you can't get out of. By applying that way, you're saying that Columbia is your first and only choice, and you're not going to change your mind.

So let's say I didn't do that, for whatever reason. Instead I just put in my application there at the regular time, by January 1st, like everybody else. The downside is I might lose the advantage of showing my enthusiasm and commitment to Columbia, and I also wouldn't know until March or April (a) whether I got in, and (b) whether I could get financial aid. So that sucks. It makes it impossible to plan.

The only upside is that if I apply the regular way, I can also apply to other schools at the same time. And so if the worst happens and Columbia doesn't accept me after all, at least maybe another few schools will. And maybe one of those schools would be Mountain State.

But can you see me going to a dinky little school like that? I mean, it's pretty there and all, but it's hardly *Columbia*. And Professor Hawkins obviously doesn't respect it—or respect Dr.

Whitfield—which might ultimately affect my career as a physicist. Just like Hannah Trong's professor said to her. So I guess that's what it comes down to: my future as a physicist, or my future for just the next few years. Yes, it might be fun to do the wacky kind of research Hannah is doing, except with physics instead of plants, but is it really worth it for me in the long run?

It has to be Columbia. Nothing has changed. I like Professor Whitfield, his college seems like a nice place, but I have to stay focused on what's right for me.

"Here's where you'll be this morning," Professor Whitfield said. "Shall we have a look inside?"

It was a small, white-walled room, just big enough for two chairs and a table. One of the chairs was big and cushioned, like something you'd have in your living room. The other one was just a regular desk chair.

"It's sound-proof," Professor Whitfield said. "We have two cameras mounted in the ceiling, and sound recorders in the walls. You'll be here by yourself most of the time. We'll be monitoring you from a nearby room."

I sat in the fluffy chair to test it out. It seemed pretty comfortable.

"Who will be watching?" I asked.

"I will," he said, "and a few of my graduate students. No one will disturb you, though. We want to make it as relaxing for you as possible."

Somehow I'd pictured myself lying flat on a gurney in something that looked like a hospital room, wires and needles sticking out of my body. I was relieved it would be just me sitting in a chair. I could handle that.

"We'll have you try a few 30-minute sessions," Professor Whitfield said, "over there and back, several times this morning. We'll see if we record any noticeable change in your vitals—heart rate, respiration, brain function—all of that."

It sounded serious. "Do you think it'll show anything?" I asked. "Like whether it's safe or not?"

"If we see something that looks wrong, we'll stop the test," he said. "It's as simple as that. Sound all right?"

I nodded.

I was feeling more nervous by the minute. I could use a little distraction. "Can we see some of the other labs?"

"Sure." The professor checked his watch. "We need to get you prepped soon, but I'll show you one more on the way."

He led me back into the hall, and down another few doors. He opened it just so I could look in.

There were machines at various stations, and a few people sitting in front of them with headphones on.

"Random number generators," Professor Whitfield said, "remote stimulus machines—we'll take a look at all this later if we have time."

"Are all of these labs part of one department?" I asked.

"No, it's a cooperative venture," Professor Whitfield said, resuming our walk down the hallway. "We all pool our grant money to do more together than we could alone."

"Is that unusual?" I asked.

"Very. Usually it's very cut-throat when it comes to lab allocations. You leave the room to refill your cup of coffee, and come back to find someone's moved into your space."

"Really?" I said.

"Not that bad," he said, "but close. It's very competitive out there—even within the same university department. There's only so much grant money and lab space to go around, and everyone's hungry for it."

"Then why is it different here?" I asked.

Professor Whitfield smiled. "Because we're rebels."

As we reached the end of the hallway, Bess hurried her pace. She obviously knew where we were going.

"And here's my particular workshop," Professor Whitfield said. He opened up another set of double doors and led me through.

There were students all around. Most of them looked a little older than I am—maybe Hannah Trong's age. And there were a few really older people, more like my mom's and the professor's age. All of them were standing around, not really doing anything, just waiting. And what they were waiting for was me.

"Everyone," Professor Whitfield said, "this is Audie Masters."

Some people gave a little wave, some said, "Hi," a few even clapped for me. It was weird. And unsettling. I don't usually like that much attention.

"This is Albert," Professor Whitfield said, introducing me to a guy in sweatpants and a lab coat. "He's going to be assisting us today."

"Hi, Audie," he said cheerfully. "Ready to get hooked up?"

My stomach felt queasy. "Sure," I said. This was no time to chicken out. I was here now, everyone was waiting—it was time for me to perform.

As Albert led me down the hall, back to the sound-proof booth, he explained some of the sensors he'd be attaching: an EKG for my heart, an EEG to monitor my brain waves, something called a pulse ox to test my oxygen level—all sorts of gadgets and equipment.

He didn't even talk about the other testing Professor Whitfield had mentioned before—trying to see whether anything changed about the room. Whether I was creating some sort of energy field or something.

"Will you be watching?" I asked. "I mean, along with Professor Whitfield?"

"Sure will," Albert said. "We'll all be in the room next door."

"How many of you?" I asked. Professor Whitfield had said it would be him and a few of the grad students. I wondered how many was a "few."

"All of us," Albert said.

"What do you mean, all of you?"

"Everyone you just met back there."

"All of those people?" I asked. "Everyone's here to see me?"

Albert seemed confused by the question. "Audie, you're a rock star."

Fifty-six

I sat in the big wide chair while Professor Whitfield and Albert fussed with some wires.

"Try to relax," Professor Whitfield told me.

"I'm trying," I said. He had attached little sticky patches to my head, my chest, my legs and my arms, and wires led from all of those to a cable that snaked through the wall to the room next door. It was a long way from just sitting alone in my bedroom, leaning up against my pillows. For one thing, here I was fully dressed.

We'd decided that since I was only going over there for short periods, I might as well dress for the weather now, instead of wearing the clothes that Halli always kept for me. So in addition to my jeans and sneakers and the navy blue Mountain State sweatshirt Professor Whitfield gave to me this morning, he had one of his students lend me a nice ski jacket to replace the warm coat I usually get from Halli. I could pop over and back in the same outfit all morning. No more need for Red to get his face in my way while I tried to lace up my boots.

"Did you bring your meditation CD?" the professor asked.

"I don't need it anymore," I said. "Halli and I can do it by ourselves now." At least we could before all this. Maybe I should have brought it anyway, just as backup. It was foolish to leave it at home.

"We're going to keep the lights on," Professor Whitfield said, "so we can observe you, but Albert has a nice selection of eyeshades for you to block it out—see whichever one feels most comfortable."

I tried a few of them on, and ended up with a padded black eyeshade made of some sort of satiny material.

"Okay, Audie," the professor said, "looks like we're all set here. Do you need anything else to feel comfortable?"

Yes! My mommy, my pillow, my own bed, solitude, privacy—

"No," I said. "I'm fine."

I had the eyeshade on, but I felt his hand on my arm. "How are you feeling?"

"Like someone is about to burn one of my leaves." My little attempt at a joke. "I mean, stressed."

"We'll leave you alone in just a minute," he said. "Then take as long as you need. You're not under any pressure here, Audie. This time is for you. Try to forget everything else and just do what you normally do."

Ha! As if that were possible.

"Good luck," Albert told me. Then I heard them both leave and close the door.

I sat there and took some deep breaths. I adjusted the eyeshade, but that made me aware of all the wires, and so then I had to breathe some more.

I wondered what time it was. I forgot to ask. Maybe Halli was already waiting. Maybe I was late.

Breathe, I told myself. Relax. Think of Daniel—don't you want to see him?

And in that quiet, strange room, I finally started to relax. And it's a credit to Halli's own powers of concentration that she was able to push through whatever blocks I had, because it wasn't long at all before I felt her tug on my sleeve.

"Heya," she said, "let's go eat."

Fifty-seven

Thirty minutes isn't a lot of time. Barely enough to greet your friends, grab a bowl of stew, sit down at a table and huddle together for warmth.

Certainly not enough time to sneak off with your parallel universe boyfriend and get in some meaningful private time.

"Now where have you been keeping all that?" Sarah asked me once we'd sat down across from each other. The sun was just going down, so there was still enough light to eat by.

"Keeping all of what?" I asked.

"Those clothes!" she said. "Very smart. Holding something in reserve for the end. All of my clothes look like I've been rolling in the dirt for days."

"And yet you still smell like a florist's," Martin said.

"I do have my standards," she answered.

Their brief moment of banter gave me time to come up with an answer. "I traded it," I said. "I met a woman yesterday who said she loved my coat, and I loved hers, so—trade."

Daniel bumped me with his thigh.

"But what about—" Sarah took a slurp of her stew and pointed with her spoon to her own neckline.

I looked down. Part of my new sweatshirt was peeking out of the coat. Jeez, that girl was observant.

"She gave me this, too," I said. I wondered if that was enough of an explanation, but I shouldn't have worried—Sarah was already on to her next topic.

"It's so nice you can finally eat with us," she said. "Although I've been telling everyone how deeply I admire your discipline."

"My discipline?"

This time it was Halli's turn to bump me with her leg. It was good I was sandwiched between the only two people who knew the truth about me, although I couldn't figure out what Halli's signal meant.

"Yes," Sarah said. "Your meditation practice. I could never forego supper, for one thing, nor could I sit for hours and hours as you do every night. My mum is always trying to get me to do something like that—"

I suddenly became aware of the time.

I bolted up off of the bench.

"I have to go," I said. "I'll be back, but right now I have to go."

There was no time for a better explanation. I took off at a run. It was stupid of me to settle in like that. Professor Whitfield would be sounding the 30-minute signal at any moment.

I was afraid I wouldn't have time to make it all the way to the hermit's hut, so instead I ran left and ducked into some trees. My heart was racing—I'd been so careless. I wasn't used to such short visits. It was so stupid of me.

Within less than a minute after I'd found cover, I heard the soft-sounding gong. That was the noise Professor Whitfield and I had agreed on: not as jarring as an alarm clock, but still a sound that would summon me back.

And back I went, into the white-walled room.

I'd left my eyeshade back at the hermit's hut, so right away the lights were in my eyes. All of the sticky patches were on the seat beneath me—they'd been ripped off when I left for the Alps.

The door opened, and I saw Professor Whitfield and Albert. Albert was grinning.

"Want to take a look?" the professor asked.

"At what?" I said.

"Something very unusual."

Fifty-eight

Albert took his seat in front of a bank of computer monitors in the observation room. There were about a dozen other people in there. They parted for me like a celebrity.

Some of them clapped, a few of them patted me on the shoulder. I was beginning to get a feeling for how it is to be Halli Markham. I could see why she doesn't always look so thrilled when strangers shout out her name.

"Can we clear the room for a while?" Professor Whitfield said to everyone, for which I was grateful. Soon it was just him and me and Albert.

The area was about three times as big as the little soundproof room I'd just been in. This place had computers and video monitors and other sorts of equipment lining all the walls. Albert sat at the wide, U-shaped desk and typed speedily on the keyboard.

"There," Albert said, pointing at the screen. The professor and I leaned in to look.

It was a colorful, blobbish-looking form, set against a dark background.

Professor Whitfield traced his finger along the top of it, where the colors alternated lavender and yellow. "Recognize her?" he asked.

I leaned closer and stared. There were no other features on the screen—no furniture or anything else to place the form in space—but yes, after a few seconds staring, I did recognize her.

"Is that me?" I asked.

"It is," the professor said. "The wave form of you. That theory of yours was correct."

"It was?"

"Look here," the professor said, pointing to the blob on the screen. "I think this answers how it is you can still receive sensory information back in your room while your body is in Halli's universe. Vapor trail, signature trail—whatever you want to call it, you clearly leave an imprint. Like a placeholder for your body to follow back."

I stared at the form again. "So I'm gone by then? I'm already over in Halli's universe?"

"Gone," Albert confirmed. "You left about five minutes before."

"Did it always stay the same?" I asked. "I mean, the colors and everything?"

"No, those fluctuated," Professor Whitfield answered. "Albert, see if you can speed it up."

The three of us watched the form I'd left behind morph from lavender and yellow to red and blue, and toward the end a little green and white thrown in.

"What does that mean?" I asked.

"I have no idea," the professor answered. To Albert he said, "Now can you pull up the overlay?"

Albert struck a few more keys, and a new set of colors emerged. A lot more reds and dark purples. You could see a hazy sort of outline, one form against the other, with the yellows in particular from the first form really standing out against the purple of the second.

"Can you give us borders?" Professor Whitfield asked. Albert traced out two separate forms, one directly in front of, and a little lower than, the other.

It was the tracing that did it. I backed away from the screen. Then I leaned forward again, just to make sure. It gave me chills. I didn't know what to think.

Professor Whitfield had been watching my reaction. "You know, don't you?" he asked.

I nodded. My mouth felt dry. I almost wasn't ready to accept it. "It's Halli," I managed to say. "She's there with me. Somehow her form is there, too—a little bit taller, broader shoulders—that's her. But . . . I don't understand."

"I don't a hundred percent, either," Professor Whitfield admitted. He looked at me. "Any thoughts?"

I was pacing back and forth now, trying to sort it out.

"What made you say it's a wave form?" I asked.

"We picked it up on a spectrograph," Albert answered. "It separates out wave frequencies."

"What are the colors?" I asked. "How did you get those?"

"They're from infrared sensors," Albert answered.

"So there was definitely something in the room," I said. "Two things. Was Halli's there the whole time?"

"Yes," Albert said. He clicked the keyboard again. "You can see here where both of your signatures show up simultaneously—right after you left."

"So what does that mean?" I said again, but the professor didn't answer. He just waited and watched me pace.

Finally the light went on in my head. I stopped pacing and looked the professor in the eye. And then I smiled, and he smiled, too. He gave me a nod. "Let's hear it."

Fifty-nine

"We're entangled," I said. "That's it, isn't it?"

"I think so," Professor Whitfield said. "At least, that was my guess."

Quantum entanglement. I've read about it, but this was my first time seeing it—if that's what was really going on. Einstein called it "spooky action at a distance." He never believed it could really happen. Quantum physicists have shown it does.

It's like this: say you have a calcium atom that emits two photons—which are particles of light—at the same time. Both of these photons are exactly the same—they have the same spin, the same velocity, everything.

Now let's say you separate those two photons into two totally different locations. Maybe one stays in Bear Creek, and the other travels miles away.

What quantum entanglement says is that even if the photons are separated and can't communicate with each other in any way, they're still connected somehow—they still sort of feel what's happening to the other one.

And that's where the observer problem comes back into play.

Because what Heisenberg's uncertainty principle says is that any time you measure a particle, you're affecting it. If you measure its spin angle, then you interfere with its velocity. If you measure the velocity, you affect the spin. That's why it's uncertain—you can never know all of the properties of a particle at the same time.

With quantum entanglement, it gets even weirder. Because when you measure the spin or velocity of one of the twin particles, the other one will change to match. Even though there's no way the two particles can communicate. That's why it's "spooky action at a distance."

And that's why Einstein hated the theory so much. Because according to his Special Theory of Relativity, nothing is faster than the speed of light. And therefore nothing should be able to communicate at a rate faster than the speed of light. But somehow the separated photons are able to communicate with each other *instantaneously*, even though there's no way a signal could reach one or the other that fast. It violates everything Einstein believed in.

Quantum physics is like that. People either hate it or they love it.

"So you really think that's what this is?" I asked Professor Whitfield. "You think Halli and I are somehow entangled?"

"It's my hypothesis for now," he said. "Ready to test it out?"

Sixty

It had been an hour since I'd abruptly left the dinner table. I had no idea whether Halli was still waiting for me somewhere, but we were about to see if that mattered.

Professor Whitfield sat across from me in the sound-proof room. Albert and whoever else might be watching were next door in the observation room.

"Describe to me how it feels," the professor said.

I closed my eyes and tried to reconstruct every single moment of what it feels like to go over to Halli's world.

"Okay. So first I have to be really relaxed. A lot of times I'll get a song stuck in my head, so I have to wait until I get rid of that. Then maybe I'll think of some phrase that came to me earlier, or something someone said to me during the day, and I have to get rid of that, too. Basically I have to get in there and vacuum out my head." I opened my eyes. "That's why the meditation CD was so good for me."

"But you haven't needed that for a while," Professor Whitfield said.

"No, not since Halli brought me over there when I was sleeping. Ever since then we seem to be able to connect a lot faster and a lot more easily."

"So what does it feel like?" Professor Whitfield asked. "When you connect?"

I closed my eyes again. "It's like a . . . tug, I guess. Like there's this soft little tug . . ."

"Where do you feel it?" he asked.

I felt around the top of my head with my hand. "I think it's up here, but maybe it's lower down, like on my shoulder—" I opened my eyes. "I'm sorry I can't pinpoint it—it's just . . . weird."

"Take your time."

I groaned and shut my eyes again. "Okay, so there's this tug—"

"Moving you to the right or the left? Or up?"

I swayed my body to test it. "Right. Definitely right. And then a little up."

We went back and forth like that a little while longer, until Professor Whitfield thought I'd given him enough information. And then he made a suggestion.

"This time," he said, "instead of being tugged, I want you to push. Think about that same body movement, the same sensations, but instead of being pulled there, push yourself."

"To where?" I asked. "Like to where Halli and I usually meet?"

"Put a destination in your mind," Professor Whitfield said. "Picture it very strongly. And try saying to yourself in a loud, internal voice, '*Go to*—' and then name your spot."

"You think that will work?" I asked.

"If it doesn't we'll try something else. This is experimentation, Audie. We don't have to get it right the first time, or even the twentieth."

That was a relief. Although I felt the pressure of a dozen or more pairs of eyes in that observation room next door, watching my every move.

I tried to put them out of my head.

"I'm going to leave now," Professor Whitfield said. "Do you want the blindfold?"

"No, I'm fine. But I'm going to try it really fast, as soon as you go. So . . ." I peeked open one eye. "Go."

He shut the door softly behind him. I shut my eyes tightly and took a few deep breaths. Then I shouted loudly in my head, "TO THE HERMIT'S HUT!"

The sensation was different. But there definitely was a sensation. A sort of slipping off to the right and up, and then a new sensation after that. Coupled with a sound.

"Oof."

"Oh, sorry!" I said.

"Don't be," Daniel said. I'd landed halfway on top of him, halfway off. And as I scrambled to take the spot next to him, he pulled me closer instead.

"Where's Halli?" I whispered.

"She'll be right back," he answered. "So we shouldn't waste any time."

Sixty-one

"So you don't need me?" Halli asked as soon as she returned. She'd gone off to bring back a few blankets. The night was very cold.

"I guess not," I said, very excited by the prospect. That might have had something to do with the fact that I'd just had five minutes alone to make out with my intergalactic boyfriend. Who was leaving in the morning. Although I tried not to think too much about that.

Even with Halli back, Daniel and I could sit side by side huddling for warmth and holding hands beneath the blanket. It sort of cracked me up—how back in the observation room at the lab, no one had a clue what was going on. They were watching an empty room, or at best, a colored blob of me on the monitor. No one would guess that what I was really doing was sitting here holding hands with a hot young Englishman.

"So what does that mean?" Halli asked. "To us?"

"I think it means it frees us both up," I said. "We don't have to schedule specific times to meet. As long as I know where you are, I can direct myself there and find you."

"But do you even need to know that much?" Daniel asked. I'd briefly explained the physics to both of them.

"What do you mean?" I asked.

"If you truly are entangled, the way you described, perhaps you have a sense of Halli in the universe, no matter where she is. You won't have to name a destination, beyond something like, 'Find Halli.'"

It was an interesting idea. One I'd be sure to share with the professor.

"My time is probably almost up," I said. I'd asked the professor for forty-five minutes this time, which he reluctantly gave me. "We have a lot of work to do," he'd said. "Please," I'd said, "just a little bit more."

I squeezed Daniel's hand. "I don't know if I'll be able to come back again before you all go to bed tonight. It might not be until the morning."

"Try to make it early," Halli said. "These guys have a long hike down to the lake tomorrow. They're going to need to catch the boat."

"Halli," Daniel said, "do you mind if we . . . just a few minutes alone, if you wouldn't mind."

"Subtle, Daniel," she said with a chuckle, but she rose to her feet anyway. "See you tomorrow, Aud."

That was Will's nickname for me. Strange to hear it for the first time coming from her. But I liked it—a lot.

Still, it felt a little weird, thinking about Will all of a sudden . . .

Although not so weird that I resisted the lips that came to mine. We pulled the blanket tighter and kept each other warm.

"Daniel," I said. "Tomorrow . . ."

"I know," he answered.

"What . . . I mean, do you think we'll ever . . . see each other again?"

"I don't know," he told me. "I hope so. One of the reasons I'm so interested in your physics lessons is I'm hoping to work that out. It doesn't seem right that this would be the end."

I sighed and leaned into him. "Although I probably shouldn't tell you this . . ."

"And now you must," he said.

I hesitated a moment more, then decided I might as well. "I am going to be seeing you, in a few weeks."

"When? Why didn't you tell me? Where shall I meet you?"

"No, sorry," I said. "It's not *you* you, it's another you. The you in my world."

Daniel sagged back against the wall. "I see."

"So it's obviously not the same," I said, "but at least I'll get to look at you."

"Brilliant for him," Daniel answered dully. "What's this imposter's name?"

"Colin."

"*Colin*," he repeated distastefully.

"Look, I know he's not you," I said, "but aren't you at least curious what he'll be like? Whether he's even a little bit like you?"

"No," Daniel said. But then he added, "Mildly."

I knew the soft gong would be summoning me back any moment. I didn't want to make the mistake again of using up all my time talking.

"I have to leave soon."

"I know," Daniel said.

"So kiss me . . ."

"Audie?" came the professor's voice from somewhere through the walls. "Everything all right?"

I lowered my arms and coughed into my hand. I wondered if they'd all just seen me obviously making out with the air.

"Fine, Professor," I said. "It worked just like you said."

Sixty-two

We took a break for lunch. Albert stayed behind in the lab, so it was just the professor and me. He walked me across campus to a Chinese takeout place.

We picked up a couple of teriyaki rice bowls, and then the professor and Bess and I found a place to sit outside. It was sunny out there, but cold. I was happy for my new sweatshirt and the ski jacket.

The professor and I batted around some more theories for a while, but then I decided I'd rather venture into another topic. Something I've been curious about for quite a while now.

"If you don't mind my asking," I said, "whatever happened between you and Professor Hawkins?"

"What makes you think anything happened?"

"I don't know," I said. "Just the way he talked about you in his book."

"Hmm." For a minute I thought that was all he was going to say. Maybe I'd overstepped my bounds by asking him such a personal question.

But finally he answered me. "I think the Hawk got scared. Our friendship's never been the same since."

"Scared about what?"

The professor set down his food.

"I showed him things that went way beyond anything he could ever imagine. At first he found it all fascinating, and invigorating—"

"That review he gave to your book," I said.

"Yes," the professor answered. "That was back in the beginning. But Hawkins likes theory—most of these physicists do. What they can't stand is when you show them that the universe really is as miraculous and mind-bending as they keep saying it is."

"So what happened?" I asked.

"One demonstration too many," Professor Whitfield said. "A few of us were out to dinner one night, talking big the way physicists like to do to each other, and I offered to let them try my latest experiment."

"What was that?"

"I'd been working on a sound recording using various tonal oscillations," Professor Whitfield said. "Experimenting with sound waves and their effects on the brain. My theory was that I might be able to change the vibration within the right and left hemispheres of the brain, and have them communicate in a way they normally don't.

"Everybody else made their excuses, but the Hawk was interested enough to try it. So after dinner we went back to my lab. I fitted him with the headphones, asked him to describe everything he saw as he went along, and then turned on the sound."

Professor Whitfield checked his watch. "We should head back now. We still have a lot to do."

"But what happened?" I asked as we started walking back to the lab.

"It took him a little while to detach from his body—" the professor started to say.

I stopped. "What do you mean, 'detach from his body'?"

And just then my phone rang. I must have forgotten to turn it off last night after I talked to my mother.

It was Lydia.

"Hey," I said, turning slightly to the side, away from Professor Whitfield. "Can I call you back in a while?"

"Nope, just passing along the message. Lasagna tonight. My mom wants to know if you're coming."

"Um, tell her thanks," I said, still hunching away from the professor. "But I have a lot of homework. Can we do it another night?"

"Gemma's going to teach us how to dance at her ball."

"Oh, ha! Well that sounds like fun. Have a good time." And then I quickly hung up.

And immediately turned back to the professor.

"Professor Hawkins detached from his body?"

The professor gave me an odd sort of look for a moment, but then he returned to his story.

"What we've found," he said, "is that certain sound vibrations encourage OBEs—out-of-body experiences. It's not that unusual, it's just not always reproducible in the lab."

"You're saying he left his body," I said. "Floated off somewhere."

"In a manner," Professor Whitfield said.

"So what happened?" I asked.

We both started walking again.

"He spent about an hour in a suspended condition," Professor Whitfield said. "Heart rate, respiration—everything on the slower range of normal, perfectly healthy. Meanwhile his consciousness, or 'prana' or 'essence' or whatever you prefer to call it, was off exploring other dimensions."

"Wait," I had to interject. "So all of this is true. It's all real."

"See, Audie, now you're getting to the problem. People don't want to believe. They see it, they experience it in the moment, but then their minds refuse to accept it afterwards. It's a form of cognitive dissonance—the brain likes to defend itself from anything that doesn't automatically fit its world view. So even though the evidence is all there, and the person knows in his heart something is true, his brain will continue to fight it by coming up with explanations like 'He tricked me,' or 'It was a hoax'—anything to avoid having to change a deeply-held, lifelong belief."

"Is that what happened with Professor Hawkins?" I asked.

"You tell me," Professor Whitfield answered. "I conducted the experiment the way I always do, keeping a voice recorder going and having the person talk to me throughout the session. Dr. Hawkins was very active—a good reporter. There were very few gaps when he wasn't talking."

"So what did he see?" I asked.

"Gray spaces, amorphous forms, light energies—same sorts of things other people have reported. But then the Hawk finally saw someone he knew."

"Who?"

"He didn't know the name," Professor Whitfield answered, "but he recognized him. Or 'it'—it was really more of an entity."

"An 'entity,' " I repeated. "Not a person."

"Not a flesh and blood human, no," the professor agreed. "But a form that was comfortable for the Hawk, and that communicated with him."

"This is so trippy," I said.

"It always is," Professor Whitfield said.

"Do you still do this experiment?"

"Sometimes," he said.

"Have you ever done it?" I asked. "I mean, be the person who has the out-of-body experience?"

"Several times."

We were nearing the lab building, but I wasn't really ready to go in. I paused beneath a big pine tree and waited to hear the rest of the story.

"This 'entity,' we'll call it," the professor went on, "seemed very happy to see Hawkins. Told him it missed him, asked him what he was doing there again. Hawk didn't have a good answer—said he was just visiting. The entity asked him if he was there for the school, and Hawk said he didn't know. It was a very confusing conversation—I could tell from the Hawk's face he wasn't enjoying it. Even in that kind of a situation, he still likes to be in control.

"So I gave him a prompt," Professor Whitfield said. "I told him to ask the person, the entity—'Ask him who he is. Ask him how he knows you.' The Hawk did, and then I waited for him to report back.

" 'He says we were schoolmates,' Hawkins told me. 'Ask him when,' I said. 'A long time ago,' Hawkins came back. 'He doesn't know the year.' It went back and forth like that for a few minutes, us trying to get more information, the entity giving us all sorts of vague answers.

"But then the Hawk had a question of his own," the professor said. "From out of nowhere he asks, 'Is she still living?' and the entity told him yes. 'Do you know where?' and the entity answered with a string of numbers. The Hawk seemed to understand it, even though he didn't explain it to me. And then the entity told him it had to leave, and the Hawk starts crying."

"Crying?"

"Like someone just told him his dog died," the professor said. "By then he looked really exhausted, and his vitals had dipped a little, so I decided it was time to end the session. I changed the sound vibrations and pretty soon he came out of it.

"Or came back into it, is the better description," the professor said. "His body jerked a little once he returned to it, then his vitals immediately went back to normal."

"I can't believe any of this," I said.

"Neither could he," the professor answered. "He remembered everything. As soon as he opened his eyes he broke down and started crying again. He was really inconsolable for a while—the whole thing was very profound for him. And then he left and that was the end of our friendship."

"Why?"

"Because again, Audie, it's the cognitive dissonance. It's the difference between having a theory and having an actual, living experience. Not everyone can handle it—you've done amazingly well. I know a lot of these experiences must be challenging for you, but you keep on taking it. You don't break the way some people seem to."

"And you think Professor Hawkins broke," I said.

"I think he did, yes. He thought—and you have to understand this, Audie, because it's not that uncommon for certain kinds of people—the Hawk thought he'd actually gone crazy. As in permanently harmed his mind. And he thought I was the person who had done it to him.

"He accused me of drugging him, of doing something surgical to his brain—it was pretty ugly for a while. He didn't want to accept what he'd really seen. Then finally enough time passed—we're talking months—and Hawkins was finally able to convince himself it had all been some fantasy his mind cooked up."

"But you don't think it was," I said. "You think he had an actual out-of-body experience."

"I do," Professor Whitfield said. "I'm fairly certain of it."

"Why are you so sure?" I asked.

"Because of . . . certain things that he said," the professor answered. "Things he wouldn't have told me in a more guarded moment. Things I'm not really at liberty to share. But I will say this: I can pretty much guarantee you'll never read about that experience in any of Hawkins's books."

Which is true—so far I haven't.

"So does he really hate you now?" I asked.

"No, I don't think he hates me," the professor said. "Dislikes me strongly? Probably."

"But he still talks to you," I pointed out. "You had lunch at that conference he wrote about in his latest book."

"You've heard the phrase, 'Keep your friends close and your enemies closer'?" Professor Whitfield asked. "I think he's afraid I'm going to tell people—expose him in some way. Tell people that the great Herbert Hawkins had what most would consider a paranormal experience, and yet he still keeps acting like he's normal."

"Isn't he?" I said. "Normal?"

"Of course he is," Professor Whitfield said. "The same as you are. Just because you've had experiences above and beyond what the average person has, doesn't make you crazy or abnormal. It just makes you better-informed.

"And by the way," Professor Whitfield added. "That whole thing about me forgetting my wallet and him having to buy my lunch? Never happened."

"He just made it up?" I asked.

"The Hawk sometimes likes to . . . embellish, to make his point."

"And what was his point?"

"That I'm a fool," Professor Whitfield said. "Not to be taken seriously."

"But then why did he put your idea in the book at all?" I asked. "Because you know that's what gave me the idea for this whole experiment."

"That's the thing about the scientific community," Professor Whitfield said. "You never know who's going to come up with the next great idea. So at least this way Hawkins can say, 'Ah, yes, Whitfield and I were discussing that at lunch.' It keeps his hand in."

"Professor Hawkins would do that?" I asked.

"Everyone does it, Audie."

"Wow. You all must end up hating each other."

Professor Whitfield laughed. "I don't hate the Hawk—not at all. I admire him for everything he's done in our field. But trust him? That's another matter.

"And speaking of trust," the professor added, "now I have a question for you."

Uh-oh.

"Tell me the truth, Audie: does your mother really know?"

Sixty-three

"I could get in a lot of trouble," he said. "You're under 18. You need a parent's permission. You really shouldn't have put me in this position."

"I know," I said. "I'm really sorry. And I'm sorry about the money for my mother's ticket—I'll pay you back."

"It isn't the money, Audie, and you know it."

I blew out a breath. "How long have you known?"

"I suspected when I picked you up at the airport," he said. "But I wasn't sure until that phone call you just had."

"But that wasn't my mom," I said.

"But you still didn't want me to hear it," the professor answered. "Which told me you've been lying to me."

There was nothing else I could say. "So what are you going to do?"

Professor Whitfield shook his head. "I don't know yet. Keep going, for now. You're here, and we've already started the tests. And I have to admit," he added, looking slightly uncomfortable, "I could have questioned you at the airport. I could have made you get right back on a plane and go home. But I didn't, did I?"

"Because you want to know," I said.

"That's right," he agreed. "So it's my own fault for letting it get this far. But Audie, you have to understand how serious—"

"I know," I said. "I really do. And I'm so sorry. But it's just that you don't know my mom. She'll completely freak out when I tell her."

"But you are going to tell her," the professor said. "If I don't have your assurance on that—"

"No, I already decided," I said. "I'm telling her as soon as she gets home next week. She really is in Philadelphia—I didn't lie about that."

The professor was not impressed.

"But I thought it would be at least a little better if I had some proof for her first," I said. "Something to show her it's not dangerous. Do you think I'll have something like that? I mean, you think it's safe, right?"

"The sensors fell off once you left," the professor said, "so all we could record was up until that moment, but yes—until then, everything seemed fine. I have no proof that it isn't safe, but I can't say I have proof it is, either."

"Then we'll have to keep trying," I said. "Because I really do need some proof. Otherwise this could be the end of all of it."

"Then are you ready to get back to work?" the professor asked.

"That's what I'm here for," I said.

We went back into the lab. Most of the grad students who were there in the morning had gone. It was just Albert and a few other people hanging around Professor Whitfield's side of the building.

Albert and I followed the professor into his office. Bess came in, too, and plopped down onto the dog bed in the corner. The professor shut the door.

I looked up at the clock and did a quick calculation. It was nighttime in the Alps—everyone would be asleep. I could have used some rest myself. Maybe curl up next to Bess on her dog bed and take a little nap.

"So," Professor Whitfield said to Albert and me, "what's everybody thinking?"

While Albert spun out some theory involving quantum entanglement and resonance fields, my mind started to wander.

First to the story about Professor Hawkins. How weird. I wonder if he really did have an out-of-body experience. And if so, why hasn't he ever talked about it? It seems like that's the kind of thing you would talk about if you were a quantum physicist. The same way Professor Whitfield and I are trying to figure out how my body goes from one universe to another in the blink of an eye.

Shouldn't scientists want to know absolutely everything about absolutely everything they can? And shouldn't we all talk about it to each other so we can learn and then go off and try other things? I thought that was the whole point of science—learning and discovery. Maybe I'm missing something.

Then my mind wandered off to other topics. I have to admit my brain was seriously fried. Too much attention this morning, too much talk, too much pressure—too much everything. I don't do that well with overstimulation. It really tires me out.

But sometimes when I'm my most tired, my brain feels more free to roam. And this time it drifted along at its own leisurely pace until it landed somewhere it felt like burrowing in.

At some point the professor must have noticed some change in my expression. "What are you thinking, Audie?"

"It's those wave patterns," I answered kind of dreamily. I'd been absent-mindedly tracing my finger across my opposite palm, picturing the two outlines Albert had shown us on the monitor.

"Remember when you were talking to me about psychokinesis?" I said. "And how maybe the observer problem is involved?"

"Yes," Professor Whitfield said.

"You said maybe it was my thoughts that got me across the gap. That Audie the observer had moved Audie the observed—right?"

"That was at least one theory," he agreed. "Although I'd say we've had a few more since then."

A few? Psychokinesis, quantum entanglement, resonance fields, wave patterns, signature trails, quantum tunneling—it seems like the longer physicists talk, the more theories they can throw at each other.

But I continued on my current line of thought. "I was thinking about Halli's wave pattern being in the room with mine. Does that mean she's doing something to put herself over here?"

"I don't know," the professor said. "Maybe."

"Why?" Albert asked.

"It's just that . . . I don't know, something is bothering me about that. But I can't figure it out. It just seems . . . wrong somehow. Like we're not really getting it."

The three of us were both silent for a moment. Then I shook my head.

"Anyway, I'm just tired—"

"Don't dismiss it," Professor Whitfield said. "Keep working on it—you might be on to something."

"Yeah," I said, "but what?"

Sixty-four

"Okay," Professor Whitfield said after about another hour. "We'll start again around 9:00 tonight. Audie, I'll take you back to the hotel now. Looks like you could use some rest."

As soon as I got in I took a hot shower, even though I'd already had one this morning. But who cares? I was a free woman in my own hotel room, no one around to tell me I shouldn't waste the water. I stood there under the spray for a long time, letting the heat coax some sort of answers out of my brain. I know I'm not the only physicist who thinks really well in the shower.

But it wasn't working. I must have been too tired. I put on my pajamas and crawled into bed for a short nap, and ended up sleeping for a couple of hours. When I woke up it was close to 6:00. I was hungry again, and thought I should probably try to figure out how to get some dinner, but first I had an idea. I decided to do an experiment.

Because it was still bothering me: why was Halli's outline in that sound-proof room? She had never physically been there, the way I had, so how had she left an imprint? Even if we were like entangled particles somehow, that wouldn't explain why her wave form was there in the same place as mine. The whole point of entanglement is the particles are connected at a distance—not that they're still glued together in one place. It didn't make sense to me.

That's why I wanted to try something.

I propped up the pillows on my bed, and got into a comfortable position. I closed my eyes and took a few deep breaths.

Then I silently called to her in my mind: "*Halli.*" I wasn't trying to go to her, I just wanted to see if she could hear me—or more specifically, hear my thoughts. I just wondered if maybe that was possible.

But nothing happened. I tried it a bunch of times over the next five or ten minutes, but I never felt or heard anything back.

So we weren't connected—not at that level. I couldn't communicate with her at a distance the way entangled particles seemed to be able to signal each other. So much for another theory.

I gave up and climbed out of bed. I really needed some food now. There was a restaurant downstairs, but I didn't really feel like sitting in there alone. The professor said he'd pay for all my meals, so I hoped it was okay if I ordered room service. Maybe just something small, like an order of French fries. And maybe something for dessert.

That's the thing about being an independent woman traveling by yourself: you can eat whatever you want. Order junk food if you feel like it and have a room service waiter bring it right to you. Sit around and watch premium cable since you can't afford it at home. Or sit there in bed racking your brain, trying to solve a physics problem that's really, really bothering you.

Which is what I did after I hung up from ordering my dinner. Sat there staring at the painting on the wall across from my bed, searching my brain for the answer:

What about all of this was I missing?

Sixty-five

It was dark on campus when we returned, and none of the grad students except Albert were hanging around the lab anymore. Either they weren't interested in the nighttime session, or the professor hadn't told them there would even be one.

He and I sat in the sound-proof booth while Albert monitored us from next door in the observation room.

"You read about remote viewing in my book?" the professor asked.

"Yes," I said. "Is that what we're going to do?"

"I thought it would be a good next step." The professor had brought in a pad of paper and a pencil with him. Now I understood why.

"I want you to remember," he said, "that remote viewing has nothing to do with being psychic or having any kind of what people would consider paranormal powers."

I remembered all that. He and his team tested all sorts of people from all walks of life, and none of them felt they had any psychic powers. Remote viewing is supposed to be this skill anyone can learn to use.

"There's something called 'beginner's success' with this," the professor told me. "A lot of people have a very high success rate on their very first try. So don't be surprised if you can do this really well."

I didn't know if that was some sort of psychological pep talk, or if it were really true. Either way I was still nervous.

"So we're just going to relax and take our time," Professor Whitfield told me. "And see what you can see."

What he wanted me to see was this: where Halli was and what she was doing in the five or ten minutes before I went over there. A kind of instant preview so I could then go over and verify that what I'd seen was real.

Professor Whitfield told me they'd done these studies with people separated in different cities across the world—one person in Colorado, another in Moscow, for instance—but no one had ever done such a thing from one universe to another.

For obvious reasons.

"You're going to be the first," he told me.

No pressure or anything.

I took a deep breath and cracked my knuckles. Then I tilted my neck from side to side to crack that. Then I rolled my shoulders, and—

"Take your time," the professor said, but he knew as well as I did that I was stalling.

I picked up the pencil. Then I closed my eyes.

"Try to draw it first," Professor Whitfield said. "You can describe it as you go, but we've found the drawing is usually easiest for people."

"But I don't really draw," I said.

"Don't worry about that," he said. "Just do your best."

And so I started drawing.

Two long lines.

"I don't really know what these are," I said, my eyes still closed, my hand moving across the page.

"Just draw," the professor encouraged softly.

Two long lines. Then a bunch of shorter lines bisecting them. Like a ladder or something.

"It might be a ladder," I said.

"Maybe," he said. "Keep going."

Then I could see Halli there, in that grid. Sitting on one of the patches, between the lines. And I could see other people around her—Daniel, Sarah, other people I didn't know.

I said all that out loud.

"Wonderful, Audie. Keep going."

I drew little squares inside the ladder-like lines.

"They're like . . . folded . . . something. Like fabric, or something."

"Can you rise up above the whole scene?" the professor asked. "Look down on it from above."

And then I could see it really clearly: Halli bent over her screen on her lap, and some sort of hologram rising above it. Daniel and Sarah looking at it, too.

"I can see them!" I said excitedly. "They're all sitting together looking at a map. One of those holomaps like Halli showed me, but this one is on her screen."

"Excellent, Audie. Now I want you to rise up even higher, and see if you can look down on the whole building they're inside. See if you can see what it looks like."

"Yes," I said in a second. "It's long and rectangular. It has a red roof."

I paused for a moment.

"And there's some white on top of it. It's . . . snow."

"Snow?" Professor Whitfield said.

"Yeah. It's coming down on the roof and on all the ground around it."

"Okay, Audie," he said, "let's stop there."

I opened my eyes.

"I'm going to leave you now. I want to hold your thoughts on that place. Do what you did before, sending yourself to find Halli. Close your eyes again. Lean back and relax."

I heard the door gently shut. I leaned back in the wide, comfy chair and tried it again—that pushing of myself, instead of being tugged. Pushing myself into the scene—

I trudged in my sneakers through the snow. I hadn't landed at the hermit's hut this time, but in between some buildings, just beyond the outside tables.

An old man stood under the eaves of the main hut, drinking from a mug and watching the snow. As I tramped toward him, he rasped, "Halli Markham!"

"*Nein*," I said, pointing to myself. "*Cousine*." At least I'd learned those two words.

I looked around at the buildings, searching for one with the red roof. I found it: a long, thin building that it just so happened Martin was coming out of at that moment.

He pulled his jacket up around his ears. "You going with Halli today?" he asked me. "Or coming down with us?"

The answer seemed obvious. "With Halli."

"You're on that suicide march, too, then, eh? Well, good luck." Before I could ask him what he meant, he patted me on the shoulder and said he'd catch up to me in a few minutes—he was off to pack some food.

I followed the stone walkway to the front of the building he had just exited. More people were just coming out.

So this was the *mattress lager*. A long building almost completely taken up by two giant bunk beds inside. Each bed frame held twelve mattresses in a row, with another frame stacked above it. A total of forty-eight people could sleep in the room.

It matched what I'd seen, even though I didn't realize what I was looking at back in the lab. Even the fabric squares made sense now: they were blankets folded at the end of every mattress.

I noticed everyone had left their shoes outside the door, so I stepped out of my wet sneakers and went inside. Red hopped off the bed as soon as he saw me and came over with a happy wag. Halli and Daniel and Sarah were there, too, huddled over Halli's screen. Just the way I'd seen them.

They all greeted me, then Halli went back to what she was saying. "You'll want to take this route," she said, pointing to an indentation between the hills. I was right—there was a holomap rising from her screen. "There's a fork here," she continued. "Go right, not left. You might see other people going left, but don't follow them. Trust me, this will be the easier way."

I joined them on the bunk bed.

Daniel reached over and gave my hand a squeeze, then went back to studying the holomap.

"The lake is here, then?" he said.

"Yes," Halli said. "The boat runs every two hours, unless the weather makes it too impossible. So the sooner in the day you can get there, the better your chances are."

Sarah looked from Halli to me. "I can't believe I won't see you every day anymore! How I'll miss the cousins!"

"We'll miss you, too," I said, and meant it more than she knew.

Daniel and I looked at each other. There was a lot more I would have said, if it were just the two of us alone.

"Think you've got it?" Halli asked Daniel.

"Yes," he said. "Thanks."

"Good," she said, putting aside her screen. "Now let's take care of that ankle."

I watched as Halli carefully rewrapped Daniel's ankle with strong white tape, smoothing it down as she made each new pass around the joint.

"How's that feel?" she asked him.

"Like it won't bend again until I can cut myself out of it."

"Good," Halli said. "It might be a little uncomfortable, but I think it will hold."

I'd been watching the whole thing in fascination. Halli was so slick and assured in her movements. She looked like a professional doctor.

"How do you know how to do things like that?" I asked.

"Ginny made me learn," Halli said. "There were so many times it was just going to be the two of us out somewhere alone, and she wanted to make sure we could take care of ourselves and each other if something happened."

"Did anything ever happen?"

Halli laughed. "Plenty of times."

A beeping sound came from Halli's screen. Lights swirled above it.

Her mood instantly plummeted. "I meant to turn that off!"

Halli picked up the screen and stepped with it outside. As the head came into focus, I heard Halli's familiar, "What."

Sarah and Daniel and I exchanged a look.

"Yes, Regina, I'm aware it's snowing. Look." Halli held the screen out in front of her. I couldn't hear what her mother said, but Halli answered, "I'll leave when I'm ready."

"Why does Halli hate her mother so much?" I whispered.

"Don't you know?" Sarah whispered back. "Didn't your parents ever talk about that?"

Daniel and I exchanged a glance.

"Not really," I said.

"Well, they abandoned her, didn't they?" Sarah said. "I even had that in the report I did for school: 'Willfully orphaned by her parents.'"

"But why?"

Daniel gave me a subtle shake of his head.

"To build their empire, of course."

"What empire?"

Daniel coughed.

"I mean, right—the empire."

Sarah looked over at Halli, who was still arguing with her mother about the weather. Sarah lowered her voice. "I should think they'd want some of the grandmother's money. Even with all their billions. Who could blame Halli for resenting them for it?"

"Right," I said. "Yeah."

Halli shut off her screen and groaned. She came back in and thumped back onto the bed.

"Why do you even answer it?" I asked innocently, but that turned out to be a big mistake.

"Why? *Why*? Because my mother is crazy," Halli said. "*Crazy*. If I don't answer, she likes to send out rescue crews. Or call my neighbors, even though some of them have never seen me in their life and don't even know I live there. And she keeps calling and calling—she's like water on a rock, wearing it down."

Sarah raised her eyebrows at me.

"Well, she's probably just worried," I tried.

"Then where was she for sixteen years?" Halli answered. "She never called me once! Where was all her worry when Ginny was hauling me all across the world? Did she *ever* try to contact me? Did she ever call me for my birthday? Did she call me when Ginny died? No! It's only now, when she wants something from me. So excuse me if I'm not thrilled to see her hideous face."

Martin stuck his head in at the door. "We all ready, then?" he called out cheerfully.

Halli bolted up from the bed. "Absolutely. Let's go."

Sixty-six

I'd negotiated with Professor Whitfield for extra time, telling him we should try it with me returning on my own. See what the readings were when I brought myself back, instead of relying on an external cue.

Of course the real reason was to buy as much time as I could to say goodbye to everyone, but the professor didn't need to know that.

The five of us stood at the trailhead, snow coating our heads. There was wind, too, which made it extra special. At least I'd traded out my wet socks and sneakers for the dry socks and boots Halli had been carrying for me.

Sarah hugged me fiercely. "Goodbye, Audie my love. Please call me when you're home again—how I would love to see your face!"

Just the idea of it—how I'd never be able to see her again—Gemma, but not *her*—nearly made me start to cry.

Martin held out his hand. "Good luck then, Audie. Hope the weather improves. Otherwise you're as mad as your cousin."

"Why? What are you talking—"

Daniel's arms pulled me in. His lips were cold against mine.

"So this is it?" I asked. "This is the last time we'll see each other?"

"Unless you have any ideas," he answered. "If not, then . . . yes, I'm afraid it is."

Now I *really* wanted to cry. It was so unfair. To finally meet someone I liked and who liked me back, and yet all we had together were a few days—and we weren't even kissing for most of those.

"Does it help to tell you I'll keep working on it?" I asked Daniel. "Night and day?"

"It helps immensely," he said. "Although somehow I wish you hadn't told me about Colin."

"I'm sorry," I said. "I guess that was a mistake."

"Just remember," Daniel said, "when I look at Halli I see Halli, not you. It's you that I'll be looking for."

How could you not throw yourself at a guy who says something like that?

We were right in the middle of one last kiss when Halli had said, "I'm sorry, Daniel, but you really need to go. I'm not sure about this weather, and you're going to have to take it slowly anyway because of the footing. I don't want you to miss your boat."

"I know, I know." He sighed and let me go.

"Wait a moment," Sarah said, "I've just had the most brilliant idea! We're having a party a few weeks from now—you both can come! It's for our dad's 50th."

"Oh, that's right," I said. "Your family's throwing a ball."

"A ball?" Sarah said with a laugh. "Hardly! I'm sure it will be just family and a few friends. Oh, you must come! Mum and Dad would be thrilled to meet you—both of you."

"You should think about it," Daniel said pointedly to me. "If you can work it out."

Halli and I exchanged a glance. I would love to go to that party, but it all depended on her. She'd have to stay in Europe a few extra weeks, then travel to England, then we'd have to work out a way for me to come and go in secret—there were more details than Sarah could have imagined.

"Um, I'm not really sure—" I started to say, but Sarah cut me off.

"I'm afraid I can't take no for an answer," she said. "You simply must come—tell them, Daniel."

"It would be *very* nice," he said to me. But I knew he understood the complications, too.

" 'Very nice,' " Sarah repeated. "Not very enthusiastic for a man in the throes of love, but let me assure you *I* would die of happiness if you two could come. Please say you will. *Please.*"

It was hard to resist her. Halli settled for, "We'll try."

"Try harder," Sarah answered. "I'll be sending you the invitation."

She looked both determined and happy as she shouldered her pack and prepared to set off. She gave Halli and me both one more quick hug, then tugged on Martin's sleeve. "Let's let Dan have a moment," she said. "Perhaps he'll return the favor when it's our turn to part." She grabbed Martin's hand and pulled him down the trail.

"Good luck," Martin called back to us. "Both of you."

As soon as they were out of earshot, Daniel turned to Halli and me. "Is it possible? Obviously I'll do whatever I can to help in any way."

It made me so happy to hear that.

"I don't know if we can, Daniel," Halli said. "I just found out I have some business to take care of, unfortunately. I'm not sure how long it's going to take."

"We'll leave it open, then," Daniel told her. "You have my comm number. Call me as soon as you know." He fixed his eyes on mine. "Try."

I nodded.

Halli helped him with his pack. "Be careful with that ankle," she told him. "Don't undo all my quality work."

"Thank you," Daniel said. "For the ankle, and—" He pointed at me. "Bringing her."

Halli smiled. "You're very welcome."

She slapped him on the shoulder, like a coach sending in a replacement. And then that was it. He turned and set off down the trail.

Halli and I stood there for a few more minutes, watching the three Brits make their way through the blowing snow. I didn't know if that was the last I was ever going to see of Daniel, or if it was just a temporary separation. Even if it were just temporary, then what? It's not like I'd solved any of the other problems. He still lived a universe away.

But I was willing to put off that complication a little while longer if it meant I could be kissing him again in a few weeks.

"I should get going," Halli said. "Karl and I need to leave if we're going to make it to the next hut by tonight."

We turned and began the walk back.

"What business do you have to take care of?" I asked Halli. I tried not to sound too pushy about it, but if there were any way she might postpone whatever it was long enough for me to see Daniel again—

Halli groaned. "Something with my parents. I don't even want to think about it right now. I'll tell you later."

Red paused for a moment to shake the snow off his fur. It seemed to be coming down harder now. I was glad I wouldn't be hiking in it like the rest of them.

Which reminded me.

"So why did Martin keep wishing me good luck and telling me what a suicide mission you're about to go on?"

"It probably would be for him," Halli said with a laugh, "but Karl and I will be fine."

She described a route they were going take, up and over the mountains to a hut several miles away. They'd stay there a few days, do some climbing and hiking in the area, then both head back to their respective homes.

"And then will you see him again?" I asked her.

"Karl? I doubt it."

"Why?" I said. "I thought you liked him."

"I do, but that's how these hut romances go. You meet, have a fun time together, then go your separate ways."

A sick feeling settled in my gut. "Is that what this was?" I asked her. "The thing with Daniel and me? Just some sort of hut fling?"

Halli gave me a sideways glance. "Audie, you saw him just now. What do you think?"

The truth is I don't really know how guys think. If I did, maybe I could have figured out how to make Will fall in love with me a long time ago. Not that any of that matters anymore, but I'm just saying.

"I guess he likes me," I said about Daniel.

"I guess," Halli agreed, bumping me with her shoulder. "Don't worry so much. I'm sure you two will see each other again."

"I hope you're right."

I could see Karl in the distance, waiting in front of the hut.

"I should probably go now," I said. "Everybody's waiting for me back at the lab."

"When will I see you again?" Halli asked.

"I don't know. Probably tomorrow morning—which is . . . tonight for you?" It was so easy to lose track. Saturday night was Sunday morning, Sunday morning was Sunday night . . . "Professor Whitfield has some experiments he wants to try tomorrow morning before I have to leave."

"Karl and I will be at the new hut by tonight," Halli said. "I'll find somewhere private for you to land."

We picked a few times when we'd try to meet, so I'd know where to look for her.

We hugged goodbye. I was still thinking about Martin's warning.

"Please be careful," I said.

Halli told me what I'd heard her tell her mother a few nights ago, but without the hostile tone.

"I'm always careful," she said. "Otherwise I wouldn't still be alive."

Sixty-seven

"Good, Audie, good," the professor said when I'd reported on everything I'd seen. I told him it was all true—the way the *mattress lager* looked, what Halli and the others were doing, the red roof, the snow—all of it.

"So now you've proven to yourself you can do it," he said. "And it was easy, wasn't it?"

"Yeah, it was," I realized. Once I stopped telling myself I couldn't really do it.

"Beginner's success," the professor reminded me. "So are you ready to take it a little further?"

"How much further?" I asked.

"You're going to like this," Albert said. He'd crowded into the sound-proof room with us to hear my report. Now he stuck around for the rest.

"You need to start by understanding something," Professor Whitfield said. "Remember what I told you about cognitive dissonance? How your brain fights against accepting something that violates its deeply-entrenched beliefs? Well, sometimes you have to fight back. You have to let go of some of your beliefs and be willing to approach the world with a fresh mind."

"Okay," I said, not really understanding what he was getting at. "In what way?"

"Some of the laws of physics aren't really laws," Professor Whitfield said. "They're just habits—habits of thinking. We believe the physical world will always act consistently in certain ways: objects will fall downward when we drop them, items like chairs and tables will feel solid to the touch, physical matter can't be moved instantaneously from one location to another just by thinking it there—all habits. You've already disproven one of those by transporting yourself from one universe to another."

He had a point there. That was definitely a habit of thinking I'd had to rethink.

"And so what you've already done tonight," Professor Whitfield said, "is discard another particular habit of thinking. You were able to see what was happening in a remote location at our same time. That shouldn't be possible, but it was. Correct?"

"Correct," I said.

"Now then," he said, "I'd like you to apply that same fresh mind to all your beliefs about time. Do you think you can do that?"

"What do you mean?" I asked.

"Can I?" Albert butted in. "So the professor's right: what you just did when you looked over at Halli's universe should technically violate the laws of physics. But you still did it. And what we've found is that you can also use the same skill not only to see a remote location, but also to see a remote *time*."

My heart sped up. "You mean, like looking ahead into the future?"

"I did it," Albert said. "It wasn't hard at all."

"Albert was a great test subject," Professor Whitfield confirmed. "We asked him to identify the person who would be sitting in seat 101, row J, in a theater in London, at a performance two weeks from when he did the experiment."

"Two weeks?" I said. "You can do that?"

"Albert's gone the furthest so far," the professor said. "Usually we ask people to look just a few days ahead—it seems more comfortable for them."

"Comfort's boring," Albert said.

"But two weeks?" I asked him. "You could really see that far ahead?"

"Described the man right down to his bald head, big mustache, and grease stain on the left side of his shirt," Albert said proudly.

"I had a colleague in London who took the man's picture," Professor Whitfield said. "Albert was dead-on."

"So . . . you think I could really do that?" I asked. I still didn't feel quite convinced.

"If you let go of your habit," Professor Whitfield said. "And know that it's possible."

"There's nothing special about time," Albert said. "Just like there's nothing special about location. It's all just information. You've heard that theory, I'm sure—that the whole universe is made up of nothing but information. We think we're seeing objects, but it's really more like pictures showing up on your computer screen. Those aren't real physical objects you're seeing—you can't hold them or touch them. They're just collections of data, translated by the computer into images we can understand. Now think about the whole universe being like that."

I wasn't sure I wanted to. Professor Whitfield was right: we do like our own habits of thinking. I liked thinking the chair I was sitting on was real. I didn't like thinking of it as just a collection of numbers and data. Although anyone who's spent any time studying physics knows solid objects aren't solid anyway—they're collections of subatomic particles vibrating and colliding and doing anything but sitting still, just being a chair. But a person can go crazy trying to live a normal life and always thinking too deeply about those things.

Still, I understood Albert's point.

"No different," I said.

"No different," Albert agreed. "If you can do one, you can do the other. And you already know you can do location."

"Beginner's luck," Professor Whitfield reminded me.

It looked like I was going to go check out the future.

While Albert returned to the observation room to set up all his sensors, the professor and I worked out a timeline.

"So how far ahead do you think I should go?" I asked him.

"It's up to you," he said. "Two days, three days, a week—whatever sounds most comfortable."

I don't know what it was—just a feeling. A prompting of some sort. But something made me choose three days.

I did the calculation. Three days ahead would be Tuesday night in my world, Wednesday morning in the Alps. "So I should sit here and try to see Tuesday night?"

"Yes, and then go over there Tuesday the way you normally would," the professor said, "and confirm whether what you saw was true."

I sat back and took a deep breath. It all seemed unbelievably wild. If I thought quantum physics was amazing before, I obviously had no clue. What Professor Whitfield and his students were doing was far more exciting—and scary—than I ever imagined. And yet here I was, about to try it for myself.

"Okay," I said. I sat up straight and held the pencil in my hand. Then I closed my eyes. "Ready?"

Sixty-eight

Snow. Lots and lots of snow.

Of course, I could be making that up. That was my main concern: that I'd just be imagining something, pretending to myself I could see the future when of course I really couldn't.

And since I knew it was snowing already, it made sense that I'd still see that.

Still, I described the scene to the professor, just like he asked me to.

"It's windy," I said. "Very, very cold. The snow is coming down much harder than . . . before." I hated to say, "three days ago," because that only reminded me how crazy this idea was. It was easier to just pretend it was all happening in the present.

"Do you see Halli?" Professor Whitfield asked.

I squinted. Even though my eyes were closed. But the snow was so thick, I had to strain to find her.

There she was. Wrapped up in her heavy coat with the hood cinched tightly around her face. Trudging slowly down the trail, really fighting against the wind.

And there was Red—poor Red! Pushing into the blowing snow, so much of it coating his face and fur it looked like he was already frozen stiff.

I didn't see Karl. Maybe he wasn't with her anymore.

But then I heard Halli shout something, and I thought I heard a male voice shout back. The wind was so loud, I couldn't make out any of the words. It looked miserable out there. I wished Halli had gone down with Daniel and Sarah and Martin three days before. I wished she were anywhere but in that blizzard.

Halli leaned over and wiped some of the snow out of Red's eyes. He shook himself, trying to fling some of the wet and cold off his body.

"What is she doing now?" the professor asked.

"She's just trying to get down the mountain," I said. "She's going very slowly—like she's trying to be careful. Oh, and now I see Karl."

He was on the hillside above her. The trail was narrow, and snaked back and forth in switchbacks. Halli and Red must have been going more quickly, just trying to get it over with, and Karl was bringing up the rear. That's who she must have been shouting to before.

"It's really steep," I said. "I'm afraid she's going to slip." I watched each step that Halli took, cringing at the idea that her boot might hit a patch of snow or ice, and send her plummeting over the edge. I wished I could have been there to help her, but at the same time I was grateful I wasn't. For all I knew, I would have been the one slipping, and she'd have to make some desperate attempt to save me.

"Can you pull back a little further, Audie?" the professor asked. "See where they are in relation to the rest of the mountain?"

Somehow I backed myself up and rose more above the scene. Professor Whitfield was right—I could see a lot more.

"There's a town down below. But it's really far. I think it's going to take them a long time, if that's where they're going."

"Do you see any shelter around them?" the professor asked. "Somewhere they can stop?"

I scanned the area, and my heart started beating faster. Nothing. There was no place for them to escape from the snowstorm. They had to keep hiking, and it looked like it might take them forever.

"I hear something," I said.

I tried to listen harder. It sounded like thunder, maybe, or a low, deep rumble. Something that almost vibrated my insides, it felt so elemental and powerful.

Then I caught sight of something out of the corner of my eye. Something that didn't look right, but that my brain couldn't process right away. It was because it didn't belong in that picture, what was happening. I think my mind wasn't ready to believe it.

It felt like it happened in slow motion, but I think it was just the opposite. Maybe the action was instant, but my brain slowed it as much as it could while it tried to catch up and understand.

I whispered the truth to the professor. "It's an avalanche."

It began high up the mountain above them. The snow simply broke off in one enormous sheet, and started thundering down the hillside.

"They're going to get hit!" I shouted out. "Run!"

Halli looked up and shouted something to Karl. They both took off in a panic, trying to outrace the avalanche before it could reach them.

But they couldn't do it. It all happened too fast. I saw Karl's feet shoot out from underneath him. He flailed his arms to try to catch his balance, but it was no use—he was already being swept along, like a swimmer pulled over a waterfall. And then the avalanche came straight for Halli and Red.

She looked up. She didn't even have time to scream. She dove on top of Red to protect him, but they were both about to die, and she knew it. She knew it, and I knew it.

"HALLI!"

"What's happening?" the professor said.

"HALLI!"

Time went so slowly, I could watch it frame by frame: the avalanche taking Karl, the roiling power of it reaching Halli, the snow just barely touching her back, and in a split-second more, it would sweep her and Red off the mountain.

Do something! DO SOMETHING! my insides screamed at me. I didn't know how to help her. There was no possible way. This was the end of everything: of Halli, of our friendship, of everything we could have been to each other in the future. All of it swept away in an instant. An instant I had to watch unfolding and knew I couldn't control.

And that's when I realized something. I may not be as physically strong as Halli, able to cross the Gobi desert or climb Mount Everest or dodge piranhas in the Amazon. I don't know how to fix a damaged ankle or speak a dozen languages. I don't even know how to make a simple order of pancakes.

But I do know something, and that's physics. And maybe I could use it to save a life.

Because finally I remembered. That thing that I'd been struggling to grasp, that idea that kept eluding me. It was something Mr. Dobosh taught us in class. Something about the properties of light.

For a long time physicists thought light was made up of particles. Then one of them showed that light was really a wave. And then Einstein showed it was both: particle and wave, depending on which instruments you used to look at it. But it could never be both a particle and a wave at the same time—in a way, it was the instruments that made it commit.

And that played into the observer problem. Because how could it be that the *scientist* could force something as impersonal as light to choose whether to be a particle or a wave?

And then Mr. Dobosh told us a strange story. Strange, in part, because it's the kind of thing I might normally read outside of class, in a book like Professor Whitfield's or one by Professor Hawkins. It was a little too fringe for Mr. Dobosh, but he thought it was so interesting he couldn't resist telling us.

There's a quasar, the center of a dying galaxy, whose light has finally reached us from something like 13 billion light years across the universe. Which means the light began its journey that long ago, and has only now reached a point close enough to us that we can see it with our best equipment.

And what scientists can see is that between our galaxy and the quasar is another galaxy, with its own gravitational field. And to get around that gravitational field, the particles of light from the quasar have to veer off either left or right, and then go back to a straight line heading toward us.

But if you watch the whole thing through an instrument that measures the wavelike properties of light, you see something very different. Instead of having to decide whether to go left or right, the light just flows around both sides at the same time, like water slipping around a rock in the stream.

But here's the part Mr. Dobosh couldn't get past: that light had to navigate around the gravitational field billions of years ago, and yet it was *now*, long after the event already occurred, when the scientists' choice of instrument made the light choose which way to behave. Someone in the present was affecting the past. It wasn't just that someone was perceiving things a certain way, he or she was *making* them be that way.

That's what all came together for me, sitting there in a quiet room watching Halli Markham about to die. If a physicist could change the past, then maybe I could change the future.

Because why was Halli's wave pattern in the room with mine when our bodies were somewhere else? Because someone was looking for waves. If they'd been looking for particles, maybe they wouldn't have found either one of us. In that moment, the entangled particles known as Halli and Audie had been off in the Alps in Halli's universe. Their waves had stayed entangled in mine.

But now Halli was over there and I was here, and there wasn't time to move our bodies around. Too much mass, I always told her. Too slow. Bodies take too long.

But maybe Albert was right: it's all just information. Nothing is real, nothing is solid, it's all just what we perceive. Habits of thought, Professor Whitfield called them. Not laws, just habits. Maybe life is more fluid than I've been thinking. Maybe I've been stuck in my ways too long.

And most of all I've misunderstood this one incredibly vital thing—everyone's misunderstood, if you just look at what they've called it. It's not the observer *problem*, it's the observer *power*. *We're* the ones who decide. We're the ones manipulating the universe. We're the ones who can make things happen.

It all washed over me in an instant—ideas, decisions, conclusions. But now Halli was out of time. In another fraction of a second she'd be dead, and I'd wonder whether I could have saved her.

I didn't have time to tell the professor. Couldn't say goodbye. Couldn't tell him to call my mom or tell her not to worry and that I loved her very much. Didn't have time to ask him if he thought it would work, but it didn't matter because it *had* to work, it was going to work, and we could sort out the reasons for it later.

The time was now.

So I gave up being a particle. Instead I became a wave.

Sixty-nine

I slammed into Halli with such velocity, I'm surprised her body didn't break apart. I felt the force of it exploding us off the mountain, into space, away from the wind and the snow and the danger, into someplace quiet and dark and warm.

I wish I could describe what happened next. I've tried to piece it together, but it's lost to me. The last thing I remember was sweeping Halli away to safety. We didn't speak. I'm not even sure we could feel each other physically there. It felt more like a pressure, like something bearing down on me or pushing me—pushing us—and I suppose that was me, the wave of me, scooping us both up and churning us the way a whirlpool catches people and holds them under the water. I know I didn't breathe for a while—didn't even think about having a body to breathe with. I was just motion and purpose, doing whatever I had to to get us both out of there and into safety.

I have no idea how much time passed. It could have been minutes or hours or days. But then finally there was light again.

And cold. But not cold like before. No wind, no snow, just a slight chill that was easy to fix. I reached down and pulled the covers up over my shoulders. And thought about going back to sleep.

I snapped bolt upright in bed. Not my bed. Not my room. Not my dog, although I was overjoyed to see him.

"Red!" He thumped his tail on the mattress and belly-crawled up to where he could lick my face. I hugged him hard. He was alive.

But I . . . I felt wrong. Like I should feel bruised and battered and exhausted by what I'd just been through, but I didn't feel any of that. I felt fine, in a way. But still wrong in a way I couldn't explain.

I pulled down the covers and got out of bed. Stepped onto the warm wood floor of Halli's Colorado house. Opened the door to her bedroom, padded out into the hall. Turned in to the bathroom, bent over the sink to splash water on my face.

I looked in the mirror.

My face, but not my hair. Not my shoulders or arms or torso. Not my strong, sturdy legs. Not my feet—my own feet still had blisters.

I stood there not believing it. But I knew it was true. The garment didn't fit. It didn't feel right. It was bigger than I'm used to, with a lot more bulk and muscle to it. And there was no denying the hair. That was Halli's hair, and would never be mine.

I pivoted toward the toilet just in time. I threw up whatever that body had eaten last. I felt ill, desperate, terrified. Red stood there and wagged his tail.

I sat on the edge of the tub and cried. My mother was gone. My life was gone. Maybe Halli—the real Halli who belonged in this body—was gone. I had screwed up in the biggest way possible. I had done something no law of physics should ever allow. I wanted my habits back. Wanted to believe the universe behaved in predictable, normal ways. One person shouldn't be able to throw another out of her body and get stuck in there herself. Impossible and horrible and wrong.

"Halli!" I shouted. But of course no one answered back.

I went to her bedroom and climbed into bed and pulled the covers up over my head. Maybe it was a dream. It had to be a dream. I'd undergone some trauma, and this was my brain's misguided way of handling it. I would just go to sleep again and wait for the dream to pass. When I woke up, I'd be back in the lab in Bear Creek, with the professor and Albert waiting for me. Halli would be . . . safe. I had to believe she'd be safe. It was all okay.

And then I sat up again. *Of course.* It was all just fantasy in the first place. I couldn't see the future—that was impossible. I'd made up the whole thing just to impress Professor Whitfield and Albert. Everything I thought had happened was still three days in the future, if it ever really happened at all. This was just a mistake. None of it was real. The future hadn't happened yet.

Such relief gushed over me, I think I fell back asleep on the spot. It was that sick sort of sleep that isn't really restful, but feels more like passing out from a fever. It feels gross when you wake up from it, like I did—not refreshing at all.

Red stood at the side of the bed, whining. I reached back to feel my hair—still long and thick and Halli's.

Red whined again and pawed at my arm.

I got up. There was nothing else to do.

I followed him to the front door, and when he whined there, I let him out. He immediately ran out into the dirt at the side of Halli's house and took the world's longest pee. Poor guy—I have no idea how long I'd kept him cooped up.

He came back in, and went straight to the kitchen. He stood patiently beside his bowl.

"Food?" I asked. "I don't know where Halli keeps that."

Red just wagged his tail and waited.

Dream or not, you still have to play your part. If it's a flying dream, you flap your arms and go. If it's a chase dream, you run until you wake up. You still have to perform your role.

So if I had to pretend to be Halli until the end of this dream, then I might as well do it right and feed her dog. I searched the drawers, the cabinets, the pantry.

"Here it is," I told Red, and he seemed thrilled. I had no idea how much to feed him, so I just filled the bowl. He attacked it like he hadn't eaten in days.

And maybe he hadn't.

How had both of us ended up back in Colorado? Had I swept him off the mountain, too? But then how did I get us back here? Why weren't we still in Europe somewhere? What were the rules? How did this whole thing work?

I sat on the kitchen floor in Halli's purple flannel pajamas and watched her dog devour his food.

"Where's Halli?" I asked him, but he just kept eating.

And where am I? I wondered—*the other I?* Was my body still out there in the cosmos, floating in the wave I created? Or had it broken apart into a million little fragments, just like I thought Halli's might have? Maybe there was just this one body now, this one universe, this one . . . being. Maybe the real Halli was gone, and my real body was gone, too, and somehow Halli's shell and I found each other in the churning whirlpool of the moment.

A physicist looks for answers. A physicist looks for clues. A physicist tries to solve the mysteries of the universe with every bit of knowledge at her disposal.

Obviously I had a lot of work to do. And no real idea where to start.

But all of that would have to wait anyway. Because just then Red lifted his head from the bowl and growled. His hackles shot up. He raced to the front door.

As he stood there barking I looked out the window to try to see what had set him off. I hadn't heard anything, and couldn't see anything that might be wrong.

But then in the distance, far up the road from Halli's house, I could see a plume of dust. A car was coming. And it was coming here.

I stood there for a second more, wondering what I should do. What would Halli do? Was I supposed to pretend to be her? I had to, didn't I? I wasn't going to suddenly start announcing that I was Audie from another planet, trapped inside Halli Markham's body.

There wasn't time to change out of her pajamas, but I remembered the robes hanging in her bathroom. I threw on the thickest one and then quickly brushed my teeth—Halli's teeth. I had to remember that as I stuck someone else's toothbrush into my mouth.

Then I went back to stand by the door. The car was almost there. Red was barking his lungs out.

And then there he was. Pulling up in front of Halli's house and getting out of the car. I watched him from the window, not believing my eyes.

He knocked on the door. Red went wild.

"It's all right," I told the dog, still feeling like I was in a dream. "He's a friend."

I opened the door. And standing there, looking even better than he does in my world—

—was Will.

*****

PARALLELOGRAM

Book 2: Caught in the Parallel

Available now!

About the Author:

Robin Brande is the award-winning author of EVOLUTION, ME & OTHER FREAKS OF NATURE; FAT CAT; DOGGIRL; PARALLELOGRAM; SECRET SECURITY SQUAD; and REPLAY. In addition to various state and national awards, her books have been named *Best Fiction for Young Adults* by the American Library Association.

She is a former trial attorney, community college instructor, yoga instructor, black belt, entrepreneur, Girl Scout leader, outdoor adventurer, and Wilderness First Responder. Her adventures range from the Rocky Mountains to Iceland to the Alps.

You can find Robin Brande on-line at:
http://robinbrande.com
http://twitter.com/RobinBrande
https://www.facebook.com/robinbrande

For Further Reading

Greene, Brian. **The Elegant Universe: Superstrings, Hidden Dimensions, and the Quest for the Ultimate Theory.** Vintage Books, 2000.

Greene, Brian. **The Fabric of the Cosmos: Space, Time, and the Texture of Reality.** Vintage Books, 2005.

Greene, Brian. **The Hidden Reality: Parallel Universes and the Deep Laws of the Cosmos.** Knopf, 2011.

Kaku, Michio. **Parallel Worlds: A Journey Through Creation, Higher Dimensions, and the Future of the Cosmos.** Anchor, 2006.

Monroe, Robert. **Far Journeys.** Broadway, 1992.

Monroe, Robert. **Journeys Out of the Body.** A Dolphin Book, Doubleday, Updated edition, 1992.

Savage, Roz. **Rowing the Atlantic: Lessons Learned on the Open Ocean.** Simon & Schuster, 2009.

Talbot, Michael. **Beyond the Quantum.** Bantam; 2nd edition, 1988.

Talbot, Michael. **The Holographic Universe.** Harper Perennial; 1st edition, 1992.

Targ, Russell. **Limitless Mind: A Guide to Remote Viewing and Transformation of Consciousness.** New World Library, 2004.

Targ, Russell and Puthoff, Harold E. **Mind-Reach: Scientists Look at Psychic Abilities (Studies in Consciousness)** Hampton Roads Publishing Company, 2005.

Targ, Russell and Katra, Jane, Ph.D.. **Miracles of Mind: Exploring Nonlocal Consciousness and Spiritual Healing** New World Library, 1999.

Thayer, Helen. **Polar Dream: The First Solo Expedition by a Woman and Her Dog to the Magnetic North Pole.** New Sage Press, 2nd edition, 2002.

Thayer, Helen. **Walking the Gobi: A 1600 Mile Trek Across a Desert of Hope and Despair.** Mountaineers Books, 2008.

Tompkins, Peter and Bird, Christopher. **The Secret Life of Plants.** Harper Paperbacks, 1989.

Wenger, Win, Ph.D. and Poe, Richard. **The Einstein Factor: A Proven New Method for Increasing Your Intelligence.** Gramercy, New edition, 2004.

Yogananda, Paramahansa. **Autobiography of a Yogi.** Self-Realization Fellowship, 13th edition, 2000.